SAMURAI

THE RING OF EARTH

Praise for the Young Samurai series:

'A fantastic adventure that floors the reader on page
one and keeps them there until the end. The pace is
furious and the martial arts detail authentic'
— Eoin Colfer, author of the bestselling
Artemis Fowl series

'Fierce fiction . . . captivating for young readers'
— *Daily Telegraph*

'More and more absorbing . . . vivid and enjoyable'
— *The Times*

'Bradford comes out swinging in this fast-paced
ure . . . and produces an adventure novel to rank among
enre's best. This book earns the literary equivalent of a
black belt' — *Publishers Weekly*

'e most exciting fight sequences imaginable on paper!'
— *Booklist*

School Library Association's Riveting Read 2009
rtlisted for Red House Children's Book Award 2009
and longlisted for the Carnegie Medal 2009

Chris Bradford likes to fly through the air. He has thrown himself over Victoria Falls on a bungee cord, out of an airplane in New Zealand and off a French mountain on a paraglider, but he has always managed to land safely – something he learnt from his martial arts . . .

Chris joined a judo club aged seven where his love of throwing people over his shoulder, punching the air and bowing lots started. Since those early years, he has trained in karate, kickboxing, samurai swordsmanship and has earned his black belt in *taijutsu*, the secret fighting art of the ninja.

Before writing the Young Samurai series, Chris was a professional musician and songwriter. He's even performed for HRH Queen Elizabeth II (but he suspects she found his band a bit noisy).

Chris lives in a village on the South Downs with his wife, Sarah, and two cats called Tigger and Rhubarb.

To discover more about Chris go to *youngsamurai.com*

Books by Chris Bradford

The Young Samurai series (in reading order)
THE WAY OF THE WARRIOR
THE WAY OF THE SWORD
THE WAY OF THE DRAGON
THE RING OF EARTH

For World Book Day 2010
THE WAY OF FIRE

For the Pocket Money Puffin series
VIRTUAL KOMBAT

THE RING OF EARTH

CHRIS BRADFORD

PUFFIN

PUFFIN BOOKS

Published by the Penguin Group
Penguin Books Ltd, 80 Strand, London WC2R ORL, England
Penguin Group (USA) Inc., 375 Hudson Street, New York, New York 10014, USA
Penguin Group (Canada), 90 Eglinton Avenue East, Suite 700, Toronto, Ontario, Canada M4P 2Y3
(a division of Pearson Penguin Canada Inc.)
Penguin Ireland, 25 St Stephen's Green, Dublin 2, Ireland (a division of Penguin Books Ltd)
Penguin Group (Australia), 250 Camberwell Road, Camberwell, Victoria 3124, Australia
(a division of Pearson Australia Group Pty Ltd)
Penguin Books India Pvt Ltd, 11 Community Centre, Panchsheel Park, New Delhi – 110 017, India
Penguin Group (NZ), 67 Apollo Drive, Rosedale, North Shore 0632, New Zealand
(a division of Pearson New Zealand Ltd)
Penguin Books (South Africa) (Pty) Ltd, 24 Sturdee Avenue, Rosebank, Johannesburg 2196, South Africa

Penguin Books Ltd, Registered Offices: 80 Strand, London WC2R ORL, England

puffinbooks.com

First published 2010
I

Text copyright © Chris Bradford, 2010
Cover illustration copyright © Paul Young, 2010
Map copyright © Robert Nelmes, 2008
All rights reserved

The moral right of the author and illustrators has been asserted

Set in Bembo by Palimpsest Book Production Limited, Falkirk, Stirlingshire
Made and printed in England by Clays Ltd, St Ives plc

British Library Cataloguing in Publication Data
A CIP catalogue record for this book is available from the British Library

ISBN: 978-0-141-33253-6

www.greenpenguin.co.uk

For Karen,
a sister to me

CONTENTS

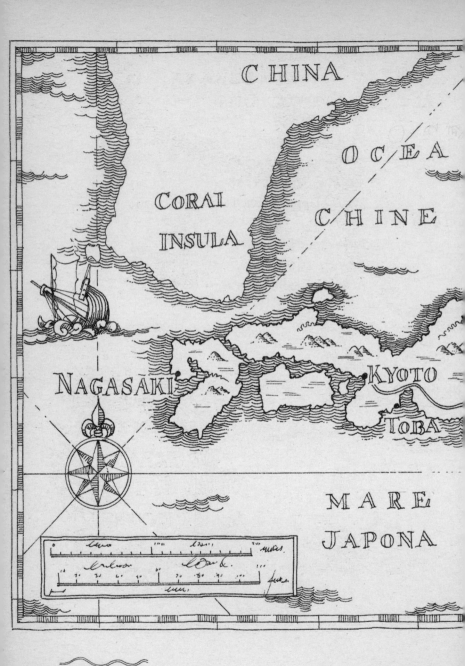

CHINA

OCEA

CORAI
INSULA

CHINE

NAGASAKI

KYOTO

TOBA

MARE

JAPONA

TOKAIDO ROAD

THE LETTER

Japan, 1614

My dearest Jess,

I hope this letter reaches you one day. You must believe I've been lost at sea all these years. But you'll be glad to know that I am alive and in good health.

Father and I reached the Japans in August 1611, but I am sad to tell you he was killed in an attack upon our ship, the Alexandria. I alone survived.

For these past three years, I've been living in the care of a Japanese warrior, Masamoto Takeshi, at his samurai school in Kyoto. He has been very kind to me, but life has not been easy.

An assassin, a ninja known as Dragon Eye, was hired to steal our father's rutter (you no doubt remember how important this navigational logbook was to our father?). The ninja was successful in his mission. However, with the help of my samurai friends, I've managed to get it back.

This same ninja was the one who murdered our father. And while it may not bring you much comfort, I can assure you the assassin is now dead. Justice has been delivered. But the ninja's death doesn't bring back our father — I miss him so much and could do with his guidance and protection at this time.

Japan has been split by civil war and foreigners like myself are no longer welcome. I am a fugitive. On the run for my life. I now journey south through this strange and exotic land to the port of Nagasaki in the hope that I may find a ship bound for England.

The Tokaido Road upon which I travel, however, is fraught with danger and I have many enemies on my trail. But do not fear for my safety. Masamoto has trained me as a samurai warrior and I will fight to return home to you.

One day I do hope I can tell you about my adventures in person . . .

Until then, dear sister, may God keep you safe.

Your brother, Jack

1

THE GAIJIN SAMURAI

Japan, summer 1614

'Hey, stranger, you're in my seat!' snarled the samurai warrior.

Jack stopped slurping his noodles. Even though there were plenty of empty benches in the dilapidated inn at Shono, a post station that served those travelling along the Tokaido Road, Jack didn't dare question the samurai. Without looking up from beneath his straw hat, he slid himself across to the next table. Then he returned his attention to the steaming bowl and took another mouthful.

'I said, you're in *my* seat,' repeated the man, his hand now resting upon the hilt of his samurai sword in a clear threat. Behind him, two other pairs of sandalled feet appeared.

Jack tried to remain calm. So far on his journey, he'd managed to avoid any serious confrontations. He hoped to keep it that way.

But with Japan in upheaval, he knew it would be difficult. Following *daimyo* Kamakura's victory in the civil war, the samurai lord had declared himself Shogun, the supreme ruler of Japan. Many of the samurai who served him were belligerent because of this. Drunk on victory, *saké* and newly acquired power, they bullied the local people and any person of lower status.

At first glance, Jack appeared to be no more than a farmer or a wandering pilgrim. He wore an unassuming plain blue kimono, a pair of sandals and a conical straw hat typical of a rice farmer or Buddhist monk. Its wide brim hid his foreign face.

Without protest, Jack moved to another table.

'*That's* my friend's seat.'

There was a snigger of laughter from the other two soldiers. Jack realized he was in a no-win situation. He would have to leave. If they discovered his true identity, he would be in *real* trouble. As a foreigner, a *gaijin*, he was a target for persecution. The Shogun's first act in office had been to issue a countrywide edict banishing all foreigners and Christians from his land. They were to leave immediately – or face punishment. For some zealous samurai, the foreigners weren't departing quickly enough. Even in his short journey from Toba to the Tokaido Road, Jack had already passed one unfortunate Christian priest, his mutilated body hanging from a tree and left to rot in the sun.

'I'll be finished soon and on my way,' replied Jack in perfect Japanese.

Too hungry to leave any behind, he hurriedly gulped down more noodles with his chopsticks. This was the first hot meal he'd had since saying goodbye to his friends four days ago.

'NO! You'll finish now!' ordered the samurai, slamming his fist upon the table.

The bowl clattered to the ground, spilling its contents across the hard-packed earth. A stunned silence filled the little inn. Its few customers began to edge towards the door. A serving girl cowered behind the counter with her father.

Forced to confront his assailant, Jack looked up for the first time.

The samurai, a burly man with a rat of a moustache and bushy black eyebrows, stared in astonishment at Jack's blue eyes and blond hair.

'A *gaijin*!' he gasped.

Jack stood up. Though only fifteen, he was taller than many Japanese men. 'As I said, I'm leaving.'

The samurai, quickly regaining his wits, barred Jack's way. 'You're not going anywhere,' he said. 'You're a fugitive and enemy of Japan.'

The other two soldiers closed rank. One was thin with a narrow pinched nose and close-set eyes; the other short and fat like a toad. Each of them carried a pair of samurai swords – a standard *katana* and a shorter *wakizashi*.

'I don't want to cause any trouble,' Jack insisted, his hand grasping his pack in readiness to make a run for it. 'I'm just passing through, on my way to Nagasaki. I'm leaving as ordered by the Shogun.'

'You should *never* have arrived in the first place,' sneered the thin samurai, spitting at Jack's feet. 'You're under arrest –'

Jack tossed his chopsticks into the man's face, momentarily distracting him, and bolted for the door.

'Seize him!' ordered their leader.

The toad-like soldier grabbed Jack's wrist. All of a sudden, the man was on his knees and crying out in pain as Jack executed *nikkyō* on him. This wristlock was the first *taijutsu* move Jack had ever been taught at the *Niten Ichi Ryū*, the samurai school in Kyoto where he'd trained for the past three years.

'Help!' whimpered the man.

The leader, unsheathing his sword, now charged forward.

Jack released the lock just short of breaking the man's arm and threw him into the path of the attacking samurai. At the same time, he reached for the *katana* strapped to his pack. As the samurai's lethal blade arced towards his neck, his own steel sword flashed from its *saya*.

The two *katana* collided in mid-air. For a brief second, no one moved.

'A *gaijin* samurai!' exclaimed the leader, his eyes wide as saucers.

'This is *the one*!' The toad-like warrior squealed as he scrambled to his feet. 'The *gaijin* our Shogun is seeking!'

'And there's a price on his head,' added the thin samurai, drawing his sword too.

All three surrounded Jack, blocking any hope of escape.

He had no choice. He'd have to fight his way out.

2

An Unfair Fight

The serving girl, a slip of a thing with a short bob of black hair, peeked fearfully over the counter. Her eyes never left Jack as he was backed into a corner.

Since it was an inn for commoners, the wooden building was a simple affair constructed mainly of bamboo and cream-coloured *washi* paper walls, with a few wooden pillars for support. The tables were rickety and worn. Beside the counter were a large cask of *saké* and several stone jars for serving the rice wine. Jack caught a glimpse of the girl's father, hurriedly stowing away the few precious china bowls he owned, and wondered if there was a back way out of the inn. The sliding *shoji* door that was his most obvious means of escape stood on the opposite side of the room, with the three samurai in between.

'Must we take him alive?' asked the thin one.

'No, his head will be good enough for the Shogun,' replied the leader.

Jack, realizing he couldn't defeat them all with a single sword, withdrew his *wakizashi*. He raised both weapons and prepared to defend himself. The two magnificent swords with their dark-red woven handles had been given to him by Akiko, his closest and dearest friend. They had been her late father's and highly prized, made by Shizu, the greatest swordsmith to have lived. This would be the first time Jack had used them in combat. But their weight felt good in his hands, the blades perfectly balanced.

The leader hesitated in his attack, taken off-guard by Jack's unusual fighting style. Most samurai only used their *katana* in a duel.

'He knows the Two Heavens!' the toad-like warrior exclaimed.

'So what?' spat the leader. 'There are three of us!'

Despite his bravado, Jack noticed the tip of the man's *katana* quivering slightly. The Two Heavens was legendary among samurai – a devastating double-sword technique taught only to the best students of the *Niten Ichi Ryū*. It was almost impossible to master, but those warriors who did were considered invincible. Masamoto, the founder of this samurai school and Jack's former guardian, had fought over sixty duels and never lost one.

'He's just pretending. No *gaijin* could know such a skill,' said the leader, pushing the fat samurai forward. 'Kill him!'

'Why me?'

'Because I order you to!'

With reluctance, the samurai drew his sword. Jack glanced at the blade. It was clean and unchipped. He guessed the man had never been in a real duel in his life.

'S-s-surrender, *gaijin*, or else!' he stuttered.

'Or else what?' Jack challenged, playing for time as he positioned himself behind a table.

'I'll . . . cut your head off,' the man replied with little conviction.

'And if I surrender?'

The samurai, stumped for an answer, looked to his leader.

'We'll *still* cut your head off,' replied the leader with a sadistic grin.

At that moment, he nodded a signal to the thin samurai.

'ATTACK!'

All three converged on Jack at once.

Jack kicked over the table and the fat one tumbled to the ground, losing grip of his sword. The thin samurai sliced for Jack's neck as the leader thrust for his stomach. Jack ducked beneath the first blade, at the same time deflecting the second attack with his *wakizashi*.

Before either of them could counter, Jack side-kicked the thin samurai in the chest, sending him flying into a pillar. There was a sharp crack as the wood splintered and the building shuddered. Spinning round, Jack now targeted the leader's head with his *katana*. The blade whistled through the air, slicing clean above the samurai.

'You missed!' he cried.

'Did I?' Jack replied as the samurai's topknot of hair slipped off his head and dropped to the ground.

Shocked at the loss of his status symbol, the leader didn't notice the creak and crack of timbers until it was too late. Jack's blade had also cut through the ties holding together a section of the bamboo ceiling. A rock-hard stem fell on to the man's head, knocking him out cold, and he was buried beneath an avalanche of bamboo.

With a scream of outrage, the thin samurai attacked once

more, thrusting for the heart. He forced Jack back towards the counter. Jack blocked the barrage of strikes, but the man was lightning fast and managed to get in a vicious slice across the belly.

At the last second, Jack jumped aside. The razor-sharp blade cut through the *saké* cask instead, cleaving the wooden barrel in half. Rice wine gushed out. The fat samurai, still on his knees retrieving his sword, was half-drowned beneath the alcoholic waterfall. An idiotic smile blossomed on his face as he gulped down several involuntary mouthfuls of *saké*.

In contrast, the thin samurai's expression was a knot of fury. He raised his sword again, determined to finish Jack off. As he did so, the serving girl appeared from behind the counter and smashed a *saké* jar across the back of his head. The samurai swayed slightly, before collapsing to the floor.

Jack stared in amazement at the girl.

'They simply can't handle their drink,' she said, smiling innocently as the fat samurai struggled in the sludge of mud and wine.

The man pulled himself to his feet, his face dripping with *saké*. Glancing round at his fallen comrades, he staggered away from Jack.

'This isn't a fair fight,' he pleaded, his sword trembling in his hands.

'It never was,' replied Jack, executing an Autumn Leaf strike.

His blade struck the back of the man's sword twice, disarming him of his weapon in an instant.

The samurai held up his hands in surrender, blubbing, 'Please don't kill me!'

In the blink of an eye, Jack sliced across the man's body with both his swords. The samurai screamed, his high-pitched cry fading into a pitiful whimper.

'I don't wish to kill anyone,' replied Jack, sheathing his swords. 'I just want to go home.'

The samurai inspected himself with amazement. He was totally unharmed, but then his *obi* fell apart and dropped from his waist to his ankles, together with the *sayas* for his swords, his *inro* carrying case and a string of coins attached to the belt.

Horrified at Jack's supreme sword skills, the samurai fled from the inn.

3

THE IGA MOUNTAINS

Jack gazed around at the destruction. The inn, run-down to begin with, was now a shambles – upturned tables, half the ceiling caved in and the floor a pool of sticky *saké*. The owner of the establishment sat in the corner, his head in his hands.

Spying the string of coins left behind by the samurai, Jack picked it up and gave the money to the serving girl. 'That should pay for the damage.'

She bowed her thanks, pocketing the coins inside the sleeve of her kimono.

'Tell me, why did you help me?' Jack asked, surprised the girl had the courage to fight, let alone come to the aid of a foreigner.

'Those three always bully our customers,' she explained. Then, sneaking an admiring glance at Jack, she added, 'You're the first to fight back . . . and win.'

From beneath the pile of bamboo the leader groaned.

'You should go,' said the girl. 'His friend will return with more samurai.'

'Will *anyone* believe a half-dressed man stinking of *saké*?' Jack jested.

The serving girl giggled, but stopped as the clang of the post station's bell rang out.

'You must leave *now*!' she urged.

Jack hurriedly shouldered his pack. Sticking his head out of the door, he saw a troop of samurai marching towards the inn.

'Come with me,' said the girl, leading him behind the counter and through a small kitchen to a back entrance. She grabbed a straw container of rice and shoved it into his hands. 'Take this and follow that trail south.'

She pointed to a dirt track that branched from the main road and disappeared into a forest.

'Where does it lead?' Jack asked.

'Into the Iga mountains.'

Jack shook his head in despair. The domain of the ninja was the *last* place he wanted to go. But a splintering crash from behind as the samurai troop kicked down the inn's door left him with little alternative.

'Stick to the main trail and beware of bandits,' the girl advised.

'Thank you,' said Jack, knowing she'd risked her own life to save him. 'But what about you?'

'I'll be fine,' she said, waving him on. 'I'll say you forced me to help.'

'WHERE'S THE *GAIJIN*?' came a gruff voice from inside the inn.

Hearing the owner obediently reply, Jack ran for his life.

'And watch out for ninja!' the girl called after him.

Fleeing from the Shogun's samurai and into the heartland of his enemy, Jack realized his escape route was suicidal. But he was spurred on by the angry shouts of the samurai. They charged up the track in hot pursuit. The serving girl was pointing furiously in his direction, screaming, 'Thief! Thief! He stole my rice!'

She's as quick-witted as Akiko, thought Jack.

Relieved she'd convinced the samurai of her innocence, he powered on and had almost reached the treeline when a crippling blow from behind knocked him to the ground. Dazed, Jack crawled feebly on. He glanced over his shoulder and saw the samurai closing in fast for the kill. He also discovered what had hit him – an arrow was protruding out of his back.

It was all over. The samurai would show no mercy.

But he felt no pain.

That was when he realized the arrowhead had struck his pack, *not* him. Scrambling to his feet, Jack lurched into the forest. A second arrow shot past his head, piercing a tree trunk with a resounding thud.

Jack didn't look back again. He ran faster, his heart thumping, his lungs burning. The trail wound through the forest, narrowing as it rose towards the mountains that ringed the notorious Iga Province.

The samurai were gaining on him.

Passing through a bamboo grove, Jack unsheathed his *katana* and sliced through the tall stems either side as he ran. Bamboo cascaded down behind him, blocking the path. The samurai were forced to stop and chop their way through.

The ploy bought him a little time. But Jack knew the samurai would eventually catch up if he stayed on the main trail. Reaching a junction of paths, he chose the smallest and least used track. Deeper and deeper he went. The light faded fast as the trees crowded in, blocking out the sky.

Jack slowed his pace and listened. The samurai's shouts were now far off and receding into the distance. He'd escaped – at least for the time being.

Catching his breath, Jack put down his pack. Hanging next to the arrow was the little red silk pouch his Zen philosophy master, Sensei Yamada, had given him. This contained an *omamori*, a Buddhist amulet that granted protection to its owner. It evidently worked. On emptying the bag, Jack discovered his father's *rutter* had saved him. The arrowhead had embedded itself in the leatherbound cover of the navigational logbook. Jack couldn't help but laugh. He'd defended this *rutter* with his life, and now it had returned the favour.

A *rutter* was the *only* means of ensuring safe passage across the world's oceans. His father's was highly sought after, since there were so few accurate ones in existence. But it represented more than a vital navigational tool. Whichever country possessed such an invaluable logbook could control the trade routes between nations and, in effect, rule the seas. His father had warned him never to let the *rutter* fall into the wrong hands. At one point it had. His arch-enemy, the one-eyed ninja Dragon Eye, had stolen it on behalf of a Portuguese Jesuit, Father Bobadillo. But with the help of Akiko and Masamoto's son Yamato, Jack had managed to get it back . . . though at the cost of his dear friend Yamato's life. With Dragon Eye and Father Bobadillo now dead, only a few people in Japan knew of the *rutter*'s existence. Unfortunately, one of them was the Shogun.

Carefully pulling out the arrow, Jack was relieved to find no more than the first few pages had been damaged. For him, the *rutter* was a means of returning home to England, of becoming a pilot like his father and providing for his sister, Jess. It was also his last cherished link to his father. After three years, Jack still felt an overwhelming emptiness in his heart. And the pain hadn't departed with the death of Dragon Eye, his father's murderer. The *rutter*, however, did ease the anguish; his father living on through the countless hand-drawn maps, personal notes and coded messages.

Rewrapping the logbook in its protective oilskin, Jack stowed his precious cargo in the bottom of his pack, along with a spare brown kimono, a string of copper coins and a couple of empty rice containers he'd been given by Akiko's mother. He added the fresh batch of rice, then checked the small wooden *inro* case attached to his hip. This contained an *origami* paper crane – a good-luck charm from his school friend Yori – and a rare black pearl he cherished from Akiko.

He missed his friends. Every day he questioned his decision to leave them, especially Akiko. It had been hardest to say goodbye to her. Ever since his arrival in Japan, Akiko had been a vital part of his life and he felt lost without her by his side. But he'd had no choice. Not only did his sister need him in England, but it was now a crime in *daimyo* Kamakura's new Japan to shelter a foreigner. If Jack had stayed in Toba, he'd have endangered all their lives.

The only safe haven was the port of Nagasaki, far in the south of Japan. This was where Jack was headed. But it was a long and dangerous journey.

Akiko had warned him to avoid the main roads and

towns, but this wasn't always possible. With no signposts and few decent roads, the going was painstakingly slow and it was easy to take a wrong turn. Besides, the need to eat and replenish his supplies had forced him to visit the Tokaido Road post station of Shono.

But these rest stops for travellers were also government checkpoints.

Having discovered the Shogun's samurai were now on the hunt for him, his hope of safely reaching Nagasaki had all but disappeared. He couldn't possibly expect to fight his way across the entirety of southern Japan.

Perhaps he should have waited to join Sensei Yamada and Yori on their pilgrimage to the Tendai Temple in Iga Ueno. Though the route was arduous and took him off course, at least he'd have benefitted from his Zen master's protection and guidance. He could imagine the old man tottering along the mountain paths, all grey beard and wrinkles. Any bandit would suffer a painful surprise if they tried to attack him. Sensei Yamada was a *sohei* – a warrior monk – his ancient appearance hiding his deadly martial art skills. But it was his wisdom that had helped Jack the most.

There's no failure except in no longer trying, the Zen master had once said. And his advice held true.

Jack knew he mustn't give up at the first hurdle. After all, this is what he'd been training for these past three years at the *Niten Ichi Ryū*. He'd always known that one day he would have to make this journey – and that as a skilled samurai swordsman he'd have the best chance of reaching his destination.

Fastening his pack, Jack got back to his feet. The forest

around him creaked and groaned, breathing with the wind. It sent a shiver down his spine. The Iga mountains didn't welcome strangers. This was where Akiko thought her little brother, Kiyoshi, had been taken by Dragon Eye, never to be seen again.

Jack decided to push on. It was still only early afternoon and hopefully he'd come across a trail looping back to the main track before dark.

Grabbing a swig of water from his gourd, he walked on through the woods and entered into a clearing. Suddenly the world seemed to spin on its axis. The trees whirled around him, the sky fell to his feet and his head struck a rock.

Before he knew what was happening, blackness enveloped him.

KING OF THE *TENGU*

Jack's head throbbed fit to burst. His right leg ached like it was being stretched on a torture rack. And his arms were heavy as lead.

Groggily, he opened his eyes. The forest was still upside down, swaying in a sickly see-saw motion. It took Jack a few moments to realize he was hanging upside down from a tree. All his belongings lay scattered beneath him. His swords, his pack, the water gourd, everything.

Lifting a hand to his face, Jack gingerly touched a patch of dried blood where his head had hit the rock. The cut wasn't large, but the impact must have been enough to knock him out for a few hours. The forest had since grown dark, the sun now close to setting.

Jack looked up. His foot was caught in a noose, the offending rope leading to a branch high in the canopy. He'd walked straight into a trap. The worrying question was, whose trap?

It was clearly designed for large prey, like a deer . . . or a man.

That meant bandits. The alternative was ninja and that

didn't bear thinking about. Whoever had set the trap, there was little point in crying out for help. He'd not only attract bandits or ninja, but the samurai who were no doubt still looking for him.

Jack had to free himself before the trapper returned. Stretching out his hand, he extended his fingers in desperation towards his *katana*. He attempted to swing himself closer. But it was no use. The sword remained tantalizingly out of reach.

Straining against his own body, he now tried to grasp the rope round his ankle. But having hung upside down for so long, his limbs had gone numb. With immense effort, he managed to grab hold of the knot. Jack took one look at it and cursed. Having been a sailor, he recognized a self-tightening knot when he saw one. Jack had little chance of undoing it with his whole body weight pulling down on the binding.

He'd have to climb the rope.

As Jack struggled to pull himself upright, he heard a rustle in the bushes. He froze, hunting for the source of the sound.

A squirrel bolted from the undergrowth and up a nearby tree.

Breathing a sigh of relief, Jack continued with his escape attempt. Then his heart stopped in his mouth as he heard another rustle, closer this time.

Someone was approaching.

In the twilight, a young boy entered the clearing. Jack guessed he was about ten years old, the same age as his sister. Dressed in a plain earth-brown kimono, he had short dark hair tied into a topknot. For a moment, they both stared at one another. The boy's eyes, as black as Akiko's pearl, showed no fear. Jack relaxed a little. With this boy's help, he could escape before the trapper appeared. Jack offered his most friendly smile.

The boy returned the smile, then punched the air in delight.

'It worked!' he exclaimed.

'What worked?' asked Jack.

'My trap!'

'This is *your* doing?'

The boy nodded proudly. Approaching his swinging captive, he turned his head to one side and studied Jack intently.

'You look funny. Your face is all red.'

'So would yours be if you'd been hanging upside down!' replied Jack irritably.

'Your hair's gone white too. Very strange.'

'It's not white. It's blond.'

'And your nose. It's huge! Are you a *tengu*?'

'No, I'm not,' said Jack through gritted teeth. His nose wasn't particularly big for a European, but it was compared to a Japanese. 'Now release me!'

The boy gently shook his head. 'I don't think so. *Tengu* are dangerous. They trick people.'

'I'm not trying to trick you,' Jack insisted. 'I don't even know what a *tengu* is.'

The boy laughed. 'Of course you don't. No demon bird would ever *admit* to being one.'

He picked up a stick and prodded Jack with it. 'You may look human, but your beaky nose gives it away.'

The boy began inspecting Jack's belongings. 'Where's your magic feather fan?'

'I don't have a fan,' Jack replied, his patience wearing thin.

'Yes, you do. All *tengu* have one. That's how you grow and shrink people's noses.'

Setting the pack aside, he spotted Jack's two gleaming swords.

'Wow! Are these yours?'

'Yes.'

'How many samurai have you killed?' he asked eagerly. Picking up the *wakizashi*, he began to swing it in mock combat.

Staring at the boy with as much menace as he could muster, Jack replied, 'Let's put it this way. You'll be next, if you don't let me down *right now.*'

The boy's mouth dropped open and he respectfully returned the sword to its *saya*. 'I know who you are,' he breathed in awe.

Finally, thought Jack. *Now we can make some progress. He must have heard about the hunt for a* gaijin *samurai.*

'You're Sōjōbō, the King of the *Tengu*. You taught the legendary warrior Minamoto the Art of the Sword. You showed him magic too! Helped him defeat his enemies and avenge his father's murder. My grandfather says you have the strength of *one thousand tengu*! I can't believe I caught you –'

'I'm *not* . . .' Jack interrupted, then had an idea. 'OK, you're right. I'm Sōjōbō.'

'I knew it!' the boy said, punching the air once again.

'As you're so clever, we should be friends,' said Jack warmly. 'What's your name?'

'Hanzo,' he replied, bowing smartly.

'Listen, Hanzo, if you let me go, I'll teach you how to fight with a sword. Just like the warrior Minamoto.'

The boy eyed him cautiously. 'My grandfather told me that *tengu* kidnap little boys. You'll make me eat bugs and animal dung until I go mad!'

'I promise I won't. I'm King of the *Tengu* and want to help you become as powerful as Minamoto.'

Hanzo's brow furrowed as he considered the offer. Then, without a backward glance, he walked off.

'Where are you going?' Jack shouted.

'I must tell my grandfather I've caught the famous Sōjōbō. I'll be back in the morning.'

'You can't leave me here all night!' Jack protested.

But Hanzo had already disappeared.

5

GRANDFATHER SOKE

'Here's a fish that could live in a tree if it wanted to,' said a voice as old and worn as the mountains. 'A real survivor.'

Jack slowly came round. His mouth was parched and he felt nauseous. His head had seemingly swollen to twice its size during the night and he could no longer feel his right leg. All his efforts to free himself had failed and he'd been forced to wait for the boy's return.

Opening his eyes, he was greeted by a wrinkled but kindly face. The old man, small of stature with spindly arms and legs, was bald save for his greying eyebrows, which appeared to be fixed in a permanent expression of surprise.

'See, Grandfather, I caught the King of the *Tengu*!' said Hanzo proudly.

'Very impressive,' the old man remarked, patting the boy with affection on the head. 'Now, why don't you give the *tengu* some water? I'm sure he's thirsty this morning.'

Hanzo lifted a gourd to Jack's mouth. Jack spluttered as more water went up his nose than down his throat.

'Thank you,' he croaked.

'A *tengu* with manners. How unusual,' said the grandfather.

'Perhaps all is not as it appears. Hanzo, I think you can release your captive.'

'But what about his magic powers?'

'Do not worry. We've got our own, remember?'

Grinning, the boy ran off into the bushes. A moment later, Jack went crashing to the ground. Groaning with a combination of relief and pain, Jack's first instinct was to escape. He rolled on to his back and undid the knot round his ankle. Grabbing his pack and swords, he got up to run away and promptly fell over.

'Give your leg a good massage. That'll get the blood flowing again,' the old man suggested as he settled himself upon a nearby log. Resting his chin on his battered walking stick, he observed Jack carefully.

Hanzo returned and sat next to his grandfather.

'So, Sōjōbō, King of the *Tengu*, are you known by any other name?' the old man asked, giving him a knowing wink.

'Jack Fletcher,' replied Jack, taking another gulp of water from the gourd as he rubbed his numb leg.

'I'm honoured to meet you, Jack Fletcher. I'm Soke. Tell me, where are you from?'

'England.'

Soke's eyebrows raised themselves even higher, seeking further explanation.

'It's on the other side of the world, across two oceans,' Jack added.

'He must be Sōjōbō!' exclaimed Hanzo. 'Only the King of the devil birds could fly around the world.'

'No, I came by trading ship. I'm a sailor.'

'Yet you carry the swords of a samurai,' Soke noted, pointing to the *katana* and *wakizashi* with his cane.

'I was trained as one, at the *Niten Ichi Ryū*.'

'Ah! The famous One School of Two Heavens.'

'You know Masamoto-sama then?' Jack asked hopefully. The great swordmaster had been banished by the Shogun to a remote Buddhist temple on Mount Iawo and Jack had heard no word of him since.

Soke shook his head slowly. 'Only by reputation – supposedly, the greatest swordmaster alive today. Did he teach you the Two Heavens?'

'Yes, he was my guardian.'

Soke blinked in surprise. A foreigner being adopted was unheard of. 'Well, that makes you samurai. Your life has as many twists and turns as a mountain stream. You're far from home, young samurai. Where are all your other *tengu* friends?'

'Dead. Killed by ninja who attacked our ship.'

'What about family?'

'My mother died of pneumonia when I was ten. My father was murdered by a ninja called Dragon Eye. The only family I have left is a younger sister in England.'

The old man, his eyes full of pity, gave a long, sorrowful sigh.

Then, looking at Hanzo, he put his arm round the boy. 'Hanzo's like you. He doesn't have a mother or father either.'

'But I have you, Grandfather!' reminded Hanzo, beaming up at him.

'Of course you do,' said Soke, smiling. He turned back to Jack and asked, 'Who are you running from?'

'No one,' replied Jack. While the old man seemed harmless enough, he didn't wish him to know the Shogun's samurai were after him.

'But the broken stems and hurried footprints along the trail suggest otherwise. Don't they teach you the Art of Stealth at the *Niten Ichi Ryū*?'

Jack, avoiding eye contact, shifted uncomfortably under the man's gaze. The grandfather may be old, but he wasn't stupid. And he was clearly observant.

'You're easy to track if you know what to look for,' Soke continued. 'The samurai patrol is bound to find your trail sooner or later.'

Jack's eyes widened in panic.

Soke smiled shrewdly. 'So a samurai has become the *enemy* of the samurai. Intriguing.'

Jack, gathering his belongings, grabbed his swords and hobbled towards a path leading south out of the clearing.

'I wouldn't go that way,' advised Soke.

Jack stopped. 'Why not?'

'Samurai.'

Turning round, Jack headed for a track going east towards the rising sun.

'Nor that way. The Iga mountains are impassable without a guide.'

Frustrated, Jack went over to a third path.

Soke solemnly shook his head. 'Bandits *and* samurai.'

Jack began to wonder if the grandfather was playing games with him. 'I'll have to take that risk.'

Stumbling down the sloping path, he tried to shake some life into his legs. Jack knew he'd been lucky the trap hadn't belonged to a bandit or a ninja, but the boy's meddling had delayed him and could have been his end. Now Jack had to hope he could elude the samurai patrol looking for him. But he hadn't got very far before he heard voices.

'Tracker! Which way now?'

'It looks like he went up slope.'

Below, Jack could see movement in the bushes. The grandfather *had* been telling the truth. As swiftly and silently as he could, Jack retraced his steps.

'Back so soon,' observed Soke, still upon the log, clearly expecting his return.

'Which way *should* I go?' Jack pleaded, the voices drawing ever closer.

Soke pointed a bony finger upwards. Hanzo was high in the branches, retrieving his rope. Though his leg was still numb, Jack realized the skills he'd acquired as a rigging monkey on-board the *Alexandria* would allow him to climb the tree.

'Why don't you just fly up?' whispered Hanzo as Jack began his ascent.

'Shh!' said Soke, putting a finger to his lips.

Jack had only just reached Hanzo when six samurai strode into the clearing.

'Old man!' demanded the lead one. 'Have you seen a *gaijin* in these woods?'

Jack immediately recognized the warrior by his rat-like moustache and lack of topknot as the one he'd buried beneath the bamboo ceiling. The soldiers accompanying him appeared to be mean, battle-hardened warriors. Two carried trident-shaped spears and another a lethal-bladed *naginata*. The samurai was clearly taking no chances this time.

One of them – the tracker, Jack presumed – was examining the ground carefully. Jack was only metres above him. If he were to glance up, it would all be over.

Soke cupped a hand to his ear. The samurai rolled his eyes in irritation. 'HAVE YOU SEEN A *GAIJIN*?' he repeated, loud and slow.

'With these eyes?' Soke laughed. 'You must be joking.'

'This is hopeless,' said the leader, angrily kicking Soke's cane away.

Then he decided to push the old man off the log for good measure. But somehow the samurai missed as Soke bent to retrieve his cane with unexpected speed. The leader lost his balance and toppled over the log himself. The troop of samurai tried to stifle their amusement.

'Are you all right down there?' asked Soke, his face crinkling in bemused concern.

Jumping to his feet, the samurai angrily brushed the dirt off his uniform. Shamed by his apparent clumsiness, he ignored Soke and waved his soldiers on.

'I'll get this *gaijin* samurai if it's the last thing I do!'

Once the troop had left the clearing, Soke beckoned Jack and Hanzo down.

'They'll be back if that tracker knows what he's doing,' said Soke. 'And there are three more patrols out looking for you.'

Though surprised at the man's knowledge, Jack was more than willing to believe him.

'Are you saying I've got no chance of escape?'

'Every path has its puddle. You just have to learn how to avoid them.'

'But how can I, when I don't know where they are?'

'Thankfully, someone else does. Come, we'll guide you through the mountains.'

'But, Grandfather,' interrupted Hanzo, 'what will Shonin say?'

'You forget, Hanzo, I'm Soke.'

Judging by Hanzo's respectful tone, this Shonin was clearly important and Jack wondered who he was.

'Besides,' continued Soke, 'our village is the only place your *tengu* will be safe. And if we look after him, perhaps he'll teach you the Art of the Sword in return.'

Realizing the old man and the boy were his best chance of escape, Jack nodded his agreement. Hanzo grinned, barely able to contain his excitement.

'But we can't let you know where the village is,' added Soke, producing a strip of cloth from the folds of his kimono.

Jack looked doubtfully at the grandfather. Was this some cunning trick? A means of leading him to the Shogun, so they could claim the reward?

'It's a matter of trust,' explained Soke.

Against his better judgement, Jack let the old man blindfold him.

6

THE VILLAGE

Jack, guided by Hanzo, had no idea where he was going. Despite the sensitivity training Sensei Kano, his blind *bōjutsu* master, had once taught him, their route twisted and turned so much that Jack could no longer tell if they were walking north, south, east or west. For most of the morning, he gauged they were headed uphill. A number of times, Soke made them hide in bushes and climb trees until one of the samurai search parties passed by.

Stopping for lunch on a ridge, they feasted on mulberries, nuts and mushrooms, together with some of Jack's dried rice.

'Where did all this food come from?' said Jack, biting into an especially juicy mulberry. He couldn't remember either of them carrying a bag.

'The woods and fields are our kitchen,' replied Hanzo proudly.

'I'm teaching the boy survival skills,' explained Soke. 'How to cook rice under a fire, recognize which berries are poisonous and trap animals.'

'But I thought it would be more fun to trap a man!'

interrupted Hanzo. 'Never thought I'd capture a *tengu*, though.'

'I'm not a *tengu*,' stated Jack for the umpteenth time. He turned to Soke. 'Must I *still* wear this blindfold?'

'I'm afraid so,' replied the old man. 'Our village's location has to remain secret.'

'But why?'

'Our very seclusion means we've avoided most of the conflicts that have blighted the rest of Japan. We wish to keep it that way. Now we must press on if we're to get there before nightfall.'

Following a stream into a valley, they scaled the opposite side. Here they remained high for a while, but Jack was tiring, dead on his feet from his sleepless night suspended in the tree.

'Not much further now,' promised Soke who, despite his age, showed no signs of slowing.

But it was almost sunset before they finally came to a halt.

'Welcome to our village,' announced Soke, removing Jack's blindfold.

Jack blinked and rubbed his eyes. On the tree-lined ridge, where he stood, was a simple Buddhist temple with a small graveyard and Shinto shrine. This overlooked a lush, hidden valley. Cradled in its bowl was a community of well-maintained thatched buildings. These were dotted within a maze of terraced paddy fields that fanned out like a patch-work quilt to fill the valley basin.

A large wooden farmhouse dominated the village's centre. Built upon a raised earthen bank and surrounded by a bamboo fence and dense thorn hedge, the building fronted an open square. To its left was a large pond fed by a mountain stream. Jack could see only one road leading into the village, but a network of narrow pathways and little bridges criss-crossed the rice fields and funnelled the farmers back to their homes. The whole setting was idyllic, a haven of peace. Jack could appreciate why they wanted to keep its location secret.

'Come,' said Soke as Hanzo raced on ahead. 'You'll need food and a good night's rest before I introduce you to Shonin.'

The sun was dropping behind the mountains by the time they reached Soke's home, two paddy fields from the main farmhouse. Surrounded by a small fenced enclosure, it was a modest affair constructed of roughly hewn timber beams and white clay walls. Soke opened the sturdy door that served as its only entrance and ushered Jack through.

Inside, the house was more like a covered yard than a room. Basic and functional, with a compacted earth floor, the entrance area appeared to serve as both kitchen and storeroom. By the wall to Jack's left was a clay furnace oven, housing two circular pots with domed lids. Next to the stove stood a wooden sink, a large jug full to the brim with water and two barrels that Jack guessed contained food. Resting against the opposite wall was a collection of farm implements: a hoe, four wooden flails and some very sharp-looking sickles. The only other items were a grappling hook attached to a length of rope, a broom and a basket for collecting firewood.

'My apologies for the mess,' said Soke. 'I've been meaning to clear up the *doma* for a while.'

33

'It looks fine to me,' replied Jack, who even after three years was still amazed at the cleanliness of Japan compared to England.

'That's kind of you to say, but it's far more pleasant through here,' said Soke, leading Jack into the other half of the house.

This area, overlooking the *doma*, had a raised wooden floor and was divided into four rooms by sliding *shoji* screens.

Slipping off his sandals, Jack stepped up to join Soke in the first room. Most of the floor was matted, though the *tatami* felt much coarser and thinner than the ones at Akiko's mother's house. But that was to be expected. A farmer certainly couldn't afford the same quality as a samurai. In the centre of the room was a sunken square hearth, above which was suspended a long iron pot hook with a lever shaped like a large fish.

'Hanzo will get the fire going,' said Soke. 'Then I can brew us some tea.'

A moment later, the boy entered with some kindling and a smouldering piece of charcoal he'd removed from the oven. Soke knelt beside the hearth and invited Jack to do the same. 'Make yourself comfortable. You're holding on to that bag like your life depended upon it!'

Jack warily put his pack to one side, along with his swords, and sat down. He expected the old man to question him further, but Soke seemed more interested in preparing the tea than discovering the contents of his pack.

With the fire built, Hanzo scurried off to the *doma* again, while his grandfather gently fanned the flames and added logs from a neat pile next to the hearth.

'Do you like *sencha*?' asked Soke.

Jack nodded. When Akiko had first introduced him to the drink, he hadn't enjoyed its bitter grassy flavour. But over the years he'd become used to it and was now quite fond of green tea.

Hanzo returned, struggling with a heavy iron kettle full of water. Jack helped him place it on the pot hook. Soke added some tea leaves, then used the fish lever to lower the kettle into the fire.

'Tell me, Jack, where are you headed?'

'Nagasaki. It's where all foreigners have been banished to.'

Soke nodded his head in sympathy. 'Such a long journey isn't undertaken lightly. But you've done the hardest part – the first step. And where have you travelled from?'

Jack saw no reason not to tell the old man. 'Toba.'

'That's on the Ise coast. Why did you not go by sea?'

'No one was willing to take me. Any person found help-ing or hiding a foreigner could be punished . . . Soke-san, I –'

The old man held up his hand. 'No, just Soke, please. That's respectful enough.'

'Soke, I appreciate all you've done for me, but I really should leave as soon as possible. I don't want to get you or Hanzo into trouble.'

'You need to rest first,' replied the grandfather firmly. 'Besides, no one will find you here. You're perfectly safe. And so are we.'

'But what if someone in the village tells the local samurai?'

Soke chuckled. 'I can assure you that won't happen.'

'But –'

'Are you hungry?' he asked, ignoring Jack's protests.

Jack's stomach growled at the mention of food.

'I'll take that as a yes.'

Leaving Jack to his tea, Soke disappeared into the *doma*. Hanzo was staring at Jack from the doorway. The boy seemed hypnotized by his blond hair and blue eyes.

'What do *tengu* like to eat?' asked Hanzo.

Jack returned the boy's gaze. He'd given up arguing about *tengu*. Instead he decided to play along.

'Little boys mostly.'

Hanzo's eyes widened in shock. Then his face brightened.

'Would you eat my friend Kobei for me? He beat me during training the other day and my arm still hurts.'

He showed Jack the bruise, a large purple patch on his bicep.

'What are you training for?' Jack asked.

'Hanzo!' interrupted Soke from the other room. 'I need your help in here.'

The boy hurried away.

A little odd for a farmboy to be involved in combat training, thought Jack as he poured himself another tea. The delicious smell of cooking wafted into the room.

After a hearty dinner of soup, rice and pickled vegetables, Jack's exhaustion finally got the better of him and he began to yawn.

'Hanzo,' said Soke. 'Please prepare a bed for our guest. He'll share your room.'

Sliding back a partition, Hanzo rolled out two *futon* mattresses, stuffed with straw, in the adjoining room.

'Thank you for your kindness, Soke,' said Jack, bowing.

'It's been an honour,' replied the old man, returning the bow.

Jack picked up his pack and swords, and joined Hanzo in the other room.

'This one's yours,' said the boy, pointing to the *futon* nearest the door.

Nodding gratefully, Jack stowed his belongings in the corner where he could keep an eye on them and carefully laid his swords beside his mattress. It had become habit to have them close to hand. As he climbed into bed, Hanzo whispered, 'When will you start teaching me the sword?'

'Tomorrow,' Jack replied, mid-yawn.

'Promise?'

'Promise,' Jack mumbled wearily, surrendering himself to sleep.

7

SWORDPLAY

Yamato hung on for dear life, one hand clasping the balcony rail. Flames engulfed the devastated tower of Osaka Castle, cannonshot shrieked through the night and the sounds of battle raged far below.

Jack stood there, watching, unable to move. Yamato's eyes were wide with fear, pleading for him to come to his rescue. But however hard he tried, his feet were immovable as stone. He could hear Akiko screaming in the darkness.

A single green eye appeared out of the shadows.

'It's all your fault,' hissed Dragon Eye.

The ninja clung to Yamato's back. One by one, he peeled away the boy's fingers.

'No!' cried Jack as his friend plummeted to the ground.

Only now could Jack move. He ran to the edge and saw Yamato's lifeless body sprawled in the courtyard.

But Dragon Eye was nowhere to be seen. A hand seized Jack's shoulder . . .

Before he'd even opened his eyes, Jack had grabbed his sword and half-drawn the blade.

'It's just *me!*' Hanzo exclaimed, his hands raised high.

Jack lay back on his *futon*, his heart racing in his chest. As the nightmare receded with the light of day, he grieved for his lost friend.

'Are you all right?' asked Hanzo.

Nodding, Jack calmed himself. He'd had the dream several times before, forcing him to relive that terrible night again and again. In truth, Yamato had made the decision himself to let go, dying with honour. But Jack still wondered if he could have saved *both* his friends. He shivered involuntarily at the thought of Dragon Eye surviving. But that was impossible. He'd fallen to his death too.

'What *were* you doing?' Jack demanded of Hanzo.

'Trying to steal your pillow without waking you.'

Jack gave Hanzo a befuddled look. The boy had a pillow of his own. 'Well, you *did* wake me. Please don't do that again. I'd hate to mistake you for a ninja.'

'Why?' said Hanzo, frowning.

'Because I might accidently cut you in half!'

Jack put the *katana* safely to one side.

'Your reactions are *so* fast,' Hanzo said in admiration. 'Anyway, you need to get up. You've missed breakfast-time. And you promised to teach me the sword.'

That was the last thing Jack felt like doing. But he'd made a promise and, as a samurai, he had to honour it. Rolling out of bed, he rubbed the sleep from his eyes and went into the next room. A bowl of cold rice and a jug of water were laid out beside the hearth.

'Where's Soke?' asked Jack as he tucked into his belated breakfast.

'Grandfather's gone to see Shonin,' said Hanzo, who

waited excitedly by the door. 'He's left some water in the sink for you to wash with.'

Finishing off his rice, Jack slipped on his sandals and entered the *doma*. Beside the sink was a wooden scoop, which he used to douse his face and hands. What he really wanted, though, was a hot *ofuro*. The habit of the samurai to bathe daily was one of the surprising pleasures of living in Japan. But Jack didn't suppose farmers had such luxuries. Anyway, five days of travel grime was nothing compared to being a sailor at sea or living in England, where washing was considered unhealthy.

Refreshed and a little cleaner, Jack stepped out into the bright midday sunshine. The glistening paddy fields were a vibrant green, the seeds planted in spring having grown into lush summer grasses. A few farmers tended the rice crop, but most appeared to be relaxing in the square. Jack could hear the laughter of children nearby and was struck by how tranquil the village was.

Hanzo tugged on his sleeve. 'So, what are you going to teach me first?'

Jack felt a twinge of nerves. How could he be a teacher, when he wasn't much more than a student himself? He didn't even have any training weapons. Looking around the yard, he spotted a stack of bamboo stems beside the outhouse. Jack selected one of appropriate length and passed it to the boy. 'Here's your sword.'

'But I want to use a *real* sword!' Hanzo protested, giving his bamboo substitute a disgruntled inspection.

Jack laughed, recalling his own impatience to wield a steel *katana*. But all that had changed when his late swordmaster, Sensei Hosokawa, had given him a harsh lesson in the responsibility of carrying such a weapon. It had involved a grain of rice, Yamato's head and nerves of steel to cut the grain in half. Jack had backed out of the challenge, straight away appreciating his teacher's point. But he had no wish to test Hanzo in such a way. Something about the boy told Jack he'd attempt the feat, whatever the danger.

'Until you have complete control of *this* sword,' Jack explained, repeating Sensei Hosokawa's words, 'you don't have the skill to use a real blade.'

Though obviously disappointed, Hanzo nodded his acceptance. 'So, what do I do now?'

Jack thought back to his very first lesson with Sensei Hosokawa.

'Hold out your arms straight in front of you,' he instructed, 'with your sword resting in both hands.'

Hanzo eagerly did as he was told. 'Now what?'

'Keep holding it like that.'

There was a small tree in the yard and Jack found a spot beneath it to observe his student. Hanzo gave him a puzzled look. 'This isn't sword fighting!'

'Yes, it is,' said Jack with a wry smile. Reiterating his *kenjutsu* master's teachings, he explained, 'If your own sword can defeat you in your own hands, what hope do you have of ever defeating your enemy?'

'Ah, it's a test!'

With renewed determination, Hanzo held out his sword. A few minutes passed and the boy's arms weren't even trembling. Impressed, Jack realized there was more to Hanzo than met the eye.

As Hanzo stood there, stock-still, three boys and a girl wandered past.

'What are you doing?' called a round-faced boy over the fence.

'Sword training, Kobei.'

'Scarecrow training more like!' he laughed.

'What would you know? You don't have the King of the *Tengu* teaching you,' Hanzo shot back, nodding to Jack in the shade.

The four of them gawped at Jack in amazement.

'I caught him,' Hanzo explained. 'And now he's set me a test to defeat the sword.'

'That's easy,' scoffed Kobei, keen to impress the *tengu*.

Suddenly the challenge was on. Jack was taken aback by the children's enthusiasm as all four grabbed a piece of bamboo and held it out like Hanzo.

Just then a young farmer approached. Strong and tanned from working in the fields, he looked tougher than many samurai. Jack judged him to be about seventeen. He had a broad handsome face with eyes brown as the earth. Discovering the children standing like statues, their faces screwed up with the effort of holding their bamboo swords, he shot Jack a questioning glance but made no comment.

'Hanzo!' called the farmer. 'Soke said to bring your guest to Shonin.'

'Yes, Tenzen,' replied the boy, hurriedly putting down his makeshift weapon.

'You lose!' said Kobei.

'I'll beat you all later,' shot back Hanzo.

Jack got to his feet and bowed. The farmer inclined his head respectfully.

As they made their way through the paddy fields, Jack's curiosity finally got the better of him. 'Who is Shonin?' he asked.

'Not who, but what,' replied Tenzen civilly. 'Shonin means the head of the village and is how you should address the leader of our clan. He's also my father.'

Walking up a rise and passing through a tall wooden gate, they entered the main square. In one corner was a set of stables. Several children were playing on the horse rail outside, attempting to walk along its beam without falling. Beyond the fence was the pond, where a group of lads were swimming, diving and play-fighting.

The villagers in the square gazed in wonder at Jack, many bowing at his approach. Jack returned the courtesy. It appeared the anti-foreign prejudice afflicting the rest of Japan had not yet reached this community. Even so, Jack overheard uneasy murmurings among the crowd about a samurai being in their village. It seemed his status was more of an issue than his race.

Tenzen led Jack over to the farmhouse. The building was far grander than Soke's and more akin to a samurai's dwelling. It had a raised veranda and shuttered windows, and was at least double the size of any other home in the village. Two men greeted Tenzen at the door and let them through. Slipping off their sandals, the three of them walked down a polished wooden corridor, passing two rooms to a set of double *shoji* doors at the far end. As they drew nearer, Jack could hear a heated conversation going on.

'Do you really think it's appropriate to have brought a samurai *here*?'

'We could learn many things to our advantage,' replied a voice Jack recognized as Soke's. 'Besides, I sense the boy has a good heart.'

'You said that last time about an outsider and we all know what happened. What if he were to draw a patrol to this valley? Need I remind you that *daimyo* Akechi still seeks to destroy our village?'

'I realize it's a risk, but the boy's as much an outsider as we are. Meet him and judge for yourselves.'

The doors to the room opened and Jack was ushered inside.

8

SHONIN

The reception room was large, carpeted with finely woven tatami mats and a raised wooden dais at the far end. To Jack's right was another set of *shoji* and on the wall behind the dais hung an ink painting of a kingfisher perched over a river.

Three men sat upon the raised floor, observing Jack's entrance.

'I thought you said he was samurai,' whispered the man in the middle. Pudgy, with a generous double chin, drooping moustache and balding head, he reminded Jack of a walrus. As first impressions went, he seemed an odd choice for a Shonin and bore little resemblance to his lean, muscular son. But as this was a farming community, Jack presumed they didn't require a toughened warrior as their leader. Or a tactful one, it seemed.

'The boy trained at the *Niten Ichi Ryū*,' replied Soke, who sat to the man's left.

'But he's foreign,' the pudgy man remarked as Jack approached.

'He's still samurai. His guardian's Masamoto Takeshi.'

'*That* at least explains why there's such a high price on

45

his head.' The man's eyes lit up with a realization. 'This boy could be used as leverage in negotiations with *daimyo* Akechi –'

'There's *no* bargaining with that lord,' Soke cut in. 'And you should be aware the boy speaks fluent Japanese.'

The man's face froze in alarm. 'You *could* have told me that before!' he hissed, forcing his startled expression into a smile.

Pretending not to have overheard the comments, Jack knelt before the three men and bowed low. Though the pudgy man was clearly two-faced, it would do Jack no favours to show disrespect. 'It is an honour to meet you, Shonin.'

'Well, our friend certainly knows the proper etiquette,' said the third man, smiling. Slim, with a handsome face and hair neatly tied into a topknot, he wore a dark-green kimono and possessed an air of supreme confidence. He studied Jack with the eyes of a hawk.

'If you know such graces, what could you possibly have done to offend the Shogun? We know he's banishing foreigners, but why is he so keen on capturing you?'

Jack decided it would be best to tell the truth to this man, who seemed more astute than the Shonin. But not the whole truth. He'd avoid mentioning the *rutter*. 'I fought against the Shogun in the war. I also defeated his sword school in a *Taryu-Jiai* contest a couple of years back. I don't think he's ever forgiven me.'

The man laughed. 'I've heard the Shogun is full of pride. Such a loss of face over his school would be hard to bear. But why are you travelling alone? Surely you still have some samurai friends?'

'Yes, but I don't wish to endanger them.'

'Very loyal of you, and brave to attempt such a journey on your own. I understand you're heading for Nagasaki. How do you expect to get through all the post station checkpoints?'

Jack shrugged. 'I've got this far. I'll find a way.'

'Courageous, as well,' commented the man. He turned to the others. 'The boy's a samurai. He clearly follows their code of *bushido*. Already he's shown four of its seven virtues. Respect, Loyalty, Courage and Honesty. I like this boy. He should stay.'

Shonin nodded his head reluctantly in acknowledgement.

The man in the green kimono addressed Jack again. 'It's an honour to meet you, Jack Fletcher. You're welcome in my village.'

Jack was momentarily taken off-guard, before realizing *this* man was actually Shonin. In Japan, it was expected that the most senior person took central position. Shonin had gone against this convention. That meant he was playing a joke on Jack – or was a very cunning man.

'Thank you,' replied Jack, now noting the man's obvious similarity to Tenzen, his son. 'But I'm not intending to stay. I appreciate Soke helping me, but I don't want to burden you or your village.'

'Jack, I'm aware you overheard Momochi–san's earlier comments,' Shonin said, respectfully indicating the man in the middle. 'But don't concern yourself. Momochi will do anything to preserve this village, even sell his own grandmother.'

'Too late! He's already done that,' commented Soke.

'And I didn't get a very good price!' retorted Momochi.

The three men laughed at their little in-joke. Jack, however, couldn't help wondering what sort of trouble their village was in.

'You're our guest,' Shonin continued, 'and I assure you we won't be handing you over to the samurai. They're not exactly our friends. In fact Soke considers it our duty to help you. I, therefore, insist you stay here and rest, at least until the search has died down.'

Later that evening, Jack joined Soke and Hanzo for dinner, a fresh pot of *sencha* steaming over the hearth.

'Shonin was quite taken by you,' said Soke, scooping up a mouthful of rice with his *hashi*.

'He's very kind,' replied Jack. 'But Momochi is right. I could attract a samurai patrol here. I don't want to add to your village's problems.'

'Please don't worry about such matters. You have enough difficulties of your own to contend with. Shonin doesn't make such decisions lightly. He's assessed the risk. There's little chance you'll be found here.'

'But what does this *daimyo* Akechi want from you? Why is Momochi so concerned about the village's safety?'

'*Daimyo* Akechi isn't popular. As lord of this region, he taxes the local villages heavily for their rice. Those who refuse to hand over their share of the crop are punished. Those who do, have barely enough left to eat. The *daimyo* knows of our village, but not its location. We intend to keep it that way.'

'But what if the *daimyo* discovered you were helping me? He'd surely do far worse than take your rice.'

48

'Jack, you know as well as I do that the samurai are scouring these forests for you. The Iga mountains are a maze of gorges and river valleys. That's why our village has yet to be discovered. If you were captured in this area, it could be disastrous for our village. At least wait a few days.'

Jack relented, bowing his head in acceptance.

'Good, that's settled then,' said Soke, smiling warmly. 'I hear you were teaching Hanzo this morning.'

Jack nodded, but before he could reply Hanzo butted in. '*Tengu*'s been showing me how to defeat my own sword. Otherwise, he said, how can I expect to defeat the enemy!'

Soke nodded appreciatively. 'A sound lesson.'

Hanzo tugged on Jack's sleeve. 'What are we going to do tomorrow?'

'Erm . . . a parry and strike,' replied Jack.

'Great!' grinned Hanzo, polishing off his meal.

Soke got to his feet. 'If you'll excuse me, I have to see Shonin before I turn in. Hanzo, he's asked to see you too.'

The boy jumped up and mock-fought his way across the room.

'See you in the morning, *tengu*!'

Jack tried but couldn't get to sleep. His mind was too full of concerns. Though Soke and Shonin had persuaded him to stay, he had yet to be convinced this was the right decision. It wasn't only his worry of endangering the village; it was a matter of self-preservation. Shonin appeared a good man, but Jack didn't trust Momochi. If the village needed to pay taxes, then Jack was surely the solution. The reward on his head was apparently substantial, maybe even enough to cover the annual rice tax several times over. This was a good enough reason why he should leave now, before Momochi persuaded the others. But, as he'd discovered, the mountains brought their own problems and dangers.

Since Soke and Hanzo hadn't yet returned from the farm-house, Jack decided to take a short walk around the village to clear his head. Sliding open the main door, he emerged into a beautiful star-filled night. The pond near the farm-house mirrored the sky, the moon floating like a silver coin in its waters.

As he wandered along a path between two paddy fields, Jack gazed up at the constellations. His father had taught him how to navigate by the stars and he knew many of them by name. Arcturus. Regulus. Bellatrix. Spica. They were like old friends.

Jack wondered if Akiko was looking at the same stars as he was. He'd once shown her Spica, one of the brightest stars in the firmament. He smiled at the memory. That had been more than two years ago in the Southern Zen Garden of the *Niten Ichi Ryū*. They'd just foiled an attempt by the ninja Dragon Eye to assassinate *daimyo* Takatomi, the Lord of Kyoto Province.

So much had changed since then. As far as he knew, the *Niten Ichi Ryū* was no more. When the students had left for war, half the school was already in ruins, the Hall of Lions just a burnt-out shell following a surprise attack by Kamakura's supporters. But even if it was still standing, there was no one left to teach there. Many of the sensei and students had died during the battle for Osaka Castle. And those who'd survived had been banished by the Shogun.

How Jack missed their friendship and guidance. And, even more, the bond that was forged between him, Yamato and Akiko in those dark times. *Forever bound to one another* had been their motto. They'd stood side by side, three friends prepared for any challenge, ready to lay down their lives for one another. Which is exactly what Yamato had done for Jack and Akiko.

But now Jack was all alone and had to make his own decisions.

Tomorrow he would leave.

Jack found himself back at Soke's house. As he turned to go inside, he noticed movement in the paddy fields. Three shadows flitted through the night towards Shonin's farm-house. For a moment, Jack thought his eyes were deceiving him. Camouflaged in black, swords strapped to their backs, the three figures moved swiftly and without sound.

Ninja!

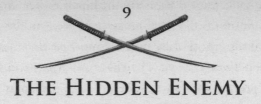

9

THE HIDDEN ENEMY

A combination of fear, anger and determination swept through Jack. Ever since the horrific attack on the *Alexandria*, ninja were his worst nightmare. Cruel faceless killers, they had no honour, no loyalty and no mercy. They cared only for payment for their services and nothing about the pain and suffering they caused.

Jack knew the Iga mountains were the stronghold of the ninja. But what were they doing here in this little farming village? Had the Shogun employed assassins to find Jack? He wouldn't be surprised. Kamakura had sunk to such depths during the war. The Shogun had even been in collusion with Dragon Eye.

But these ninja ignored Soke's abode where Jack was staying. They were headed straight for Shonin's farmhouse. It seemed the trouble the village was in with *daimyo* Akechi was enough for the samurai lord to hire assassins himself. Jack had to warn Soke. Running back inside, he knocked on the old man's door.

'Soke?' he called, but got no answer.

Sliding opening the *shoji*, he found the room empty, the

futon unmade. Hanzo wasn't in the house either. They must be with Shonin still – that meant *both* were in danger.

Grabbing his swords, he ran out into the night. The pathway between the paddy fields was narrow and wet, and in the darkness proved treacherous. He cursed as his foot slipped into the muddy waters. Why couldn't the farmers make proper-sized paths?

Stumbling on, he reached the road. The three ninja had already entered the square and had disappeared from view. Jack dashed up the slope and through the gate. The square was deserted, but oil lamps, burning inside the farmhouse, cast orange bars of light across the hard-packed earth.

The main door to the building was ajar. Jack carefully approached and placed one eye to the crack. The corridor was deserted. Drawing his *katana*, he slipped inside and headed for the reception room. He could hear voices and prayed he wasn't too late.

As he passed the first *shoji*, it opened and a ninja stepped out, eyes wide with alarm. In an instant, the assassin had drawn the sword strapped to his back. The *ninjatō*, with its trademark straight blade and square handguard, flashed through the air. The speed with which the assassin struck took Jack by surprise, but his years of samurai training kicked in. He deflected the attack and retaliated with a cut across the chest.

The ninja leapt aside with cat-like agility. But Jack kept up the pressure, driving the intruder down the corridor. Their swords clashed and locked against one another. In that moment, the ninja attempted to throw something into Jack's eyes. Jack, familiar with *metsubishi* blinding powder, turned away and managed to avoid the worst of it, but realized he'd been compromised. In a desperate move to regain the advantage, he didn't retreat. Instead he drove forward, pushing the ninja back and crashing through the double doors.

The framework cracked and the paper ripped as they tumbled into the reception room. Shouts of alarm broke out from the assembled villagers. Through eyes streaming from the *metsubishi* powder, Jack spotted Hanzo in the corner.

'Get out of here!' he screamed.

But he was too late. The other two assassins were already in the room, *ninjatō* drawn and making for Shonin and Soke.

Before Jack could do anything to save them, he was flung head over heels by the assassin pinned beneath him. He crashed to the floor, losing grip of his sword. Jack scrambled after it, but the ninja was already to his feet, bearing down on him, sword raised high, aiming to plunge the steel tip into his back.

'NO!' he heard Hanzo shout.

The ninja hesitated, and in that moment Jack rolled away. As he did so, he kicked the ninja's ankles, sweeping him to the floor. In a final bid to defend Soke, Jack snatched up his sword and confronted the other assassins.

The first ninja, flipping back to his feet, closed in from behind.

Jack was surrounded. *But why weren't Soke, Hanzo and the others escaping while they had the chance?*

Outnumbered, Jack knew this was his last stand. Blinking away the remains of the pepper powder, he withdrew his *wakizashi* and raised both swords into the Two Heavens guard.

'STOP!' commanded Soke.

Immediately, the three ninja backed away. Jack, swords still in hand, stared in astonishment at the old farmer.

'But . . . they're ninja!' he exclaimed.

Soke calmly stepped forward and laid a hand on Jack's shoulder.

'So am I.'

10

MIYUKI

Jack stared at Soke in disbelief, his blood running cold at the idea. Meanwhile Shonin, sitting on the dais, was quietly chuckling to himself, enjoying the shocked look on Jack's face.

'Put down your swords,' urged Soke. 'We're *all* ninja here.'

'But I thought you were just a farmer,' said Jack.

'I am that too.'

The realization hit Jack. The old man had been playing him like a puppet all along. Enticed by the promise of escape, he'd let himself be led straight into the heart of the ninja's domain. He was now trapped in their secret village, caught like a bug in a web. Jack tightened the grip on his swords. The ninja may have tricked him, but he wouldn't surrender without a fight.

'There's no need for that,' said Soke gently. 'You're our guest.'

'*Our guest?*' exclaimed the ninja standing behind Jack.

The girl's voice took Jack by surprise. The assassin he'd been fighting pulled off her hood. The girl was perhaps sixteen, pretty with a spiky bob of black hair. She stared indignantly at Jack with eyes as dark and deadly as the night.

'Yes, Miyuki. Our guest. So please treat him like one.'

Ignoring the request, she pointed the *ninjatō* at Jack's throat. 'He's no guest. He's a samurai!'

'He's a *tengu*!' corrected Hanzo, running to Jack's defence. 'I caught him. And he's my friend.'

Miyuki shook her head in disbelief. 'I should have guessed *you'd* be involved. Why didn't anyone tell me?'

'You were away on a mission,' explained Soke.

'Well, your *tengu's* lucky I didn't kill him,' she sneered.

'No, *you're* lucky I didn't kill *you*,' corrected Jack, the tension giving way to a warrior's pride.

Glaring at him, she took a step closer. 'The only good samurai is a dead one.'

'No, Miyuki,' interceded Shonin, holding up his hand. 'Not in this case. He's a foreigner and the Shogun's samurai are hunting him. His enemy is our enemy. That makes Jack one of us.'

Miyuki laughed coldly. Nonetheless, she relented, sheathing her *ninjatō* with more force than necessary. 'As you command, Shonin.'

'Your weapons too, Jack,' reminded Shonin. 'You're making me and my ninja very nervous.'

Jack didn't trust Shonin. He no longer trusted *anyone* in the room. Soke, Hanzo, Tenzen, they'd all been deceiving him. The idea he was their guest was laughable. The truth was he was their prisoner. And as a samurai, Jack could never allow his swords to fall into the hands of his sworn enemy. The time to escape was now . . . or never.

Jack shook his head. 'I won't surrender to you.'

'Very well,' said Shonin. 'Soke, please persuade him.'

'We're not your enemy, Jack,' insisted Soke, gripping him reassuringly on the shoulder. 'We're trying to help you.'

Jack glanced towards the door. Tenzen blocked his way, but there was still a chance he could fight his way through.

Without warning, Soke dug his thumb into Jack's neck. A bolt of pain shot through Jack's body and his legs collapsed beneath him.

Jack was unconscious before he even hit the floor.

11

Running in Circles

Hearing voices nearby, Jack cautiously opened his eyes. He was back in Soke's house, laid out upon his *futon*. Rubbing at the dull throb in his neck, Jack sat up. He found himself alone and otherwise unharmed. The old man had used some form of *Dim Mak* on him. Jack recognized the pressure-point fighting technique, having once been a victim of it courtesy of Dragon Eye. No longer would he underestimate Soke.

Jack's only thought now was of escape. He wouldn't allow himself to be held prisoner by the ninja, not if he could help it. His pack was in the corner as he'd left it, the *rutter* still safely tucked inside. But his swords were nowhere to be seen.

Silently, he moved to the *shoji* and peeked through. The hearth room was empty. Grabbing his pack, Jack slid open the door and tiptoed through to the *doma*. The voices grew louder. The ninja were right outside the entrance.

'The boy's more trouble than he's worth,' hissed a voice Jack recognized as Momochi's.

'You can't deny he's a skilled fighter.' It was Tenzen. 'I've never seen Miyuki so riled.'

'That makes him more dangerous. He's not to be trusted.'

59

'As I said,' interrupted Soke, 'I'll deal with him in the morning.'

Jack had no intention of staying until then.

He hunted the house for his swords, but they weren't anywhere. As much as it pained him and went against the samurai code, he'd be forced to leave without his weapons. It would be simply too risky to search an entire ninja village.

But he needed *something* to defend himself with. Among the farm tools he found an old knife and tucked it into his *obi*. Then he searched the *doma* for a means of escape. The single shuttered window was clearly too small; the thatch roof too compact to break through. That left the entrance door as the only exit. Then he noticed the candle in the *doma* flickering as if caught in a breeze. But the window was closed. Ducking down, Jack spotted a missing wall panel under the raised timber floor through which the breeze was entering. He crawled under the boards, pulling his pack after him.

The gap opened on to the paddy fields behind the house. He shoved his pack through, but the hole proved too small for him. Furiously, Jack dug away at the earth. He knew he didn't have much time. Someone was bound to check on him soon. With great effort, he pulled himself through. Shouldering his pack, he darted along the edge of the nearest paddy. If he could just reach the treeline, they'd have little chance of catching him.

Weaving his way up the slope, he headed for the temple. With no direct route through the terraced fields, the going was tortuously slow and he'd barely made the village boundary when he heard Hanzo shout.

'Grandfather, the *tengu*'s gone!'

Jack stumbled on to a wide path and ran for his life. His lungs burnt for oxygen as he climbed the steep valley side. Reaching the temple, Jack took one final glance back. He couldn't see any ninja following him, but that didn't mean they weren't there, hidden by the darkness.

The forest was pitch-black and Jack had to rely on all his other senses to navigate his way through. He tried to remain calm, but his panicked mind imagined ninja at every turn. Trees transformed into devilish apparitions. Shadows pursued him. Invisible assassins revealed their presence in the snap of a twig or the rustle of leaves.

But no one materialized to stop him.

After an hour, he was forced to rest. Thankfully, dawn was approaching and the sky was getting brighter. In spite of his paranoia, he hadn't seen or heard any pursuing ninja. Miraculous as it seemed, he'd escaped.

Swigging the last of the water from his gourd, Jack realized he was ill-prepared for a long journey. He'd lost his swords, possessed only a little rice, and had no idea of his location.

Guessing that Soke had taken him south from Shono into the Iga mountains, Jack judged his best chance now was to head west. Hopefully, he'd find a road leading to the town of Iga Ueno. Two years ago, Jack had visited the Tendai Temple there for the Circle of Three challenge. The monks would surely remember him and be willing to provide sanctuary. If his luck was in, Sensei Yamada and Yori might even be there by now.

With a destination in mind, Jack's resolve strengthened. He looked to the sky. It was hard to gauge east accurately with the mountains still obscuring the rising sun. But as long as he had the morning light to his back, Jack knew he would be heading in the right direction. He set off, determined to get as much distance between himself and the village as possible

But Jack soon discovered his chosen route wouldn't be easy. The rivers cutting down through the mountain range didn't allow for straight lines. Sometimes impassable gorges forced him to turn back altogether, then valleys bent his path the wrong way and, to add to the confusion, the thick forest canopy diffused the sun so it became impossible to judge his direction.

It was mid-morning when Jack spotted footprints. They were fresh.

Jack looked fearfully around at the trees and bushes. He knew the woods not only harboured ninja and samurai patrols, but mountain bandits too. In spite of his tiredness, the threat sharpened his senses and he noticed something odd about the prints. No Japanese had feet that big. It was then that Jack realized they were *his* footprints. He was going round in circles.

Cursing, Jack kicked a tree in frustration. He was well and truly lost.

He decided he'd just have to follow a river valley until he came across a well-used track, and take his chances. Half a mile down he stumbled on to just such a path. Jack almost laughed out loud with relief. Either direction looked as promising as the other, so Jack threw a forked stick into the air and left the decision to chance.

Fate sent him right.

He'd only taken a few paces when someone seized him from behind and dragged him into the undergrowth. Before he had a chance to react, Miyuki had him pinned to the ground, a knife to his throat.

'Let me go!' protested Jack.

'Be quiet!' she hissed. 'Or I'll slit your throat.'

The sound of footsteps could be heard. Miyuki pressed closer to Jack, pulling the undergrowth around them.

'I don't like it in this forest,' said a man's voice.

'Scared of ghosts?' taunted another.

Through a small gap in the bushes, Jack saw a patrol of four samurai come into view.

'Yes. There are bad spirits in these trees. Shadow warriors. People disappear.'

'There are bandits too,' piped up the smallest of the samurai, glancing around nervously.

'The sooner that *gaijin* is caught, the better. What's so special about this one, anyway?'

'The Shogun wants him. He's a samurai. Fought for the other side.'

'Don't make me laugh. A *gaijin* samurai!'

'I wouldn't laugh if I were you. He knows the Two Heavens.'

'If you believe that, then you'll believe anything!'

When the samurai had gone, Miyuki retracted her blade and let Jack go.

'Have you been following me all this time?' he demanded.

'It's not hard,' she replied. 'An elephant leaves a smaller trail than you.'

'But why save me?'

'I didn't. Soke ordered me to bring you back. Alive.'

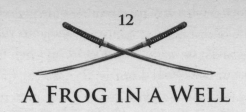

12

A Frog in a Well

'A host doesn't paralyse their guest with *Dim Mak*!' protested Jack, who once again found himself in Soke's house.

When Miyuki had first tried to escort him back to the village, he'd run. But the ninja girl moved so effortlessly through the forest, she soon caught up. They'd fought hand-to-hand, matched in skill. He'd pulled his knife, but she disarmed him with alarming speed. Jack was convinced only his fatigue allowed Miyuki to beat him. Binding his hands and hobbling his feet, she'd dragged him home like a wild dog.

'My apologies,' Soke replied, offering him some *sencha*, 'but you left me no option. *Now* we can talk sensibly.'

Jack took the tea, but didn't drink it. The ninja were masters of *dokujutsu*, the Art of Poison.

Soke poured himself some tea, returned the kettle to the pot hook and took an appreciative sip. 'Ahhh, a perfect brew! Now, as I was saying, we're your friend, not your enemy.'

'No ninja can ever be a friend of a samurai. And I feel the same,' Jack replied. 'The ninja Dragon Eye murdered my father. Yamato, who was like a brother to me, sacrificed his life because of that assassin. Ninja will *always* be my enemy.'

Soke bowed his head low, his eyes full of grief. 'I'm truly sorry for your father and dear friend, and I can understand why you must hate us. But a frog in a well does not know the great sea.'

Jack stared blankly at Soke, bewildered by the man's bizarre choice of words.

'Your understanding of the ninja is misguided. Like the frog, you're judging things from one narrow perspective, that of the samurai. All you know is what *they've* told you and from your own regrettable experience of Dragon Eye. But just as a single tree doesn't make a forest, nor does one ninja represent all *shinobi*.'

Jack gave a hollow laugh. 'Since meeting you, Soke, I've been hung from a tree, tricked into entering a ninja village, knocked unconscious and now kidnapped. My opinion of ninja has *not* changed.'

'That is one truth, but I see another,' said Soke. 'Good fortune caught you in that tree. Our meeting meant I could guide you to safety. At Shonin's house, I rescued you from yourself, avoiding unnecessary bloodshed. Finally, Miyuki prevented you being captured by the samurai patrols.'

Jack found Soke's words unexpectedly persuasive, but ninja were known for their ability to deceive. 'Why should I believe you? Unlike samurai, ninja have no code of conduct.'

'True, we do not follow the seven virtues of *bushido*. Instead we cultivate the spirit of *ninniku*. A compassionate heart, one that doesn't harbour grudges and always seeks peace and harmony. The essence of a ninja is a pure heart.'

'Yet you *still* assassinate people.'

'Occasionally the ninja are employed for such work by the samurai and their *daimyo*. But the single life of a leader can sometimes save thousands of soldiers' lives on the battlefield. Is that not better?'

'That depends upon who you kill.'

'A fair point,' agreed Soke, putting down his tea. 'And that is why assassination is not our preferred means. Our true skills lie in espionage and strategy. The information we gather allows an enemy to be defeated, not by direct combat, but by using such intelligence to undermine and weaken our enemy's position. So you see, while the samurai seek open warfare, we, the ninja, seek to avoid conflict through our actions. We only engage in combat as a last resort.'

'But you're mercenaries without honour,' argued Jack.

'That is what the samurai would have you believe. In truth, we are farmers, merely trying to survive and preserve our way of life. The Iga clans have been persecuted by the samurai for generations. Thirty years ago, that warlord Oda Nobunaga almost wiped us out. Even though our village survived, it's still a target for *daimyo* Akechi. Did you know that Hanzo's parents were murdered by samurai?'

Jack sadly shook his head.

'The ninja may be as opposite to the samurai as the moon is to the sun,' continued Soke, 'but we're not the devils you think we are. And samurai are not the saints you imagine.'

'That may be your truth,' accepted Jack, 'but it isn't mine.'

'I realize it'll take time to convince you. But tell me, Jack, who is hunting you now . . . and who is protecting you?'

They both knew the answer.

'From the beginning, I said it's a matter of trust,' Soke continued. 'I will trust *you* now by returning your swords. I know how important they are to a samurai.'

Soke retrieved the *katana* and *wakizashi* from his room and, bowing, placed them before Jack.

'I'm free to go?' queried Jack in surprise.

'By all means, leave,' Soke said, indicating Jack's pack, untouched, by the door. 'But you're clearly of great interest to the Shogun. I'd be surprised if you survive more than a day.'

Jack picked up his swords. 'It's a risk I'm willing to take.'

'You do have another choice,' said Soke as Jack headed to the door.

'And what is that?' Jack asked cautiously.

'Stay here until the samurai move their search elsewhere. You still have a long journey ahead and if you were to learn a few ninja skills, you might just reach your destination alive.'

'Me? Train as a *ninja*!'

Soke smiled. 'Only by becoming one will you truly comprehend the Way of the Ninja.'

13

TREE FIGHT

Jack walked out.

Shouldering his bag, he strode off towards the one and only road in the village. The old man was out of his mind. How could Soke suggest that *he* become a ninja? It'd be going against his father's memory to even contemplate such an idea. The *shinobi* were dishonourable assassins. Murderers.

Or were they?

Soke had put a seed of doubt in his mind. *A single tree doesn't make a forest.*

As he passed through the village, Jack was struck by how normal everything appeared. People bowed at his approach. Farmers tended their fields. Children played in the square. They looked like ordinary families, not killers.

A young girl ran up to him. 'Where are you going, *tengu?*' she asked.

Jack recognized her as the little girl who'd taken part in sword training the day before. 'Home.'

'Don't you like it here?'

'It's very peaceful,' Jack admitted, 'but I have to return to my sister.'

'What's her name?'

'Jess. She's only ten.'

'Like me!' the girl squealed. 'I'm supposed to give you this, by the way.'

She handed Jack a small orange fruit.

'What is it?'

'A *mikan*. Try it.'

Jack went to take a bite, before realizing it might be a trick.

'It's very tasty!' she insisted, producing one of her own. 'But Soke said you need to peel back the skin to discover the real fruit.'

The girl skipped off towards the square, happily devouring hers.

Jack examined his *mikan*. What was Soke up to now? The gift looked innocent enough and didn't appear to have been tampered with. Carefully removing the skin, he found a fleshy, segmented fruit inside. He tentatively popped a slice into his mouth. Its intense sweetness brought a smile to his face and Jack thought he understood Soke's message. Having had to figure out so many of Sensei Yamada's *koan*s and riddles while at the *Niten Ichi Ryū*, Jack was used to such obtuse teachings. He presumed the *mikan* was meant to represent his view of the ninja, the skin being his false impression and the edible fruit inside the truth.

Then again it could be just a piece of fruit.

But Soke had got him thinking. Maybe he was being too rash in his judgement. Perhaps the ninja *were* trying to help him, after all. The question was, why? They might share a common enemy, but there had to be another reason. And he would never know unless he stayed.

Then there were the problems of negotiating the mountains, avoiding the samurai patrols and getting past every checkpoint thereafter along the road to Nagasaki. The idea of acquiring some ninja skills was appealing. Miyuki had moved through the forest as silent as a shadow. Dragon Eye had stolen in and out of guarded castles with the ease of a ghost. The ninja were masters of the Art of Stealth. With those same skills, Jack could elude the samurai rather than have to fight them.

But it seemed disloyal to his guardian Masamoto to contemplate learning such dark arts. The swordsman had brought him up to be a true and noble samurai. The man had fought against ninja all his life. But then hadn't Akiko trained as a ninja – under the explicit instruction of Masamoto himself?

In order to know your enemy, you must become your enemy.

Perhaps this is what he should do. Jack still found it hard to justify training with the ninja. Then the Lord's Prayer came into his head . . . *Forgive us our sins, as we forgive those who sin against us.* As a Christian, he'd always been taught to forgive. But how could he forgive those responsible for his father's death?

A realization hit him. Dragon Eye hadn't been a ninja to begin with. He'd been born a samurai. Circumstance of war and a twisted poisoned mind had turned him towards the ninja. Although it was those skills that made him the terror he became, Dragon Eye's heart had *never* been pure.

If Jack was to stay true to his own samurai teachings, he

must follow the first virtue of *bushido*, Rectitude, to be fair and equal to all people. This demanded that he give the ninja a chance to prove themselves, before judging them all to be like Dragon Eye.

It wouldn't delay me greatly to stay a few days, thought Jack. *And I might learn a few things to my advantage.*

But should he decide to stay, he'd have to be on his guard at all times.

Lost in thought, Jack found himself wandering beside the edge of the pond. As he neared a large maple tree, he heard Hanzo shouting.

'*Tengu!* Up here!'

Jack saw the boy hanging from a branch high above the water.

'What are you doing?'

'Training,' he replied, as if it was the most obvious thing in the world.

'For what?'

'Holding on. You need to be strong to climb walls. Sometimes you might have to hold on for hours before you can escape. I bet you can't hang on as long as I can!'

Jack smiled. There was something compelling about the boy's enthusiasm, and also something very familiar. Hanzo reminded him a little of his good friend Yori. Deciding he'd had enough of thinking, Jack put down his swords and pack, and climbed the tree. Shimmying along the branch, Jack dropped down beside Hanzo and clung on with his fingers.

'So how long do we do this?'

Hanzo grinned. 'Until one of us falls in.'

As they both dangled over the pond, Miyuki appeared.

'You've decided to hang around then?' she smirked.

'For a little while,' Jack replied. 'Thanks for saving me this morning.'

'Don't thank me. I was under orders. I'd have left you to your fate.'

'No, you wouldn't,' said Hanzo, shocked. 'Shonin said Jack's one of us.'

'He's *not* a ninja,' replied Miyuki dismissively. 'A samurai doesn't have the skill or pureness of heart to be a *real* ninja.'

'Of course he does. Jack's King of the *Tengu*!'

'Is that right?' she mocked.

'Apparently,' Jack replied, swinging nonchalantly from the branch, his old skills of hanging from the yardarm as a rigging monkey quickly coming back.

Miyuki glared up at him. 'You think what you're doing now makes you a ninja? That's kids' training.'

Still smarting from his defeat at hand-to-hand combat, Jack felt compelled to challenge Miyuki. 'You're just scared I could beat you.'

'No!' she shot back. 'Samurai always think they're so superior.'

Miyuki leapt cat-like into the tree and climbed on to the branch next to Jack's. She positioned herself opposite him.

'You think this is easy. The real test is whether you could do this under the pressure of battle.'

'Why would I be hanging from a tree in the middle of a fight?' asked Jack.

Miyuki rolled her eyes in irritation. 'It could be a castle wall or a rock face. Whatever, you wouldn't last a minute.'

Jack thought of Yamato clinging to the balcony in Osaka,

while he'd been desperately holding on to the rope from which Akiko dangled. He'd been faced with an impossible choice, but he hadn't let go. 'What makes you so certain of that?'

Miyuki lifted her leg and kicked Jack in the stomach.

Taken by surprise, he couldn't avoid the attack. The foot connected and a blast of pain rocketed through his midriff. Absorbing the impact, he somehow managed to cling on to the branch with his fingertips. Miyuki tried again, this time roundhouse-kicking him in the thigh. But Jack had regained his hold and was ready for her. He raised his knee, blocking the attack, then swung both his feet at Miyuki.

She let go with one arm and swayed out of the way. Using her free hand, she reached over and hammered Jack's knuckles with her fist. Jack was forced to release his grip, grabbing further down the branch. It began to bend under his weight.

Meanwhile, Hanzo was laughing in delight at the acrobatic tree fight.

Miyuki swung herself across to another bough to get a better angle of attack on Jack. The two of them fought in mid-air, each trying to gain the advantage.

Scissor-kicking him, Miyuki wrapped her legs round Jack's waist. She tugged on his body, trying to dislodge him. Jack struggled to keep hold, his strength now rapidly fading. As a last-ditch effort, he released one hand and grabbed for Miyuki's wrist. He yanked her grip loose at the same time as she pulled him from his branch. They both tumbled through the air, entangled in one another's grasp, and fell into the water.

Jack came up gasping, Miyuki beside him. She stared daggers at Jack.

Hanzo dropped from the tree on to the bank. 'I win!' he shouted with glee.

Miyuki ignored the jubilant Hanzo.

'You should leave, *samurai*,' she seethed. 'Before you really get hurt.'

'You've just convinced me to stay,' Jack replied, smiling amiably. 'You make a fine sparring partner.'

'Great!' said Hanzo, oblivious to Miyuki's horrified reaction. 'You can train with us every day.'

Dragging herself out of the water, Miyuki fixed Jack with an icy glare.

'I'll be watching you,' she said. 'I don't trust samurai.'

And I don't trust ninja, thought Jack.

14

GRANDMASTER

'Back so soon,' observed Soke as Jack, dripping wet, entered the yard with Hanzo.

Jack could see that the old man had been expecting him. Three bowls of rice and a pot of tea were set out upon the bench in the yard.

'Hanzo persuaded me to hang around,' Jack replied, putting his pack inside the *doma*.

Soke nodded. 'He's a fruit that won't ever fall. It's no wonder you lost.'

'I was actually shaken from the tree,' Jack admitted. 'By Miyuki.'

'Why am I not surprised?' laughed Soke, indicating for Jack to join him on the bench. 'She has a wild spirit, that one.'

Soke handed Jack a bowl of rice, and all three tucked into their dinner as the evening sun slowly dropped behind the mountains.

'Can Jack train with me tomorrow?' asked Hanzo eagerly.

'That depends upon whether the Grandmaster will allow it,' Soke replied.

'The Grandmaster?' said Jack.

'Yes, he's the protector and overseer of our school of *ninjutsu*. The Grandmaster holds the key to the eighteen disciplines of our martial art.'

'*Eighteen!*'

'Yes. A ninja must learn them all. Hand-to-hand combat. Weapon skills like the *shuriken*, *shuko* and *kusarigama*. Evasion techniques of disguise, concealment and stealth-walking. The mystical arts of explosives, poisons, mind control and *kuji-in* magic. *Ninjutsu* is about becoming a total warrior, one who is independent, invincible and – most importantly – invisible.'

'So the Grandmaster is the teacher of all this?'

'Yes, but there is only ever one Grandmaster at a time,' explained Soke, finishing his rice. 'He carries all the knowledge with him. He alone possesses the *densho*, the scrolls that contain the secrets of our art.'

'But what happens when he dies?' asked Jack.

'It's the Grandmaster's duty to ensure the knowledge is passed on from generation to generation. Tradition dictates that he'll have chosen a student and trained that person in preparation for the role. Upon his death, the pupil will inherit the scrolls and become the next Grandmaster.'

'That's some responsibility,' observed Jack.

'Yes, it is,' Soke agreed. 'And only the Grandmaster has the authority to change the techniques or traditions of our art. Only he can decide if you, Jack, a foreigner and a samurai, should be permitted to learn our secrets.'

Jack stopped eating. He'd become excited at the prospect of learning such extraordinary skills. He'd never imagined there was so much to being a ninja. And since leaving the *Niten Ichi Ryū*, he missed the challenge and thrill of training. But now Soke had raised doubt as to whether he would be taught at all.

'When do I get to meet this Grandmaster?' asked Jack tentatively.

Soke smiled at him. 'You already have.' He raised his cup to Jack. 'Pour me some tea, will you?'

Jack stared dumbfounded at the old man.

'Soke is my title; it means Grandmaster.'

Jack knew he shouldn't be so shocked. His Zen teacher, Sensei Yamada, had been ancient, yet still a deadly force to be reckoned with. Soke was no different. To master the eighteen disciplines of *ninjutsu* would undoubtedly take a lifetime. Jack picked up the pot and filled Soke's cup with a trembling hand.

Straight away, Soke poured the tea on to the ground.

'Is something wrong?' asked Jack, concerned he'd offended the Grandmaster.

'The usefulness of a cup is its emptiness. If you are to train as a ninja, you must forget *everything* you've learnt as a samurai.'

15

THE FIVE RINGS

'Are you ready for your first lesson?' asked Soke.

'Now?' said Jack, both eager and apprehensive at the idea.

'Time flies like the wind. You must catch it while you can.'

Picking up his walking stick, Soke stood and beckoned Jack to follow him. Hanzo remained behind to clear up. The summer evening was warm and pleasant, the sun shimmering off the mountain peaks in a halo of golden light. Soke led Jack through the paddy fields to a small rise overlooking the village.

'In order to understand *ninjutsu*, you must first understand the Five Rings,' Soke began, using his cane to draw five interlocking circles on the ground. 'These are the five great elements of our universe – Earth, Water, Fire, Wind and Sky.'

With the tip of his stick, Soke wrote the *kanji* symbols for each element into each one of the circles.

地　　水　　火　　風　　空
Earth　*Water*　*Fire*　*Wind*　*Sky*

'The Five Rings form the basis of our approach to life. As ninja, we recognize the power of nature and seek to be in harmony with it. Each of the Rings represents different physical and emotional states:

'Earth stands for stability and confidence.

'Water is adaptability.

'Fire is energy and commitment of spirit.

'Wind is freedom, both of mind and body.

'Sky is the Void, the things beyond our everyday existence, the unseen power and creative energy of the universe.'

Jack listened intently, nodding, trying to appear as if he understood what the old man was talking about.

Soke smiled, chuckling to himself. 'I can read your mind as clearly as a reflection in a pond. Let me show you the Five Rings in action.'

Soke swept his hand around the valley.

'The Five Rings are in everything we do. They're the inspiration for a ninja's techniques and tactics. See how the village is laid out. We've applied the principles of the Ring of Earth here.'

Jack looked, but all he saw was an ordinary farming village. 'Where?' he asked.

'A ninja without observation is like a bird without wings,' Soke chided. 'Look harder. If you were to attack our village, what problems would you face?'

Jack studied the lie of the land through an invader's eyes. 'You're in a steep valley,' he began. 'That makes it much harder to launch a mass attack.'

'Good,' said Soke. 'What else?'

'There's only one road in and out. Otherwise there are just lots of paths in between the rice fields.'

'Yes, and notice the paths are very narrow . . .'

'So that only one person can pass at a time?' hazarded Jack.

'Exactly!' said Soke, striking his stick upon the ground with satisfaction. 'Everything has been designed to make the village as difficult as possible to penetrate with an army. The Shonin's farmhouse is in the middle of our rice fields, which are a maze in themselves, and when flooded act as a massive moat. We've created natural defences both to his quarters and the square by raising them upon an earthen bank. The bamboo fence and thorn hedge form another barrier. So you can see we've exploited the surroundings and environment to our advantage. That's one way a ninja can use the Ring of Earth.'

Jack gazed in astonishment as the scene before his eyes transformed from an innocent-looking village into a disguised fortress.

'Follow me,' said Soke, heading in the direction of a small stream. 'The Ring of Water gives rise to an entire discipline of *ninjutsu*, known as *sui-ren*. Water training. Not only must a ninja be able to swim, but he must learn to use water as a weapon, as a way of escape and a means of survival. You'll encounter these techniques in due course. But first you need to understand the Ring of Water's key principle.'

He pointed to a log on the ground. 'Place that across the stream.'

Jack lifted the log into position until it blocked the channel.

'What's that done?' said Soke.

'It's stopped the stream.'

'Are you so sure?' he challenged.

They watched as the water backed up against the log. Then it ran around the ends and spilt over the top.

'What does that teach you?' asked Soke.

Jack thought for a moment. 'I need a bigger log.'

Soke shook his head. 'That's samurai thinking. If something doesn't work, more power, more men, bigger swords. But however large you build that dam, water adapts and will always find a way.'

He pointed to a leaf that floated down the stream, around the log and into the pond. 'What I've demonstrated is the principle of *nagare* – flow. From now on, apply this to your thinking. If something doesn't work, change your strategy. Use it in your *taijutsu*. When an opponent blocks or resists a technique, simply flow into another. Follow *nagare* and eventually you'll catch your opponent out.'

Soke indicated for Jack to pull the log from the stream.

'Like a river flowing down a mountain, whenever you encounter an obstacle, move round it, adapt and continue on.'

Now Soke led Jack into the village square and over to a building that resounded with the rhythmic clang of hammer on metal. Here, Soke introduced Jack to the bladesmith Kajiya. He passed Soke a newly forged *ninjatō* for inspection. The blade glinted in the light of the blazing furnace.

'I'm aware the samurai consider the sword to be their soul,' said Soke, glancing at the *katana* and *wakizashi* on Jack's hip. 'But for a ninja, it's just another tool, a means to an end.'

He returned the sword to Kajiya with an appreciative nod. Then both he and Jack watched as the bladesmith fanned his furnace to an intense heat, removed a glowing orange blade and resumed his hammering.

'Fire is energetic, forceful and fast-moving,' explained Soke. 'Our weapon techniques are closely associated with the Ring of Fire. But this element also influences other areas of *ninjutsu*, in particular the discipline of *kajutsu* – the Art of Fire. This can be as subtle as spreading a rumour. Or –'

BANG!

Jack dived to the floor as the ground exploded in front of him and a cloud of smoke rose into the air. Rolling to his feet, he drew his sword. He didn't know whether they were being attacked, or if the furnace had exploded.

Then he heard the two men laughing.

'Did you *see* him jump?' chortled Kajiya, tears of laughter streaming down his face.

As the smoke dispersed, Jack noticed the remains of a small container of gunpowder lying on the ground.

'Very funny,' said Jack, grinning along with the joke as he resheathed his sword.

'Kajiya likes to prove a point,' said Soke, patting the bladesmith on the shoulder. 'As I was saying, *kajutsu* can also be as blatant as an explosion. A ninja must learn to use gunpowder and fire for destruction, for diversion and if necessary for dealing death. But the Ring of Fire shouldn't be considered an aggressive element. Its essence is motivation.'

Soke pointed to the hilltops. 'Up there, we have hidden woodpiles. On the approach of an enemy, they're lit by lookouts and these smoke beacons give the village advance warning of an attack.'

Bowing their respects, they left Kajiya to his work. Soke now guided Jack up the path towards the Buddhist temple. The sun had disappeared behind the mountains and dusk was fast approaching. Halfway up, they stopped beside a small Shinto shrine surrounded by wild flowers.

'I'm curious to know,' said Soke, 'what you consider your best sword technique to be.'

'I suppose in terms of speed, *kesagiri*, a double diagonal cut.'

'Show me,' said Soke. 'I'll be your target.'

Jack gave the Grandmaster an uncertain look as the old man positioned himself in front of him. 'I don't want to hurt you . . .'

Soke smiled. 'Don't worry about me. I need to see your skill up close.'

'Well, don't say I didn't warn you,' replied Jack, preparing to attack. In a flash, he drew his *katana* and sliced through the air, cutting up through Soke's waist and then down diagonally across his chest.

Both times, Soke moved out of the way.

'Impressive,' he said, nodding approvingly. 'How about your best kick?'

Jack sheathed his sword, then launched himself into a flying front kick.

Soke waited until the last second before moving aside.

'Good. And your best punch?'

Jack turned round, flicking out his arm and delivering a spinning backfist to the head. Soke ducked beneath.

'You're very fast,' he acknowledged. 'Now, how about –'

'Why not show me *your* best move?' said Jack, breathless from the unexpected exertion.

'I already have,' replied Soke. 'The best move is simply not to be there.'

'This is the Ring of Wind, isn't it?'

'Now you're learning!' said Soke. 'The Ring of Wind embodies the spirit of *ninjutsu*. Evasion is far better than engagement. Silent walking, escape running and shallow breathing to feign death, all derive from this element. See how the leaves in the trees above us move.'

Jack's eyes were drawn to the sway of the branches. Only now was he aware of an evening breeze rising up from the valley.

'Wind can be light or tear a house apart,' explained Soke. He bent down to pick a dandelion from beside the shrine. 'The Ring of Wind teaches us to be open-minded. To respond to any situation and be ready for any attack as it occurs. In other words, to go where the wind blows.'

Holding up the dandelion, Soke blew at its snow-white head and the seeds drifted away on the breeze.

'A ninja's presence should be like the wind – always felt but never seen.'

By the time they reached the temple, night had fallen and the stars shone bright in the heavens. Jack could hardly make out Soke's face in the darkness.

'This is one of the few places along the ridge from which you can see our village,' said Soke, pointing to the distant glow of Kajiya's furnace.

At the entrance to the temple, Soke lit a stick of incense

and bowed before an effigy of the Buddha. Jack did the same. Though he was Christian, he'd come to respect the teachings of Buddhism. But he also followed the rituals so as not to draw attention to himself. Sensei Yamada had advised that the more he appeared a Buddhist, the more likely people would be willing to help him on his journey.

'We've nearly reached the end of your lesson,' said Soke. 'Only the Ring of Sky remains. This is the most powerful of the elements. And the hardest to obtain. As I've explained the Sky is the Void, the unseen power of the universe.'

'If you can't see it, how do you know it's there?' asked Jack.

Soke looked up. 'Tell me, is the sky empty?'

'No, it's full of stars.'

'Likewise, the Ring of Sky isn't empty either. And though you cannot see the stars during the day, they're still there. The Ring of Sky is the basis for *mikkyō*, our secret teachings – meditation, mind control and *kuji-in* magic.'

'Magic?' questioned Jack.

'Yes. The ninja's spiritual origins lie in Shugendo, an ancient religion that teaches us to connect with nature and harness its power. A ninja trained in these arts can invoke *ki*, the spiritual energy of the void, and bend it to his will.'

Having experienced the power of *ki*, when Sensei Yamada once knocked him off his feet solely using the secret art of *kiaijutsu*, Jack could well believe the ninja were capable of magic.

'The Ring of Sky also symbolizes the ideal of a clear mind. A ninja attuned to this element can sense his surroundings and act without thinking – without using his *physical* senses.'

'You mean like *mushin*?' said Jack, who'd been taught the concept of 'no mind' by his swordmaster Sensei Hosokawa.

'Good, you're beginning to understand,' replied Soke. 'From now on, everything around you – even the mountains, rivers, plants and animals – should be your teacher.'

Soke had all but disappeared into the darkness. Only his voice remained.

'Master the Five Rings – learn to endure like the Earth, to flow like Water, to strike like Fire, to run like the Wind and be all-seeing like the Sky. Then, young samurai, you'll be a ninja.'

THE ART OF STEALTH

'Come on!' insisted Hanzo. 'We don't want to be the last.'
Jack finished fastening the ties of his trousers round his knees
and slipped on his long *tabi* boots. Over a shirt with close-
fitting arms, he'd donned a jacket and secured it with an
obi. He left the face-scarf and hood on the bed as they
weren't required for training sessions.

Standing up, Jack took a look at himself. He never imagined that one day he'd wear the *shinobi shozoku* of the ninja.
It sent a chill through him as if the ghost of Dragon Eye
had possessed him. Jack prayed his father up in Heaven
would forgive him and also that Masamoto would *never*
find out.

In this instance, each piece of *shinobi* clothing was dyed
the same dark green. *To blend in better with the fores*t, Soke
had told him.

Folding his own clothes and putting them next to his
pack, Jack remembered the *rutter* inside. He wasn't happy
about leaving it so vulnerable, but he didn't really have a
choice. His only reassurance was that Soke had shown no
interest in his belongings. Jack felt sure the Grandmaster

didn't know anything about the *rutter* and he wanted to keep it that way. With little alternative, Jack stuffed his clothes on top. They would prevent a casual observer from finding it, but certainly wouldn't stop a determined thief.

'Let's go!' said Hanzo, pulling on Jack's arm.

They hurried down the main road and out of the village. Hanzo scampered ahead along a narrow track that twisted through some woods towards the bottom of the valley. It was barely dawn, the birds just beginning their morning chorus. Wiping the sleep from his eyes, Jack caught up with Hanzo in a small hidden glade where a brook lazily wound its way through the trees.

Soke was already waiting for them. He welcomed Jack with a bow. 'I trust it's not too early for you.'

'Not at all,' replied Jack, bowing and yawning at the same time.

'Dawn and dusk are the times to see and not be seen. Perfect conditions for training and missions.' Soke glanced over Jack's shoulder. 'Good, now that we're all here, we can begin.'

Jack looked around, but apart from Hanzo, the glade was deserted. Having been used to formal classes at the *Niten Ichi Ryū*, he was somewhat surprised there were no other students.

Soke smiled ruefully. 'Today's lesson will focus on the Art of Stealth, perhaps the most crucial set of skills you need to master.'

All of a sudden, a rock unfolded into Tenzen. A boy emerged from a clump of bushes. Two *shinobi* appeared from behind trees. Materializing out of the grass, more ninja students revealed themselves. Jack almost jumped out of his skin when Miyuki dropped down beside him, silent as a ghost.

'Easily spooked, aren't you?' she said.

Regaining his composure, Jack smiled amiably. 'I certainly won't be playing hide-and-seek with you!'

'They were practising *gotonpo*, the Art of Concealment,' explained Soke. 'Since *ninjutsu* is primarily about evasion and escape, the best way to achieve this is not to be seen in the first place.'

Soke indicated for Tenzen to return to the edge of the clearing.

'By applying the Ring of Earth, a ninja blends with the environment. See how Tenzen becomes one with the tree and disappears.'

Even though Jack knew where Tenzen was, he could hardly make him out. The ninja merely looked like a bulge in the trunk.

'Or if there's no immediate coverage,' Soke continued, 'you must break up your body's outline. A human form is too easily recognizable. So learn to lose your shape. Watch Tenzen become a rock.'

Emerging from behind the tree, Tenzen squatted down into a ball, folding his arms round his body, and became perfectly still. In the shadowy light of dawn, Jack wouldn't have given Tenzen a second glance.

'Now you try it,' instructed Soke.

Jack went over and crouched beside Tenzen. Adopting the same posture, he tried not to move. After a few moments, he heard sniggering from one of the students. Jack looked up. It was the boy who'd hidden behind the bushes. He was about Jack's age, skinny with close-cropped hair, pencil-thin lips and tight, mean eyes.

'He can't do it!' jeered the boy. 'He looks like a big white *daikon* radish in the dirt!'

'You've made your point, Shiro,' stated Soke, giving the boy a stern look. 'Jack, your blond hair does give you away. You need to cover it in future. Also, never look directly at your enemy during concealment. Otherwise their instinct will sense your presence.'

Jack nodded, all of a sudden self-conscious about his appearance. Maybe he was more suited to being a samurai than a ninja. Soke beckoned him and Tenzen to rejoin the group.

'It's possible to hide anywhere – behind walls, beneath bushes, inside water barrels, below floors and even in plain sight. Have I told you of the time I was caught out in an open field, a troop of samurai in hot pursuit?'

'How did you escape?' asked Hanzo on cue.

'I pretended to be a scarecrow, of course!'

The students all laughed and Jack realized it was a well-told story. 'Samurai are so stupid,' he heard Miyuki mutter. As much as Jack wanted to defend their honour, he thought it prudent to keep his silence among the ninja. But it occurred to him that Miyuki fostered a surprisingly deep hatred of the samurai.

'Yet the best place to hide, as you know, Jack,' continued Soke, 'is above – in a tree or on a roof. People seldom look up.'

Soke now addressed the whole class.

'But we can't hide all night. So a ninja must learn *shinobi aruki* – stealth-walking. Miyuki, please demonstrate.'

Miyuki sank low and began to cross the glade in short, prowling steps. She made no sound at all, even as she passed through the long grass.

'Notice how Miyuki keeps her foot pointed, placing her toes down first. That way she can feel for any obstacles. Her weight then gradually shifts on to her toes, thereby ensuring she makes no noise. Lastly, she lowers herself on to the side of her foot, until the heel touches the ground and she's ready to take the next step.'

Miyuki entered the stream and Jack was amazed. She barely made a ripple.

'When dealing with water crossings,' Soke explained, 'not only must your foot enter straight like a spear, but remember not to drag the back one. Lift it high and clear before placing it. Now I want you all to practise this. Find a partner and try to steal up on them without being detected.'

The ninja paired up, very obviously avoiding Jack. He got the impression he wasn't exactly welcome among their ranks. Once again, he was in the position of having to prove his worth, just as he'd had to as a *gaijin* samurai at the *Niten Ichi Ryū*.

'Do you want to train with me?' suggested Hanzo.

'That would be good,' said Jack.

'I'll go first. You wait on the other side of the stream.'

Hanzo ran off to the edge of the glade and waited for Jack to take up position. Turning round, Jack listened intently for the boy's approach. He didn't expect Hanzo to get very far. Sensei Kano had taught Jack how to hear sound shadows. But there was no reason to tell Hanzo about that skill. Not yet, anyway.

The glade was quiet, the stream too lazy to make much noise. This would be easy. 'Ready when you are,' Jack called out.

'Your turn!' Hanzo replied, his grinning face right next to him.

For the second time that morning, Jack almost jumped out of his skin. How on earth had Hanzo crept up on him like that? For a brief moment, he thought the boy had cheated. But Hanzo's trouser legs were clearly wet.

Shaking his head in disbelief, Jack crossed the brook for his attempt. Sinking into a low back stance just as Miyuki had done, Jack lifted his front foot and took a step. His toes touched the ground, but as the rest of his foot made contact there was a sharp snap of a twig.

'Heard you!' said Hanzo. 'Try again.'

Miyuki gave Jack a sorry shake of the head.

'You need to feel with your toes first,' observed Soke. 'Then transfer your weight little by little. That way you can stop if you begin to make a sound.'

Jack warily tested the ground ahead. He edged slowly across the glade, the other ninja passing in silent speed. Halfway across, his leg muscles began to ache. He wasn't used to such painstaking movement. As he entered the long grass, Jack lost his balance and his lead leg brushed against the seed heads.

'Heard you!' cried Hanzo. 'Last chance.'

Jack now felt the pressure. Everyone else was watching him. Concentrating on each foot placement, Jack somehow managed to reach the stream without further mishap. But as soon as he stepped into the water, he made a loud splash.

'Heard you *again!*' said Hanzo, turning round. 'You're not very good for a *tengu*, are you?'

'*Tengu* are better at flying,' Jack retorted, much to the amusement of the others.

'It wasn't bad for a first attempt,' said Soke. '*Shinobi aruki* takes time to master. Practise your stealth-walking in the paddy fields every day until you can cross them without making a single ripple.'

Soke now summoned all the students into a circle.

'However refined your stealth techniques are, sometimes you'll be discovered. Other times you may need to deliver information quickly. In those instances, escape running is essential. This is where we combine the Ring of Wind and the Ring of Water. Not only must you run fast, but you have to avoid and overcome obstacles. So I'm going to split you into teams of three and set you a challenge.'

Soke put Jack in a group with Tenzen and Miyuki, much to her annoyance.

'The first team to get back to the village is the winner,' declared Soke. 'But you cannot use the road. For the purpose of this exercise, it's patrolled by samurai. That means your route must be through the forest. You'll encounter a number of barriers on the way. Use teamwork and jumping skills to get past these.'

The students readied themselves.

'You'd better fly fast, *tengu*,' cried Hanzo. 'We're going to beat you!'

'Big talk for a small boy,' shot back Tenzen on his team's behalf.

Miyuki turned to Jack and whispered, 'I hope you run better than you walk. I don't like losing.'

'Neither do I,' replied Jack, her comment rousing his samurai spirit.

Miyuki scowled at him, but had no opportunity to reply.

'You've been discovered,' announced Soke. '*Escape!*'

17

DRAGON BREATHING

The ninja students charged out of the glade.

Jack was soon left behind by Tenzen and Miyuki. They flew through the forest, bounding over logs and weaving between trees like young deer. Jack was fit, but not as amazingly agile as these ninja. He had to clamber over a fallen tree his two partners had jumped in a single leap. The dense undergrowth clawed at his clothes, while Tenzen and Miyuki appeared to glide through unscathed.

'Keep up, samurai!' demanded Miyuki.

Jack, his heart pounding in his chest, raced after them. He sensed a couple of the teams were trailing behind them, but he needed to prove he was as good as the best of the ninja. Putting on a burst of speed, he pursued his receding team members.

'Ditch!' warned Tenzen.

Jack jumped, only seeing it at the last second.

But he didn't leap far enough. His foot missed the far side, he slipped and tumbled to the ground. Thankfully, his *taijutsu* training kicked in. Throwing out an arm to protect himself, Jack rolled to his feet in one fluid motion.

He was up and running before he'd even registered the fall.

Glancing back, Tenzen gave Jack an approving nod at his *ukemi* skills.

The next obstacle they encountered was the valley's river. Too wide for them to leap across unaided, the ninja were using long staves and vaulting it. Miyuki was already on the other side.

'Come on!' she called, tossing Jack a pole.

Jack hesitated. He'd never done this before.

'I'll show you,' said Tenzen.

Taking the pole, he ran at the river. As he reached the bank, Tenzen buried the tip of the stave into the middle of the waterway and leapt high into the air. He flew up and over, vaulting to the opposite side where he landed lightly upon his feet.

'Your turn!' he said, throwing the pole back.

Plucking up his courage, Jack gripped the wooden stave and lifted it off the ground. He charged towards the river, driving the pole into the water. But he hadn't counted on the pull of the current. As he buried the tip into the river-bed, the pole was yanked off-line. Too late to correct his mistake, he launched himself and hoped for the best.

Jack soared into the air, then lost all momentum.

For a moment, he hung suspended over the river. Then, like a felled tree, he slowly toppled sideways into the water with a loud splash. Jack came up gasping and swam hard for the opposite bank. Miyuki didn't bother waiting for him.

'You'll never cross a moat like that,' said Tenzen, dragging him out of the river. 'Next time, throw your body weight forward as you jump.'

Bedraggled, Jack clambered to his feet as Tenzen ran on.

Jack eventually caught up with them both at a small rock face. It was the perfect natural barrier for the village further up the valley. *The Ring of Earth in action*, thought Jack.

One of the teams was already at the top, Hanzo waving at him.

'Fly, *tengu*, fly!'

Jack couldn't believe it. The boy wasn't only an expert at stealth-walking, he was fast too. Then Hanzo disappeared with his team.

The other ninja groups were at various stages in the climb. Miyuki was halfway up, Tenzen not far behind. Jack realized this was his chance to prove himself. All his years as a rigging monkey would pay off once again. Throwing himself at the rock face, Jack clambered hand over hand with practised ease. He soon levelled with Tenzen and then, to Miyuki's utter astonishment, passed her too.

At the top, Jack turned round and waited, taking the opportunity to catch his breath.

'Gruelling, isn't it?' commented Shiro, the boy who'd laughed at Jack's earlier attempt to conceal himself. He was waiting for the last of his team to join him. 'Soke does this *every* glade lesson. I don't know why we can't just walk back for once.'

'That wouldn't be any fun!' said Kobei, clambering over the lip.

Shiro rolled his eyes at the boy, then ran on.

Noticing Miyuki haul herself up the last few metres, Jack

offered his hand. But she ignored the gesture. Tenzen, however, clasped Jack's outstretched arm and pulled himself alongside.

'There's ninja blood in you!' he said, grinning. 'I've never seen anyone climb that fast.'

'Let's go!' interrupted Miyuki. 'We've still two teams ahead of us.'

Running on, they emerged from the woods and out on to open grassland. The village was now in sight at the top of a long slope. Jack could see the other teams not far ahead. Tenzen and Miyuki broke into a sprint, determined to catch them. Jack did his best to keep up, but he soon lagged behind. He simply couldn't maintain the ninja's pace. For every step he took, they seemed to take two.

Miyuki forged on. But Tenzen, noticing Jack struggle, dropped back.

'Try Dragon Breathing,' he suggested.

'What's that?' gasped Jack.

'It's a secret cyclic breathing pattern. Follow my rhythm. *Inhale – exhale – exhale – inhale – exhale – inhale – inhale – exhale*. Repeat.'

Jack copied Tenzen. It took him a few tries, but as soon as he got the hang of it, the running immediately became easier. More air reached his lungs and the process focused his mind. Now he seemed to fly up the slope. The Way of the Ninja certainly contained some surprisingly effective techniques.

They passed Shiro's team and powered on to the village, neck-and-neck with Hanzo's group. But there was still one more obstacle to go – a high boundary hedge. Miyuki was beside it, ready to boost them over.

'Come on, Jack!' she cried encouragingly.

With victory in sight, Miyuki had apparently put aside her malice towards him.

If we win this, Jack thought, *I may just win her over too.*

Jack sprinted up to Miyuki, put his foot in her hands and she threw him high into the air. Only as he passed over the top, did he register the devious grin on Miyuki's face.

But by then it was too late.

18

BLOWING ZEN

'Always look before you leap!' said Miyuki, peering over the hedge with an expression of utmost innocence.

Unable to stop his descent, Jack had landed face first in the village manure heap. As he floundered in the rotting compost, he heard the arriving ninja teams burst into laughter. Jack was fuming – though more with himself at trusting a ninja like Miyuki. Now he was a laughing stock.

Tenzen nimbly jumped over the hedge, suppressing a grin as Jack wiped dung from his eyes.

'Every new ninja falls for that old trick,' he said, offering Jack a helping hand

Jack swallowed back his pride. He couldn't allow Miyuki to think she'd got under his skin.

'An old and rather *dirty* trick!' he replied, to which Tenzen laughed good-naturedly.

'Think yourself lucky,' shouted Miyuki, her face creased with amusement. 'I was going to put thorns in, just to make a point!'

'I don't think Miyuki likes me very much,' commented Jack through gritted teeth.

'It's not you,' replied Tenzen under his breath. 'She just doesn't like samurai. Being born in the winter, she was named "Beautiful Snow". But sometimes Miyuki can be as cold as her name. She'll thaw given time.'

'I hope so,' replied Jack, taking a look at his manure-covered clothes with disgust.

'Miyuki taught you a good lesson. Another time it could be a pit, a moat or even some samurai's spear. You'll never make that mistake again.'

Jack had to agree. He'd also be far more wary of Miyuki in future. Flashing her a breezy smile to show he could take a joke, he headed back to the river to wash himself down, while the other students returned to their homes for the day's chores.

Despite immersing himself several times, Jack still couldn't shift the acrid tang of manure from his hair. He reckoned it would be a day or so before that faded, though the embarrassment of the prank would linger on far longer. He'd already heard Miyuki nicknaming him 'the Smelly Samurai'. Not that the name-calling bothered him that much. He'd suffered far worse at the *Niten Ichi Ryū*. His class rival Kazuki, along with his Scorpion Gang, had taken particular pleasure in persecuting him for being a foreigner. But at the samurai school Jack had had his friends to turn to. Here, among the ninja, he was alone.

As he made his way back to Soke's house, Jack heard a haunting, soulful sound drift through the air. His curiosity roused, Jack followed its plaintive song across the open grassland and into the trees that bordered the valley's mountains. Reaching a steep slope, he found a narrow pathway winding up the valley side towards the sound's source.

Jack climbed, rising above the treeline, until he arrived at a cave that looked out over the valley in the direction of the village. Inside he found Soke, cross-legged before a Shinto shrine, playing a long bamboo flute. A slow languid melody rose and fell in time with his breathing, echoing off the walls to create a never-ending waterfall of sound. The old man's eyes were closed and he appeared lost in meditation.

Jack sat down at the cave's entrance and waited patiently for Soke to finish. He studied the old man, his wrinkled timeworn features at odds with his role as a deadly ninja Grandmaster. Yet again Jack wondered why Soke was so committed to helping him.

The Grandmaster put down his flute. 'This shrine is in honour of our mountain god, Yama-no-kami,' he explained, as if he'd been expecting Jack. 'I play to appease him.'

'Your god should be very happy then,' replied Jack. 'It sounded like an angel singing.'

'I appreciate your compliment, but there are far better players than me,' said Soke, humbly bowing his head. He held up his flute. 'This is a *shakuhachi*,' he explained. '*Komusō*, the Monks of Emptiness, use it as a spiritual tool to attain enlightenment. Have you practised meditation before?'

Jack nodded. 'Sensei Yamada taught us *zazen*.'

'Well, this is the art of blowing Zen. Instead of sitting and contemplating a *koan* riddle, you focus on the playing of a song.'

Soke reached behind and produced a second instrument. 'You look like you'd benefit from some *suizen*.'

Passing Jack the flute, he taught him to hold it vertically like a recorder. Then he showed Jack how to position his fingers over the five pitch holes.

'You blow across the top of the flute like this,' he instructed, placing his lips at right angles to one end of the bamboo. A clear note sang out. 'By changing the angle, you can also change the sound.'

Jack wet his lips, placed them against the flute and exhaled. The instrument squealed like a strangled bird.

'Don't blow so hard,' said Soke, suppressing a grin. 'Gently, as if trying to move a feather.'

Taking another breath, Jack tried again. This time the flute gave out an unsteady but tuneful note.

'Good. I'll teach you a basic *honkyoku*. This song is called "*Hifumi hachi gaeshi*". It's a favourite of the *komusō*. They play it when begging for alms.'

Settling himself into a comfortable position upon the cave floor, Soke began a simple beseeching melody. Having performed the whole song, he then repeated the opening phrase several times, showing Jack the finger positions of each note.

'Now you try.'

Jack made a faltering attempt, but soon ran out of breath.

'Focus on breathing from the belly, not the chest,' advised Soke, 'just as in normal meditation. The melody should flow as effortlessly as the air from your lips.'

Jack spent the remainder of the morning practising the introduction to the song. As he played the tune over and over, his breathing extended and became more natural. He began to float with the melody. By the end, his mind was as calm and still as the midsummer day.

'You've made excellent progress,' Soke commended. 'I'll teach you the whole piece over the next few days.'

'Thank you,' replied Jack. 'But what does this have to do with *ninjutsu*?'

Soke raised his eyebrows, as if to say *You tell me*.

Jack thought for a moment. 'The Ring of Wind?'

Soke smiled. 'Exactly. Learning the flute has other advantages besides meditation for a ninja. As you'll have discovered, it helps you control and extend your breathing. Which is what my next lesson is about.'

On cue, the other students began to turn up. They sat in a semi-circle at the entrance to the cave, overlooking the valley.

'There you are!' exclaimed Hanzo, taking his place beside Jack. 'I've been looking for you everywhere.'

Miyuki sat as far from him as possible, on the opposite side of the semi-circle. Next to her, Shiro began to sniff the air and wave his hand in front of his nose. This encouraged a round of sniggering. Rather than ignore it, Jack played along. He sniffed the air too, then pointed at Hanzo and held his nose, grimacing at the supposed stink. This caused more amusement. At this point Hanzo farted and the whole class erupted into laughter.

Soke, grinning too, held up his hand for silence. 'A good laugh is like manure – it doesn't do any good until you spread it around. But we should make a start. Now that Jack's been *initiated*, I trust you'll all support him in his training.'

The gathered students gave a courteous bow in Jack's direction. His good-natured acceptance of the joke seemed to have won him some support. Miyuki, however, kept her eyes on Jack as she bowed, challenging his presence. She wasn't so willing to accept him.

'This morning we focused on concealment and escape,' Soke continued. 'But hiding isn't only about not being seen, it's about not being heard.'

'Or smelt!' Shiro added.

Soke shot him a disapproving look and the boy offered a half-hearted bow of apology in return. 'On occasion, a ninja must be able to hold their breath for a long time. You might have to conceal yourself close to your target and the sound of your breathing could give you away. Other times you might be forced to stay underwater, or even feign death. Breath control is a subtle but crucial ninja skill.'

Jack listened intently. Having experienced the power of Dragon Breathing, he was eager to learn other ninja tricks.

'In order to hold your breath for a long time, begin by breathing in and out slowly and deeply from the belly,' explained Soke, demonstrating a long drawn-out inhalation and exhalation. 'Clear your lungs completely, then take a large gulp of air and hold it.'

A few of the students copied Soke, Shiro looking as if he was about to explode.

'How many times have I told you?' said the Grandmaster despairingly. 'Don't take in so much that you're straining.'

Shiro let out his breath in one big whoosh.

Soke, ignoring the boy, continued with his instruction. 'You need to relax every muscle in your body. Combine this with meditation, slowing down your heartbeat, and it's possible to hold your breath for several minutes.'

Jack was astounded by this revelation. When he and Akiko had escaped Osaka Castle by swimming through a well tunnel, he'd barely managed a minute and had almost died drowning. Only Akiko's kiss of life-giving oxygen had saved him.

'To achieve this feat is as much about mastering the mind as the body,' said Soke, tapping a finger to his temple. 'You have to consciously suppress your need to breathe. The best way to do this is to think about something else, something pleasant. I want you all to practise this now.'

As the circle of students began deep breathing in preparation for the task and filled their lungs, an unspoken challenge arose among them. No one wanted to be the first to have to take a breath.

They sat in silence, some with eyes closed, all of them in meditative postures. Jack focused on relaxing his body and slowing his heartbeat. To begin with, the task was easy. But as the first minute approached, the instinct to breathe grew from mild requirement to desperate need. His stomach tightened and his lungs cramped, but he fought the urge.

Remembering Soke's advice, Jack thought of his sister Jess. He imagined returning home to her, seeing her pretty face shining with joy at his long-awaited return. He tried to picture how her appearance would have changed in all the years he'd been away.

This helped him past the initial burn and the challenge became easier. Jack was aware that several students had already given up. But he kept going. He wanted to prove he was as capable as the best of them.

Another minute passed. Jack now felt a little light-headed and somewhat detached from his body. The urge to breathe was once again building, like water up against a dam. More students succumbed, gasping air back into their oxygen-starved lungs.

Miyuki wasn't one of them. She remained calm and focused, her eyes fixed on Jack. He returned her gaze, and a personal battle of wills was taken up.

Jack was determined to beat Miyuki. She seemed unfazed by the task. But a vein pulsed in her neck, the muscles of which twitched under the strain. She was struggling too.

This gave Jack hope as they entered the third minute. Although he'd never attempted a feat like this before, he understood the principles that allowed the body to achieve the seemingly impossible. During the Circle of Three challenges the year before, he'd learnt the only limits were those of the mind. Akiko had proved this when she stood beneath a freezing waterfall for longer than the burning time of three sticks of incense and hadn't gone into thermal shock.

The body can keep going as long as the mind is strong, the Tendai priest had said.

Jack concentrated on his memories of Akiko. Seeing her smiling face before him, remembering their times together beneath the *sakura* tree, feeding off the strength of their relationship.

Forever bound to one another.

There were now only three students left – Tenzen, Jack and Miyuki.

'Look! His face is red as a Daruma Doll!' exclaimed Shiro.

Jack barely registered the comment, the voices distant and detached. Darkness was seeping into the edge of his vision, but he was too close to winning to give up now. His samurai pride was at stake.

Tenzen submitted and took several relieved breaths. Now only the two of them remained: Miyuki and Jack locked in silent combat.

'Come on, *tengu*!' encouraged Hanzo, unable to control his excitement.

The other students took up a whispered chant of 'Miyuki! Miyuki! Miyuki!'

Miyuki's whole body was trembling now.

I'm going to beat her, thought Jack. *I'm going to beat her.*

19

CONSTANT THREAT

'I can't believe you passed out!' exclaimed Hanzo, his face creased with laughter. 'I thought you'd *died*!'

'Just concentrate on your cutting exercise,' snapped Jack, holding up his shaft of bamboo as a target.

As likeable as the boy was, he could be infuriating at times. Jack was attempting to give him a sword lesson in the yard before dinner, but Hanzo was unable to get over Jack's dramatic defeat in the breathing challenge.

Hanzo lowered his weapon, his brow suddenly furrowing into a worried expression. 'But *tengu* can't die, can they?'

Jack shook his head, though he was thinking, *This tengu can!*

Determined to beat Miyuki, Jack had stopped breathing until his oxygen-starved brain blacked out. Thankfully, his body instinctively started breathing again and, coming to, he'd been greeted by the Grandmaster's concerned face. 'That was a remarkable first effort,' Soke had said. 'But an unconscious ninja is as good as dead. A lesson for you all: recognize your limits.'

Even though he'd lost to Miyuki, Jack had gained respect

from the other ninja who'd been impressed by his astounding willpower.

The rest of the lesson had been devoted to shallow breathing techniques: first controlling the sound of their breathing; then recognizing the difference between someone asleep and someone pretending; and finally learning how to feign death.

'This evasion technique should only be used as a last resort, as it leaves you exposed to your enemy,' Soke had explained. 'But by pretending you're dead, or mortally injured, you can lure an enemy into a vulnerable position for attack.'

They'd all attempted the technique, but it had proved far more difficult to appear dead than anyone had imagined. Many of the younger students burst into fits of giggles, Tenzen sneezed and Jack struggled to maintain a vacant dead stare without blinking. But Hanzo had been disturbingly convincing – he hadn't even reacted when the Grandmaster prodded him twice with his cane.

'Dinner's ready,' announced Soke from the doorway of the *doma*.

'Great, I'm starving!' replied Hanzo, bowing hurriedly to Jack and dashing inside.

Jack smiled, wondering how Hanzo had managed to keep still long enough to feign death. The boy was so full of life.

After dinner, Soke suggested Jack should practise his stealth-walking in the paddy fields, Hanzo having gone off to play with his friend Kobei. The evening was pleasantly warm, the sun glinting like liquid gold off the waters. Rolling up his leggings, Jack entered the field behind the house. The mud was soft and yielding beneath his feet. Remembering how he must spear his foot and lift the back one high and clear, Jack began to make his way to the other side.

Each step sent large ripples through the reflected sky. But as he progressed, the disturbances upon the water's surface became less and less. Jack discovered balance was crucial in helping him place his lead foot. With careful adjustment and by pointing his toes, he managed to enter the water almost without sound, the ripples now far less noticeable – the only problem being that his progress was slower than a snail's.

Halfway across, Jack couldn't help laughing at the absurdity of what he was doing. Here he was in Japan, ankle deep in a paddy field, a former rigging monkey turned samurai warrior attempting to walk like a ninja! He could just imagine what his friend Saburo would say if he ever found out. Not that he intended to tell *any* of his samurai friends. Jack still felt very uncomfortable at the idea of training as a ninja. But it was a matter of necessity if he was to get to Nagasaki safely. Refocusing, he continued with his stealth-walking practice.

The sun was clipping the mountaintops by the time Jack finally returned to his starting point. He was about to clamber back on to the path when he heard two people engaged in a tense discussion.

'I understand you're teaching *ninjutsu* to our *guest*,' said a voice disapprovingly.

'Yes, I believe he has an aptitude for it.'

Silently lifting his feet one by one out of the water, Jack stealth-walked to the back of the house and peeked round the corner. The second-in-command, Momochi, was having tea with Soke under the tree.

'You're disclosing our innermost secrets to *him*,' seethed Momochi, his moustache twitching with annoyance.

'Not all, just the ones he needs to survive his journey.'

'But he's a samurai! *And* a foreigner! This goes against the doctrine of the scrolls. It must stop.'

Soke shook his head. 'It's *my* decision as Grandmaster who can or cannot be taught our Art. By all means, take it up with Shonin. But I think we owe it to the boy to help him, considering all he's been through with Dragon Eye —'

'I won't see our village risked for the sake of some misplaced guilt,' Momochi interrupted, his anger bubbling to the surface. 'The boy's a constant threat to our village. Samurai patrols are on the increase. I can soon arrange to hand him over to *daimyo* Akechi, then our village would be safe.'

'I've already told you, there's *no* bargaining with that lord,' said Soke firmly. 'Akechi is bent upon wiping the *shinobi* out, just as General Nobunaga almost did. Delivering the boy will only strengthen his influence with the Shogun. I don't want Akechi persuading him that ninja are a threat in times of peace. With the Shogun backing him, we wouldn't stand a chance.'

'But our outposts report that Akechi is preparing for an offensive with or without the Shogun's support. I've got word he's planning to raise a second battalion at his castle in Maruyama.'

'All the more reason to keep a low profile.'

'*All* the more reason to hand over the samurai boy. We don't know where his loyalties lie. He could betray us for his own freedom.'

'I doubt that,' Soke replied, putting down his teacup. 'Jack may be samurai, but he is honourable and has a pure heart worthy of a ninja.'

'You place too much faith in this *gaijin*, Soke. I *will* speak with Shonin. Maybe he can make you see some sense.'

Bowing curtly, Momochi strode off in the direction of the farmhouse.

Jack waited for the Grandmaster to go back inside.

Why did Soke feel so compelled to help him?

Jack got the sense the old man somehow blamed himself for his predicament. Or perhaps Soke knew about the *rutter*, and was trying to work his way into Jack's trust so he could acquire the code. But isolated by choice within this valley, Soke and his clan could have no connection with Dragon Eye or the political ambitions of the man who'd hired him, Father Bobadillo.

Soke had said, *A single tree doesn't make a forest*. In the short time he'd been living and training with the ninja, Jack was starting to appreciate that. And whatever the Grandmaster was up to, he was just glad the man was willing to teach him their skills – they'd be vital to his survival on the journey ahead.

Though he had no reason to trust *any* ninja, he had some sympathy for their situation. The samurai lord sounded a tyrant and Jack certainly didn't want to attract further trouble to the village by staying. At the same time, if he left now, he'd be caught and do just that. He was trapped by circumstances. As agreed with Soke, it would be best to wait until the samurai gave up their search.

In the meantime, he'd have to be very wary of Momochi. Without doubt, *that* ninja would sacrifice him at the first opportunity.

20

SIXTEEN SECRET FISTS

Jack grimaced in agony. Miyuki had him on his knees, pain paralysing him. All she was holding was his thumb – and she was compressing it into an excruciating lock. To add insult to injury, the young ninja was standing on his toes.

'*That's* how you do the technique, samurai,' she said, releasing him.

Over the past two weeks, Jack had not only continued practising evasion and escape tactics, but had been introduced to the ninja's version of *taijutsu*. Initially surprised at how different the unarmed combat training was from that of the *Niten Ichi Ryū*, he now appreciated the effectiveness of their style and found it appealing. The aim behind their *taijutsu* wasn't necessarily to kill, but to fight their way through to a means of escape. And while the samurai rigorously drilled their moves to perfection, the ninja rarely practised a technique more than five times in any session.

'A rigid system is open to attack,' the Grandmaster had explained in their first *taijutsu* lesson. 'Any formal structure has weakness inherent within it. That's the flaw in the samurai's fighting art. Take the foundations from the house and it collapses.'

Soke had demonstrated this on Jack, asking for a classic samurai attack. Neatly evading his cross-punch, Soke had stepped on Jack's lead foot, then knocked the back of his knee to take away his balance. Jack was so distracted by this that, before he could retaliate, Soke had him in a painful armlock and was sweeping him to the ground.

'There's no right or wrong way in *ninjutsu*,' the Grandmaster had gone on to say. 'It only has to work. Each attack you'll encounter is unique in terms of distance and timing, so each response should be unique in its own way. Learn the basic principles, then apply them with a flexible mind.'

Every *taijutsu* lesson so far had been a painful experience. But none more so than today when Soke had partnered him with Miyuki to run through the most crippling locking techniques.

Jack stood up, massaging his throbbing thumb. The morning sun was now filtering through the trees into the glade, but the lesson was far from over. The other students were tirelessly practising different hand-to-hand strikes.

'Good work, Miyuki,' said Soke, nodding with approval at her execution of the thumb lock. 'I think it's time you taught Jack the Sixteen Secret Fists of the ninja.'

Miyuki stared at Soke, taken aback by his suggestion. 'Does he *really* need to know them all?'

Soke nodded.

'As you wish, Grandmaster,' she said, reluctantly bowing to his request.

'Jack,' said Soke, 'you may be familiar through your samurai training with a few of these techniques – the use of the fist, edge of the hand, elbow or knee to strike with. But the ninja don't limit themselves to this. We see the whole body as a weapon. Miyuki, please demonstrate Demon Horn Fist.'

Without warning, Miyuki charged head first into Jack. Her forehead struck his ribcage, knocking him to the ground. Jack landed heavily, wheezing for breath.

'I admire your eagerness, Miyuki, but that may have been a little *too* hard,' cautioned Soke.

'I held back,' she protested, raising her hands in innocence. 'I didn't break his ribs, did I?'

You weren't far off it, thought Jack, knowing Miyuki was trying to assert her dominance again.

'It's all right,' said Jack as he took a breath and brushed himself down. 'I should have been in a stronger stance.'

'Very well,' said Soke. 'Continue demonstrating the rest of the techniques. But be careful, especially with the Eight Leaves Fist.'

He gave Miyuki a stern look before wandering off to check on the other students' progress.

'What's the Eight Leaves Fist?' asked Jack.

Cupping her hands, Miyuki slapped Jack either side of the head on his ears. Even though the attack was relatively soft, Jack reeled from the unexpected strike. His legs buckled momentarily and he lurched to one side.

'Done *properly*,' Miyuki explained, smirking as Jack had to lean against a tree to steady himself, 'the Eight Leaves Fist can cause loss of balance *and* deafness in your enemy.'

'I can understand why,' said Jack, his ears still ringing.

'This one's called Extended Knuckle Fist.'

Folding her fingers at the second knuckle, she raked them down the centre of his chest. In spite of himself, Jack cried out. The attack was excruciating. Before he could recover, she went on to the next.

'This one's Finger Needle Fist.'

Standing in front of Jack, Miyuki closed her right hand to leave only the little finger protruding.

'What are you going to do with *that*?' asked Jack warily. The digit appeared too fragile for any meaningful strike.

'It's for soft targets. Like the eyes or . . .'

Reaching over, Miyuki inserted her little finger into his left ear and pressed deep into the canal. Before he knew it, an arc of pain like lightning coursed through Jack's body.

'That hurts!' he exclaimed, standing on tiptoes to relieve the agony.

'It should do,' she said calmly. 'I've targeted a *kyusho* point.'

'*Please*, that's enough!'

'But how are you going to understand the effectiveness of these techniques if you don't experience them for yourself? Some samurai you are!'

She removed her finger, releasing the nerve point, and the pain instantly stopped. 'Perhaps we should end the lesson.'

'No!' shot back Jack.

'Then stop complaining.'

'I just have an aversion to unnecessary torture, that's all,' argued Jack.

'Well, you're clearly not man enough to be a ninja,' she retorted.

Riled by the implication, Jack *did* stop complaining. But by the end of the session, he felt bruised and battered all over. Miyuki hadn't held back in her demonstration of any of the Sixteen Secret Fists – even to the point of knocking him temporarily unconscious with Fall Down Fist. Yet, in a single session, her phenomenal skill had helped him understand how to apply the different fists and their effectiveness in combat.

'Excellent work, both of you,' commended Soke, drawing the training to a close. 'Jack, you've been extraordinarily fast in grasping the principles.'

'I've had a very *dedicated* teacher,' Jack replied, smiling coolly at Miyuki.

'I'm sure she was,' said Soke, a knowing smile on his face. 'Why else do you think I chose her!'

As the Grandmaster went to dismiss the class formally, Miyuki whispered out of the corner of her mouth, 'Soke may be pleased, but I'm not so easily impressed. Don't outstay your welcome, samurai. You're *not* a ninja, and you *never* will be.'

Miyuki turned and strode off in the direction of the village.

Jack was taken aback by her continued animosity. The other ninja were beginning to accept him and he couldn't think of any reason to deserve such spite. Recalling his training with Akiko at the *Niten Ichi Ryū*, Jack wondered how two warrior girls could be so different.

Akiko and Miyuki were like fire and ice.

Training had been a pleasure with Akiko. With Miyuki, it was a trial. If Soke hadn't held her in so much esteem, Jack would have sworn Miyuki was the ninja sister of Kazuki. Though a gifted martial artist, Miyuki acted as hard and unforgiving as a rock and was almost as malicious as his old school rival.

Akiko was equally talented, possessing an inner strength like the steel of a samurai blade. But she had a gentle side, a warmth and a compassion for others that knew no bounds.

Jack missed her deeply.

21

RICE PAPER

Hanzo shot by the house at full pelt. Close behind was Kobei, followed by two other boys. Wondering what the urgency was, Jack stopped his stealth-walking practice in the paddy field and watched them hurtle down the road. But as they sprinted past the other villagers, nobody seemed alarmed at their haste. When the four boys reached the pond, they rounded the large hanging tree and raced back up the road. Approaching the house once more, Jack noticed they all wore straw hats on their chests.

'What *are* you doing?' cried Jack.

'Speed . . . training,' gasped Hanzo, drawing nearer.

'But why the hats?'

'*Makes-you-go-faster,*' replied Hanzo, zooming past without stopping. 'Can't . . . let them . . . fall.'

Hanzo disappeared up the road towards the shrine, a trail of dust following in his wake. Kobei was still hot on his heels, but the other two boys now lagged far behind. This at least explained Hanzo's remarkable pace in the escape run.

'Impressive, isn't he?'

Jack turned round to see Soke, his bright eyes gazing proudly in Hanzo's direction.

'He's certainly full of surprises,' agreed Jack. 'After barely a few lessons, he's skilful enough to wield a real sword. It's as if he was born with it in his hands. Where does he get it from? His parents? Or you?'

'No, no, no . . . He's a natural. Much like yourself.'

'Me?' said Jack, surprised by the compliment.

Soke nodded. 'I was concerned your samurai training would be a barrier to *ninjutsu*, but you've mastered the basic principles very quickly. Even more impressive, you've already become quite adept at *shinobi aruki*,' Soke commended. A wry smile then graced his old worn face. 'Certainly better than when you tried to sneak up on me and Momochi having tea the other week.'

Jack's face flushed with shame.

'Don't worry. Spying is *exactly* the sort of skill you should be refining as a ninja.'

'Maybe it's time I left,' said Jack, mortified at being caught. 'I've already delayed more than I should.'

'Nonsense,' said Soke, waving his hand dismissively. 'You've only taken your first steps in comprehending the Five Rings. It would be irresponsible of me to let you leave half-trained.'

'But Momochi —'

'Momochi is just being paranoid,' Soke interrupted. 'But that's a good thing. It's important that somebody questions matters. Momochi's suspicious nature has paid off on many occasions. He has a nose for trouble.'

'I *should* go then,' Jack insisted. 'I have no wish to endanger the village more than I have.'

Despite his noble words, Jack didn't really want to leave. He felt protected within the valley. Granted, he was worried by Momochi's intentions, but he was more concerned about the samurai who hunted him. Not that he wanted to stay any longer than necessary among the ninja; it was just that the *ninjutsu* lessons were increasing his chances of reaching Nagasaki alive.

Soke laid a reassuring hand upon Jack's shoulder. 'Momochi's wrong in this instance. Shonin and I have spoken and he is of the same mind. The searches are dying down, but the samurai are still patrolling the borders. You should stay a while longer. Patience is not only a virtue; it can be a lifesaver for a ninja.'

Jack was relieved at the Shonin's decision, though he knew Miyuki wouldn't be thrilled at his continued presence and would most certainly try to make his life with the ninja as uncomfortable as possible.

'Follow me. It's time we perfected your stealth-walking,' said Soke, leading Jack back inside the house.

Laid out across the floor of the *doma* were long sheets of thin rice paper. They stretched from the doorway to the raised wooden floor and had been dampened with water.

'Your task is to cross the room without tearing the paper.'

Jack didn't think this was possible – the sheets looked awfully fragile.

'You'll need to master *uki-ashi*,' explained Soke. 'Floating feet technique.'

The Grandmaster stepped on to the paper with his tiptoes and very gently lowered his feet. 'Imagine each step is as light as a feather.'

Jack couldn't believe what he was seeing. The Grandmaster appeared to almost hover above the paper's surface. As Soke crossed the room, he didn't leave a single mark or footstep. To the untrained eye, it looked like magic.

'Now you try,' said Soke, mounting the raised wooden floor to observe his student.

Taking a breath, Jack carefully placed his toes down on the paper just as the Grandmaster had. So far, so good. Lowering the sole of his foot to the ground, he took a second step. But when he lifted his back foot, he heard the undeniable rip of paper.

'Call upon the Ring of Wind,' Soke advised. 'Float, don't walk.'

Jack tried again, summoning up feelings of lightness and imagining he was a feather. His balance was much improved from all the paddy-field practice, but still his feet tore the rice paper every time.

At that moment the door opened and Hanzo, hot and out of breath, charged in.

'Floating feet!' he cried. 'I love this!'

Kicking off his sandals, he joined Jack in the task. 'Bet I can reach the other side before you do, *tengu*!'

'It's not a race, Hanzo,' chided Soke gently. 'If you're not careful, one day your impetuosity will be your downfall.'

As if to prove Soke's point, there was a sound of tearing as Hanzo tried to overtake Jack.

'It's only a *little* rip,' defended Hanzo, bringing his thumb and forefinger close together to show how insignificant it was.

Soke shook his head. 'A tear is a tear. Even the slightest

error of judgement can ruin a mission. Remember that. Your life may depend upon it.'

'Yes, Soke,' replied Hanzo, abashed.

'*Uki-ashi* takes patience to perfect,' instructed Soke. 'But once you master it, you'll be able to cross any surface without making a sound.'

'Even a Nightingale Floor?' Jack asked.

Two years ago, *daimyo* Takatomi, the lord of Kyoto Province, had invited Jack to his castle and demonstrated this remarkable security feature for preventing an assassination – a wooden floor constructed on metal hinges that trilled like a bird with the pressure of a single foot. No one could walk across it without alerting the guards – supposedly, not even a ninja.

'That is the most challenging of crossings to train for,' admitted Soke. 'I know of only one man who has achieved such a feat.'

'Will you show me how, Grandfather?' asked Hanzo eagerly.

'When you're able to steal the pillow from beneath my sleeping head, then you'll have truly mastered *uki-ashi*. And only then will you have the necessary skill to cross a Nightingale Floor.'

Giving the boy an affectionate pat on the head, Soke settled himself in front of the hearth and started the fire for dinner.

Hanzo glanced up at Jack, frustration etched across his face.

'It's impossible,' complained Hanzo under his breath. 'I've tried, but he *always* wakes up!'

22

SHURIKEN

'How's the *shakuhachi* playing coming along?' enquired Soke.

Jack looked up from his breakfast of rice, miso soup, pickles and broiled fish. He'd virtually forgotten the taste of barley bread, butter and cheese that formed the staple ingredients of his breakfast back in England. In fact, his previous life was little more than a faded memory. Jack often wondered if he'd even recognize England when he eventually found his way home. More to the point, would his sister recognize *him*?

'To be honest, I haven't practised much,' Jack admitted, feeling a little guilty. Another week had passed and, although he'd found the flute a pleasant enough pastime, he considered his energies better spent on skills more relevant to being a ninja and helping him on his journey to Nagasaki. 'I've been concentrating on *uki-ashi* and the Secret Fists.'

'You really should practise everyday.'

'I've kept up my breath-control training,' Jack added quickly.

'The *shakuhachi* is more than meditation and breathing exercises.'

Soke picked up his flute and began to play. His soulful melody lulled Jack, who leant against the wall to respectfully listen. Partway through the tune, Soke raised the bamboo flute and pointed it in Jack's direction.

All of a sudden, there was a sharp *phut*.

A black dart shot out from the end of the flute and pierced the wooden pillar beside Jack's head. Jack was too startled to say anything. Hanzo, his mouth full of rice, spluttered with laughter.

Soke lowered his flute. 'As I was saying, you *really* should keep up your practice.'

'It's a *weapon*?' exclaimed Jack, regaining his composure.

Soke nodded. 'A blowpipe in disguise.'

Putting down the flute, Soke stood and retrieved his walking stick. 'If a ninja is going to travel freely, he has to carry weapons that don't arouse suspicion.' Soke tapped his cane. 'As innocent-looking as this is, my walking stick makes a very effective *hanbō*. I can use the staff to strike, restrain or even throw an enemy.'

He twisted the head of the bamboo stick.

'With a slight *shinobi* adaptation, it becomes even more lethal.'

Swinging the cane round his head, a short length of chain shot out and whipped through the air, its weighted end passing a hair's breadth from Jack's nose. For a second time, Jack swallowed back his shock. This wasn't turning out to be the relaxed breakfast he'd expected.

Slipping the chain back inside his walking stick, Soke then pointed to the various farm tools that lay around the *doma*. 'For a ninja, anything can become a weapon. We've adapted the rice flail into the *nunchaku*; the sickles we use for harvesting become deadly *kama*; the grappling hook is a *kaginawa* for both climbing and hooking an enemy. In fact, the more common the item, the better.'

Soke picked up one of the *hashi* he'd been using for breakfast. With a flick of his wrist, he threw the chopstick at Jack. It penetrated the wall like an arrow, the quivering shaft directly in line with Jack's eyeball.

'With the right technique, a *hashi* can become a very effective *shuriken*,' explained Soke.

Jack pulled out the chopstick and examined it in amazement. He'd never take a *hashi* for granted again.

'Come,' beckoned Soke. 'We'll find Tenzen. He's one of the best at *shuriken-jutsu*.'

The three of them wandered over to the village square, where they found Tenzen with Kajiya in his forge. They bowed their greetings to one another and Soke invited Tenzen to introduce Jack to the Art of the *Shuriken*.

'*Shuriken* are a simple, but versatile weapon,' explained Tenzen as Kajiya laid out a selection of throwing blades – some were straight iron spikes; others were flat and star-shaped; some looked like needles; others like knives.

'As you can see, most are small enough to conceal in your hand. This gives us the element of surprise in a fight.'

Tenzen picked up an eight-pointed throwing star, a hole through its centre.

'Although they can kill,' he said gravely, 'we mainly use *shuriken* to distract the enemy.' He pointed to various parts of Jack's body. 'Targets are the eyes, face, hands or feet. Basically any area not protected by a samurai's armour.'

'Are these poisoned?' Jack asked, recalling Dragon Eye's devious tactics.

Tenzen shook his head. 'You *can* poison the tips for a more lethal effect, but you have to be very, very careful when handling them yourself. I'd advise against it until you've become more skilled.'

Jack gazed in dread fascination at the varied array of *shuriken*.

'What's that one used for?' he asked, pointing to a large *shuriken* with a spiralled cord attached.

'It's a little invention of mine,' answered the bladesmith, grinning with pride. 'Inspired by the Ring of Fire. I've attached a fuse, so the *shuriken* can be lit and thrown to start a fire. Tenzen's been testing it out for me.'

'I've heard it works rather well,' said Soke, giving Kajiya a congratulatory pat on the back. 'Tenzen, will you show Jack the three main techniques for throwing a *shuriken*?'

Bowing, Tenzen selected several of Kajiya's *shuriken* and took up position in the square. At one end were three fence posts driven into the ground. Even at this distance, Jack could see the wood was pockmarked and guessed they were regularly used for target practice.

By now, some of the villagers had gathered round to watch the display.

Choosing a straight spiked *shuriken*, Tenzen threw it over-arm at the target. It struck the first post with a resounding *thunk*. Then he selected a flat-bladed *shuriken*, flinging this one underhand. The weapon pierced the second post, sending a splinter of wood flying. Finally, he flicked a star-shaped *shuriken* sideways from waist level. The silver star flashed through the air to penetrate the third post. Each attack was effortlessly executed and devastatingly accurate.

'Now *ikki goken*,' instructed Soke.

Hanzo nudged Jack excitedly, whispering, 'The "five blades in one breath" technique! Tenzen's the only one who can do it.'

Fanning out four throwing stars in his left hand, Tenzen weighed-up the first *shuriken* in his right hand and took aim.

In the blink of an eye, Tenzen launched the first *shuriken*. His arm moved in a blur as he threw the other four in quick succession. The attack was so fast that before the first star had even hit the middle post, the other four were all airborne. They struck the wood one after the other like a pepper of gunfire.

There was a round of applause from everyone and Tenzen gave a humble bow. He turned to Jack and handed him a four-pointed star.

'You have a go.'

Jack reluctantly accepted it. The *shuriken* was lighter than he'd expected and the edges viciously sharp. He felt very uneasy holding the trademark weapon of the ninja, having witnessed first hand the damage they could inflict. His father had been wounded by one, the cook at Akiko's house had been killed with one and Yamato's brother had been poisoned by one. And now *he* was about to learn how to use this weapon himself.

Tenzen mistook Jack's uncertainty for a lack of confidence.

'Hold it between your thumb and forefinger. Not so tight,' he advised, adjusting Jack's finger positioning. 'Grasp it lightly as if holding a swallow's egg. You need to allow the *shuriken* to slide from the fingers.'

Jack did as he was told and lined himself up with the first post.

'Now throw it sideways, flat, as if you're skimming a stone. At the moment of release, tense your fingers and wrist so you get a straight accurate pitch.'

Jack brought back his arm, winding up to throw. As he straightened his arm, with a flick of his wrist he let the metal star go.

The *shuriken* shot through the air and struck the target dead-centre.

Tenzen and Hanzo stared in amazement at Jack, while Soke's eyebrows shot up with surprise. Jack couldn't believe it himself.

'Beginner's luck,' he said by way of an explanation.

Tenzen wordlessly passed Jack a second star.

Jack went through the motions again. But the pressure was on this time and he released the *shuriken* too late and with too much force. The star veered wildly off target, shooting between the posts, towards the village well.

A dark-haired girl let out a surprised yelp as the *shuriken* shattered the clay water pot she was filling. Soaked to the skin and looking around furiously for the source of the attack, Miyuki spotted Jack.

She gave him a deadly stare.

Tenzen, trying to stifle a laugh behind his hand, whispered, 'I *think* you need more practice.'

23

THE INVISIBLE NINJA

'Please be seated,' said Shonin, indicating for Jack to take his place between Soke and Hanzo.

Jack had been invited with his hosts for dinner at the farmhouse. Miyuki, Tenzen and a grumpy Momochi sat cross-legged opposite. Shonin was at the head of the table.

Two young girls bearing trays entered the room and began to set out dishes. Although the food wasn't as varied and fancy as the samurai banquets Jack had experienced in Kyoto, it nonetheless looked extremely tasty, with miso soup, purple eggplant, pickles, omelette and grilled fish, as well as several bowls of steaming rice.

'Tell me, how are you finding life as a ninja?' asked Shonin as they ate.

Jack thought for a moment. 'Challenging!' he replied.

But Jack didn't mean this solely in terms of the intense diversity of his *ninjutsu* training. Or how it conflicted with what he'd learnt as a samurai warrior. He was struggling with his opinion of the ninja themselves. He'd been in their company a month now and, like the skin of the *mikan*, his views regarding the ninja had slowly been peeled back to reveal a different truth.

They were no longer the faceless assassins he'd fought against. They were farmers, villagers, children and even training partners. Poles apart as they were from the samurai, this didn't mean the *shinobi* were without virtue or principles. The spirit of *ninniku* was apparent in every aspect of their lives. Bounded by compassion and guided by the Five Rings, they possessed a philosophy and way of life equal to that of the samurai's *bushido*.

And, dare he admit it, Jack *enjoyed* training as a ninja. Their arts, dark and mysterious as they were, made a great deal of sense to him – especially considering the long and dangerous journey ahead. Yet he'd sworn since his father's death that the ninja would *always* be his enemy. *But were they?*

His experiences were leading him to question this belief. The ninja were shielding him from the samurai and, in the main, had treated him with kindness and respect. He even considered a few, like Soke, Hanzo and Tenzen, were becoming his friends and mentors. But the ninja had been his foe for so long that, despite everything, it was hard to let go of his old convictions. Too much water had passed under the bridge to suddenly start trusting them now. He still was no closer to understanding their true intentions or their reason for helping him. So, like Momochi, he remained suspicious and on his guard.

His life as a ninja was indeed challenging . . . *challenging* everything he stood for and had come to believe.

Shonin nodded sagely, as if reading the conflict in Jack's mind.

'How would you assess his progress, Soke?'

'Jack's taken to *ninjutsu* like a duck to water – you should see his *shinobi aruki* in the paddy fields,' he replied, giving Jack a good-natured smile. 'Though he's a touch hit-and-miss with his *shuriken-jutsu*.'

Jack glanced guiltily in Miyuki's direction and caught her scowling at him. She still hadn't forgiven him for breaking her pot and soaking her.

'But he's learning fast, Father,' said Tenzen.

'Good. I'm sure he will under your guidance,' replied Shonin, beaming proudly at his son. 'And, Miyuki, I understand you've been teaching Jack the Sixteen Secret Fists. Does he know them *all*?'

'Yes,' she replied, tight-lipped.

I should do, thought Jack. *She's demonstrated them on me enough.*

'Now, Jack, you've no doubt wondered why I agreed to Soke's request to teach you – a samurai – the art of the ninja,' said Shonin.

'That has crossed my mind.'

'Well, I'm counting on an exchange of skills. I hear you've introduced Hanzo to the basics of samurai swordsmanship. But I'm intrigued to know more about the Two Heavens. I've heard it's invincible. What can you tell me?'

Jack hesitated. Masamoto *only* divulged his secret of the Two Heavens to those few *Niten Ichi Ryū* students he deemed worthy enough in mind, body and spirit. Even if he could have requested Masamoto's permission to reveal such knowledge, he already knew the answer: *Never reveal your secrets to the enemy*. Yet the ninja had openly shared many of their own secret techniques with him. It was surely unreasonable to refuse – and disrespectful.

Caught in a dilemma, Jack wished he had Sensei Yamada around to advise him. Then he recalled an allegory the old Zen master had given Yori a few days before Jack left Toba: *The cat taught the tiger how to fight. The tiger became very strong. One day the tiger turned on the cat and the cat ran up a tree. That is the one secret the cat never taught the tiger.*

Jack was in danger of teaching a tiger. But as long as he kept to basic principles and didn't reveal the inner secrets, surely he could tell Shonin about the Two Heavens.

'You do know it?' said Shonin, his tone firm and expectant.

'Of course,' replied Jack, smiling. 'The Two Heavens is a double sword method. The moves are designed to allow attack and defence simultaneously. Masamoto-sama believed that if your life is on the line, you need all your weapons to be of service.'

'A wise man. Go on.'

'While the two swords are the core to this technique, the essence of the Two Heavens is the spirit of winning – to obtain victory by any means and with any weapon.'

Shonin nodded appreciatively. 'Much the same principle as in *ninjutsu*. I'd very much like to speak with this samurai – even if he is our enemy.'

'I'm afraid that won't be possible. Masamoto-sama's been banished by the Shogun,' said Jack.

'That is most unfortunate,' replied Shonin. Then a smile curled the edge of his lips. 'Perhaps *you* can give me a demonstration of the Two Heavens?'

Jack had only envisaged giving a verbal explanation of

the principles – not to demonstrate it. Though uneasy at the idea, Jack felt he had little choice but to agree. After all, what real harm could it do? The technique took years, if not a lifetime, to master. A single demonstration couldn't teach the tiger how to climb.

'I'd be honoured,' said Jack, inclining his head.

'Excellent. Soke will arrange a time and place. Now, I have some welcome news. The samurai patrols have been called off. At least in these mountains.'

Jack could immediately feel the invisible noose round his neck loosening. Finally, he could continue on his way to Nagasaki.

'I do realize you'll want to continue your journey,' Shonin acknowledged. 'However, I'd advise extreme caution as all checkpoints and samurai outposts have been ordered to capture you, dead or alive. You may, therefore, wish to complete your training with Soke before leaving. Now, is there anything else we can do for you?'

'Make me invisible!' said Jack, thinking of the countless patrols and post stations he'd have to negotiate.

'That can be arranged.'

Jack laughed. But his laughter petered out when he saw the Shonin's deadly serious face.

'All ninja learn the art of invisibility,' stated Shonin, matter-of-factly.

'But that's impossible.'

'I ask you, how many people are here now?'

Jack looked round the table. 'Seven.'

Shonin shook his head. 'You forgot Yoko.' He pointed to the serving girl who'd been standing still and silent in the corner. 'Being invisible isn't about not being *seen*. It's about not being *noticed*.'

'That could be a little more difficult for me,' said Jack, indicating his blue eyes and blond hair.

Shonin dismissed this obstacle with a wave of the hand. 'Soke, please explain.'

The Grandmaster turned to Jack. 'Invisibility is often a question of patience and agility. By combining concealment techniques with stealth-walking, a ninja essentially becomes invisible.'

'But I can't hide *all* the way to Nagasaki,' said Jack.

'True. So sometimes the best place to conceal yourself is right under the samurai's nose,' he said, pointing to Jack's.

'What do you mean?'

'A ninja must be a master of disguise and impersonation. *Shichi Hō De* is the "seven ways of going" –'

'Shonin, with all due respect,' interrupted Momochi, 'do you *really* think it's right to be revealing such a deep secret?'

'This one's essential to his survival,' insisted Soke.

'Jack's agreed to show us the Two Heavens. It's a fair exchange,' pronounced Shonin.

Momochi bowed his head in reluctant acceptance.

'As I was saying, *Shichi Hō De* is the "seven ways of going". A ninja may appear as a samurai, a farmer, a *sarugaku* dancer, a *yamabushi* priest, a *komusō*, a merchant or a strolling player. Disguised as such, a ninja can travel freely and without detection. By impersonating an official, we can even gain access to forbidden areas.'

'But I'm not Japanese and never can be.'

'You've been practising your *shakuhachi*?'

Jack nodded.

'Good. This will help make you invisible. The only people officially allowed to play that instrument are the *komusō*. These Monks of Emptiness also have permission to travel freely through Japan.'

'I still don't understand,' said Jack. He'd been impressed that the instrument was a weapon, but it was no magic flute.

'Yoko!' beckoned Shonin. 'Bring in my *komusō* garments.'

The girl slid open a *shoji* and returned a few moments later with some blue priest's robes in a large round wicker basket.

'Please show Jack how the *komusō* dress.'

Slipping on the robes, together with a white *obi* and a golden shoulder shawl, Yoko then put the basket right over her head.

'They wear the *basket*!' exclaimed Jack, laughing out loud with amazement.

'It's a symbol of their detachment from the world. And it's the *perfect* disguise for you.'

24

DIVING DEEP

'The Five Rings teach us how to use nature to our advantage,' explained Soke, who sat surrounded by his students upon the bank of the village pond. 'Earth can be used for concealment. Wind for covering our tracks. Fire for destruction . . .'

Jack screwed up his eyes, suddenly forced to look away by a blinding flash of light.

'. . . or distraction.'

Concealed in Soke's hand was a polished silver *shuriken* angled to reflect the bright summer sun.

'But, of all the elements, a ninja should choose water to be his closest ally,' the Grandmaster revealed. 'Nothing is softer and more yielding than water, yet not even the strongest may resist it. Water can flow quietly or strike like thunder. It can be a weapon, a defence, offer camouflage or provide transport. For example, we've all heard of the Koga ninja using wooden water spiders on their feet to cross moats. I prefer a boat, of course – far drier – but this method has struck terror into the hearts of the samurai, who now believe ninja can walk on water!'

There was some suppressed laughter at this. Jack, however, didn't join in. He'd been fooled by this very tactic during the assault on Osaka Castle. He was somewhat relieved to discover the truth behind this supernatural ability.

'Now tell me, what ways can we turn water into a weapon?'

Tenzen raised his hand. 'You could block and divert a river to cause a flood or wash away bridges.'

Soke nodded. 'Excellent. Such a tactic avoids direct engagement with the enemy. However, it requires careful planning and the terrain may limit you. Other options?'

'You can poison a castle's water source,' Miyuki suggested.

'Ah . . . yes, very effective. But this may kill innocent people too.'

'Then just the drinking cup of your enemy.'

'Better,' Soke acknowledged.

Jack made a mental note *never* to accept a drink from Miyuki.

'So how about camouflage?' asked the Grandmaster.

Hanzo thrust up his arm. 'You can hide in barrels, urns, wells, ponds, rivers –'

'Yes, yes, thank you, Hanzo, we get the idea,' cut in the Grandmaster, gently waving the boy's enthusiasm down. 'Your breathing training will enable you to conceal yourself for short periods of time. But occasionally you'll need to stay submerged for longer.'

Getting to his feet, Soke approached a clump of reeds and plucked a long thin stalk from the waters.

'A hollow reed like this will allow you to breathe under-water. It also has the benefit of blending in with its environment, making it harder for the enemy to detect you. But what if there isn't one to hand?'

'You can use your *saya*,' said Shiro, who sat beside Miyuki, picking distractedly at the grass.

Tenzen, noting Jack's puzzled frown, picked up his *ninjatō* and showed Jack the end of the scabbard – where Jack's samurai *saya* was rounded and solid, the ninja's had a small breathing hole in it.

Soke continued. 'Finally, water can be used as a defence. You can draw your enemy into a river and force them to fight in the water. A samurai's armour will weigh them down, giving you the advantage. To improve your water-fighting skills, you'll practise your *taijutsu* and weapon work later in the pond.'

Jack hoped he wasn't partnered with Miyuki again. She was more than likely to drown him – 'accidentally', of course.

'Water can also act as a shield. Tenzen, I require you for this demonstration.'

As Tenzen stripped down to his loincloth, Soke went over to the hanging tree where a bow and quiver of arrows rested against the trunk.

'You may be under fire when making an escape, so it's vital you learn how to avoid the arrows and gunshot of the enemy.'

To Jack's utter amazement, the Grandmaster picked up the bow, nocked an arrow and took aim at his student.

Diving into the pond, Tenzen swam hard beneath the surface. Soke fired at him, the arrow lancing through the water. It appeared to strike Tenzen, but he kept going. As Soke launched another two arrows, Tenzen swam on, emerging unharmed on the opposite bank.

'Your turn, Jack,' shouted Tenzen.

'*Me?*' replied Jack, alarmed at the idea. Tenzen may have made it unscathed, but *he* knew what he was doing.

'Go on,' urged Hanzo. '*Tengu* can't die!'

Jack gave Hanzo a doubting look.

'The samurai's too scared,' Miyuki taunted.

Jack realized that if he wasn't to lose face, he had no real choice. Stripping off, he approached the bank.

'Bet the water's cold as ever,' mumbled Shiro as Jack prepared to dive in.

The Grandmaster already had an arrow nocked.

'Remember to swim deep,' advised Soke, pulling back on the drawstring and taking aim.

The old man *really* meant to shoot him.

Jack, taking three deep controlled breaths, dived into the icy waters of the pond. The chill shocked him initially, but he soon began to pump his legs when he caught a glimpse of an arrow shooting past his head. He had to go deeper.

As he swam, he felt an arrow strike his back. Luckily, he was deep enough for the initial momentum of the weapon to have been lost. Even though it didn't pierce his skin, it was a painful reminder of how dangerous the training exercise was.

Not willing to risk surfacing, he kept swimming. But the exertion was putting considerable strain on his lungs. He desperately needed to take a breath. Suppressing the instinct as he'd been taught, he forced himself onwards.

Another arrow glanced off his leg, much softer this time.

The dark shadow of the bank drew nearer and Jack exploded to the surface, gulping in a lungful of air. Clambering out, he collapsed on the ground, breathless and horrified by the experience.

'Well done,' said Tenzen, patting him on the back.

'Soke is crazy!' gasped Jack.

Tenzen nodded. '*Usually* he blunts the arrow tips.'

The two of them waited together on the far bank while the other students made the perilous crossing. As Jack lay there drying in the sun, he noticed there were no farmers in the fields.

'When do you *do* any farming?' he asked.

Tenzen smiled.

'Summer's the best season to be a rice farmer,' he explained. 'Having planted the seedlings in spring, nature takes over. Aside from a bit of weeding and irrigation, we can sit and watch the rice grow. That is when we're not training as ninja. But come end of summer, we'll be working dawn to dusk, harvesting the crop.'

'And that's no fun!' moaned Shiro, flopping down next to them, breathless from his swim. 'Won't be long now until we're threshing the rice till our arms drop off.'

Jack was suddenly aware how quickly time had slipped by. If he didn't move on soon, summer would be over and he'd be travelling through the autumn. The days would be shorter, the nights colder and the journey longer. It was time to go.

Hanzo surfaced and swam over in his direction, a broad grin on his face.

'Told you *tengu* can't die!'

Jack realized it would be sad to say goodbye to Hanzo. Despite the boy's irritating refusal to call him by his name, Hanzo's enthusiasm was infectious. His easygoing nature and openness were refreshing and in contrast to the typically reserved temperament of most Japanese. Over the course of their sword lessons together, the boy had proved a quick learner and dedicated student. As a result, Jack had grown fond of the lad.

Hanzo pulled himself out and sat upon the edge of the pond, his feet dangling in the water, as he watched Miyuki prepare to cross.

'Hanzo . . .' began Jack, then he tailed off, his mouth dropping open in astonishment.

Jack couldn't believe he hadn't noticed it before. But this was the first time they'd been swimming together.

'What is it?' asked Hanzo.

'Erm . . . nothing.'

But it *wasn't* nothing.

There, on Hanzo's lower back, was a small cherry-red birthmark in the shape of a *sakura* blossom petal.

Just like the one Akiko had described on Kiyoshi, her long-lost brother.

25

A SILENT MIND

That night Jack lay on his *futon*, unable to sleep, his mind whirling with the prospect that Hanzo might be Akiko's little brother.

Akiko had once told him that the boy had been snatched as a child by Dragon Eye during the assassination of Yamato's older brother, Tenno, five years earlier. Though many thought Kiyoshi had been killed, Akiko always believed her brother was still alive. Why else would the ninja have taken him?

In spite of a prolonged search by Masamoto and his samurai, the boy was never found. But Akiko didn't give up hope. She'd heard a rumour about a boy of samurai status entering a ninja clan in the Iga mountains, and had convinced herself that it must be Kiyoshi.

This was one of the reasons Akiko had agreed to Masamoto's plan for her to train as a ninja. She'd intended to infiltrate the *shinobi* and discover the whereabouts of her lost brother. But Dragon Eye was the only one with certain knowledge of Kiyoshi's fate. When the ninja had died, the secret died with him. And so had Akiko's hopes.

Until now.

Jack had once asked Akiko how she'd recognize her brother after the passing of so many years. She'd informed him that Kiyoshi had a birthmark like a petal of *sakura* blossom on his lower back. Just like Hanzo.

It could be a complete coincidence. But Hanzo was the right age. There were aspects of his nature that were very familiar to Jack. His passion for life, his independence and his gentle spirit were all reminiscent of Akiko. And, like his sister, the boy was a natural martial artist.

How many other young ninja would have such a distinctive birthmark?

'Are you asleep?' came a whisper from the other side of the room.

Jack didn't answer, caught up in the possibilities surrounding Hanzo. Or could it be Kiyoshi?

'I know you're awake. I can tell by your breathing.'

A shaft of pale moonlight filtered through the bars of the room's little window. Jack turned to face him. In the half-light, he thought he could picture Akiko in Hanzo's features. The high cheekbones. His easy smile. The eyes, black as the pearl she'd given him.

He dearly wanted him to be Kiyoshi. For Akiko's sake.

'Shall we try and steal Soke's pillow?' Hanzo whispered.

'Hanzo, what do you remember of your parents?'

Hanzo blinked. 'My parents?'

Jack nodded.

'Only what my grandfather told me. They died when I was five.'

'Do you remember if you had any brothers or sisters?'

145

The boy pondered this question carefully, his brow furrowing deeply. 'Sometimes I dream of a nice lady who calls me *kachimushi*, "her little dragonfly". But Grandfather's never mentioned I had a sister.'

That was a problem, Jack realized. Soke had told him that Hanzo's parents had been killed by samurai. But Akiko's mother, Hiroko, was alive and well in Toba, while her father had been tragically killed in the battle of Nakasendo ten years ago. So they couldn't be Hanzo's parents. Even if the boy's past was wrong, Hanzo's grandfather was Soke and he wasn't of samurai origin. How could he be the grandfather of Akiko *and* Hanzo?

Despite the birthmark, these facts denied the possibility that Hanzo could be Kiyoshi. It was just conincidence and wishful thinking on Jack's part.

'Let's go and steal the pillow,' insisted Hanzo, getting quietly out of bed.

Jack gave in to his enthusiasm. Pulling back the covers of his *futon*, he joined Hanzo crouched by the *shoji*. Cautiously sliding it open, they both stealth-walked across the hearth room to Soke's door.

Jack reached for the handle of the *shoji*. Hanzo stopped him. Then, producing a small bottle of vegetable oil, he ran it along the bottom edge of the frame.

To stop the squeaks, he mouthed.

Jack smiled at Hanzo's ingenuity. *The boy certainly has Akiko's cunning*, he thought.

Putting his hand to the door frame, Jack pulled on the *shoji*. It slid silently open. Soke was fast asleep on the far side of the room, his head resting upon the pillow. Jack wondered how they were going to remove it without waking the old man.

They crept closer, quieter than mice.

Yet, before they were even halfway across the room, the Grandmaster opened his eyes.

'You need to silence your mind too!'

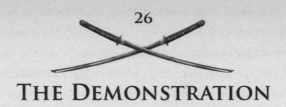

26

THE DEMONSTRATION

The blade of the *ninjatō* almost took Jack's head off.

Ducking beneath it, he retaliated with a devastating cut to the midriff. Miyuki blocked it with her sword and drove forward to skewer him. But Jack wedged his blade against hers, sparks flying as the two weapons ground against one another. Deflecting the *ninjatō*, Jack aimed his sword's *kissaki* at her throat, the razor-sharp tip stopping short of piercing her neck.

A perfect Flint-and-Spark strike.

Her attack halted, Miyuki glared at Jack before retreating to safety.

A murmur of respectful appreciation arose from the crowd gathered round the village square. Shonin, who sat to one side beneath a large parasol, observed Jack with increasing admiration. His eyes never left the young samurai as Jack raised both his swords into a high Two Heavens guard and waited for Miyuki's next assault.

The challenge was supposed to be a 'friendly' one, for the benefit of Shonin to witness the Two Heavens in action. But the fight had quickly escalated in ferocity, becoming more of a duel than a demonstration. Miyuki was determined to beat Jack – to prove the Two Heavens was flawed and show that the ninja were more skilled than the samurai.

Equally, Jack wasn't willing to lose face at the hands of Miyuki. Not only was the reputation of Masamoto's technique at stake but Jack's personal honour too. Having been defeated in hand-to-hand combat during his escape attempt, Jack had no intention of letting her do the same with the sword.

The hot sun beat down and, like Miyuki, Jack was breathing hard from the exertion of combat. Blinking away the perspiration running down his forehead, he tried to manoeuvre himself so that his back was to the sun and Miyuki would be forced to look directly into its glare. His opponent being such a skilful fighter, Jack needed every advantage he could get.

So far Miyuki had tried every ninja trick – throwing dust into Jack's face, feigning surrender, and even standing on his toes during one particularly close encounter. But she'd been unable to break through his defence.

Miyuki had one third and *final* chance to defeat him.

What would her strategy be now?

She squinted into the bright sunshine, looking for a gap in his guard.

'Two can play at that game,' she said, bringing up her blade and angling it so the sun reflected into Jack's eyes.

Momentarily blinded, Jack had to rely upon the blind fighting skills Sensei Kano had taught him. Hearing the scuff of Miyuki's feet and the *swish* of her sword cutting through the air, he instinctively blocked her incoming strike with his *wakizashi*, then brought his *katana* round in a counter-attack. Miyuki neatly evaded it and came at him from the opposing angle, her sword cutting down towards his neck.

Only then did Jack notice the subtle but crucial shift in her fighting style. She now wielded her *ninjatō* left-handed!

Jack was almost caught out, her blade slicing dangerously close to his right ear. He rapidly retreated across the square. But Miyuki's attacks were even faster now. As he blocked her barrage of strikes, Jack suspected she was naturally left-handed and had hidden this fact in order to surprise him with her true skill.

He was now literally fighting for his life.

Miyuki didn't let up and nearly penetrated his defence on several occasions. Then Jack spotted his chance. Miyuki over-committed to an attack, her sword remaining extended a little too long. Jack swiftly executed an Autumn Leaf strike, twice hitting the back of her blade.

The *ninjatō* clattered to the ground.

Disarmed, Miyuki fumed at Jack as the crowd applauded his supreme skill. Jack bowed in humble acknowledgement.

But Miyuki wasn't finished. Striding over to Kajiya's forge, she snatched a *manriki-gusari* chain hanging from a beam. Spinning the weapon above her head, Miyuki threw the weighted end at Jack. Out of the corner of his eye, he spotted the surprise attack and managed to block it with the back of his *katana*. But the links wrapped round the blade and Miyuki jerked the sword from his hand.

Now Jack had only the *wakizashi* to defend himself with.

Whirling the chain again, Miyuki called out, 'What are you going to do now, samurai?'

Without hesitation, Jack flipped the sword over in his hand and threw it at her — just like Masamoto had once done to him.

The short sword flew like a *shuriken* through the air. Miyuki, in mid-swing, her arms above her head, was an easy target. The *wakizashi* struck her dead-centre in the chest, and she was knocked to the ground.

Mountain-to-Sea technique. To attack in a manner that wouldn't be expected.

A gasp of astonishment was followed by more applause, everyone realizing that if the sword had been thrown point first, the result would have been fatal. Jack, glad as he was to beat Miyuki, hadn't wanted to hurt her. He walked over and offered his hand. 'You fought well.'

'*You* were lucky!' she growled, ignoring his outstretched hand as she got to her feet.

'Samurai skills, more like,' said Jack, retrieving his swords.

Miyuki looked daggers at him. Shonin approached with Momochi and Soke, the Grandmaster beaming with approval at Jack's performance.

'That was most enlightening,' said Shonin. 'Thank you.'

Bowing, Jack readied himself for the inevitable onslaught of questions about the Two Heavens. He'd have to be careful not to reveal too much to the tiger.

'Masamoto-sama must not only be a great swordsman but a great teacher,' Shonin acknowledged. 'The Two Heavens is a truly remarkable sword style. But I wouldn't say invincible.'

With a brief nod of his head, Shonin strode off to the farmhouse, engaged in deep conversation with Soke.

Jack stared after the two ninja, open-mouthed.

'I thought Shonin wanted to *learn* the Two Heavens,' said Jack, more to himself than anyone in particular.

Momochi heard him and laughed.

'Shonin didn't want to learn how to *do* the technique,' he said, a sly grin on his face. 'He wanted to learn how to *defeat* it.'

Jack's heart sank as he realized the implications. A tiger as intelligent and cunning as Shonin could work out how to climb the tree for himself – or simply cut it down.

'Shonin was looking for weaknesses in the technique,' Momochi went on, gloating at Jack's evident alarm. 'That demonstration has just saved many a ninja's life.'

Momochi swaggered off to join Shonin and Soke.

Jack bitterly regretted his decision to display the Two Heavens. He could only pray Masamoto would forgive him for this serious error of judgement. At least the ninja were only intending to use their knowledge for defence, rather than to attack samurai.

'You were amazing!' exclaimed Hanzo, scampering over excitedly. '*Tengu* technique! I can't wait to learn it.'

'Very impressive,' Tenzen agreed.

'I had a good teacher,' replied Jack, allowing himself a smile as Hanzo mock-fought with two imaginary swords. 'Masamoto-sama's the greatest samurai swordsman in Japan. Courageous, noble –'

Miyuki laughed scathingly. 'A samurai, noble?'

'Yes!' said Jack defiantly. 'He taught me *bushido*.'

'*Bushido!*' spat Miyuki, squaring up to Jack. 'You believe in that *lie*?' Miyuki's defeat in the demonstration had evidently roused her anger. 'You need to be told the *truth* about the samurai and their precious code of conduct.' She prodded Jack hard in the chest with her finger. '*Bushido's* their excuse for killing, a way of absolving their guilt. The samurai are all murderers! Tyrants! Devils!'

'That's not true,' countered Jack, taken aback by the hatred blazing in her eyes.

'Really?' she challenged. 'My family were *murdered* by samurai!'

So *this* was the source of Miyuki's rage, realized Jack, and immediately understood the pain she was suffering. 'I know how you feel –'

'How can you? Let me tell you what samurai are capable of. Then you'll see them in their true colours. Have you heard of the great General Nobunaga?' she said, her tone thick with sarcasm.

Jack nodded, recalling Akiko telling him about the warrior's famous battles of thirty years ago.

'Well, that "brave" samurai sent forty thousand troops against just *four* thousand Iga ninja. Then he ordered them to burn all the villages to the ground and massacre every man, woman *and* child. What part did the samurai's code of *bushido* play in that?'

Nose to nose with Jack, a thunderous expression on her face, Miyuki didn't wait for his reply. 'And he's not the only one! *Daimyo* Akechi follows in his footsteps, laying waste to any ninja clan he finds. Where's the rectitude in destroying whole villages? What honour is there in killing a defenceless woman, *like my mother*? How much courage does a samurai need to kill a child? My brother was not yet five!'

A tear ran down her cheek, her whole body trembling with emotion.

'Miyuki, calm down,' interjected Tenzen, stepping between them. 'Jack's not to blame —'

'Calm down? Samurai like *him* are the cause of all our troubles.' She turned her attention back to Jack. 'Do you know there were nearly a hundred ninja clans in these mountains? Now they can be counted on the fingers of one hand!'

Miyuki thrust her hand in Jack's face to emphasize the point.

'So don't tell me you know how I feel. You're a samurai at heart. And always will be. I hate *everything* you stand for.'

Her rage suddenly spent, Miyuki began to sob uncontrollably. 'I lost my mother . . . my brother . . . my father . . . everyone . . .'

'I'm truly sorry,' said Jack. 'But I *do* understand how you feel. My father was murdered too.'

Miyuki stared at him through her tears, her eyes a mixture of shock and suspicion.

'By the ninja Dragon Eye,' explained Jack, to both Tenzen's and Miyuki's astonishment.

'Maybe you do know a little of how I feel,' she relented, shaking her head in dismay. 'But Dragon Eye was never a *true* ninja. No matter how hard Soke tried, he was a lost cause.'

'Soke *knew* him?' said Jack, the heat of the day suddenly turning icy cold.

'Knew him?' replied Miyuki. 'Soke taught Dragon Eye *everything* he knew.'

27

SOKE'S STUDENT

Clouds were gathering on the horizon, and the sun appeared like a blood-red eye peering over the mountaintops when Jack confronted the Grandmaster outside his house.

'Is it true?' he demanded.

Soke leant heavily upon his cane and sighed deeply, the weight of the world seeming to rest upon his bony shoulders. He looked at Jack with eyes sorrowful and full of regret. For once, the Grandmaster appeared as frail and old as his age.

He nodded slowly. 'Yes . . . Dragon Eye was a student of mine.'

'Why didn't you tell me?'

'Would you have stayed if I had?' asked Soke.

'Of course not.'

Jack had considered leaving the moment Miyuki had told him. How could he trust the man who'd taught his arch-enemy? The one who'd been the source of the deadly arts that had killed his father?

'Then you have your answer,' replied Soke, seating himself on the bench in his yard.

Jack was confused. Was the ninja playing some cruel game with him, like a cat taunting a mouse until it died of fright? The Grandmaster surely knew of the *rutter* and its importance. He was just biding his time to strike.

'What do you *want* from me?'

Soke smiled kindly. 'Only to help you.'

'But why?'

'Please sit,' said Soke, patting the bench beside him. 'Then I'll explain everything.'

Reluctantly, Jack sat down, keeping a wary distance from the Grandmaster.

Soke took a deep breath and began, 'Dragon Eye, or should I say Yoshiro as he called himself then, came to our village much like yourself – alone, a fugitive of the samurai. He'd been a farmer until his village was ransacked during the Nakasendo War. He'd lost his eye in an arrow attack. Out of compassion we took him in –'

'Yoshiro wasn't his name,' Jack corrected. 'And he wasn't a farmer. He was Hattori Tatsuo, a samurai lord. The defeated *daimyo* of northern Japan. And he pulled the eye out himself.'

Soke blinked, his eyebrows shooting up in surprise. Then he gave a hollow laugh, thumping the ground with his walking stick. '*That* explains a great deal. I had my suspicions the man was more than he claimed to be. He was a master of deception, possibly the most talented student I've had the honour of teaching.'

Jack visibly recoiled at the praise the Grandmaster had just heaped on his enemy.

'*Only* in respect of his skill,' Soke added quickly. 'Dragon

Eye *never* embraced *ninniku*. He didn't understand the importance of a pure and honest heart to being a true ninja.'

'So why teach him at all?'

'I didn't realize what a rotten core he had. And he was such a natural at *ninjutsu* I even contemplated him succeeding me as Grandmaster!' Soke shook his head in disbelief that he of all people could so easily be deceived.

'But then I saw his true nature on missions – his cruelty, the pleasure he took in killing. I hoped to change him, guide him back on to the true path. But it was too late; he'd learnt all he needed and left to form his own ninja clan.'

'*You* created that devil,' said Jack, his words more a statement than an accusation. Angry tears welled up in his eyes as he thought of all the pain, the suffering and devastation that Dragon Eye had wreaked upon his life and those of his friends.

'Most regrettably,' Soke admitted, his eyes downcast. 'So I feel responsible for your predicament. As soon as you told me of the fate of your father, I wanted to make amends.' He gripped Jack's arm in earnest. 'I thought if I could teach *you* the ninja skills you need to get to Nagasaki . . . in some small way, I'd gain absolution. And maybe you'd find it in your heart to forgive me.' Soke let his hand fall and bowed his head, like a sinner in prayer.

Jack had never seen the Grandmaster appear so vulnerable. He seemed truly repentant. Even though it was the old man's teaching that had made Dragon Eye the deadly ninja he became, Jack couldn't blame Soke for his student's evil deeds. Dragon Eye himself, along with Father Bobadillo, were the ones truly responsible for his father's death.

'It wasn't your fault,' insisted Jack. 'And your teaching *has* given me hope for the journey ahead.'

Soke raised his head with relief.

'I just can't believe Dragon Eye could fool someone like *you*, a Grandmaster.'

'Dragon Eye was very cunning,' said Soke through gritted teeth. 'Any time I became reluctant to teach him, he'd show signs of *ninniku*. I saw these as indications of progress. But he was merely tricking me into unlocking more ninja secrets – even *Dim Mak*. He played me like a *shakuhachi*!'

The two of them sat there in silence as the setting sun blinked shut behind the mountains. The ghost of Dragon Eye seemed to hang over them in the encroaching darkness.

'Once I really thought he'd changed,' said Soke, clearly relieved he could talk through his guilt. 'The man performed a compassionate, courageous act, something wholly in the spirit of *ninniku*. He saved a boy.'

'Who?'

'Hanzo,' Soke revealed, smiling happily for the first time that night. He lowered his voice so that Hanzo couldn't hear them from the *doma*, where he was preparing dinner. 'In truth, he's from another ninja clan. Five years ago, his home was attacked by samurai. Dragon Eye rescued Hanzo from certain death and then asked me to look after him.'

Jack stared, open-mouthed, in astonishment at Soke. 'Hanzo isn't your grandson?'

'No, he's an orphan. But it made it easier for him to think I was.'

Jack couldn't believe what he was hearing.

Hanzo had been taken by Dragon Eye. So had Kiyoshi. Both five years ago. And both had the same birthmarks. There were just too many coincidences.

Hanzo's no orphan, thought Jack. *And he's no ninja either. He's samurai.*

28

THE PILLOW

A light summer rain was falling across the valley. Jack, sheltering beneath the eaves of the farmhouse, listened to the paddy fields ripple and resound to a million raindrops.

Soke and Hanzo had both gone to bed, but Jack couldn't sleep. The revelations of the day played upon his mind. Although he'd found the Grandmaster's explanation convincing, he felt uneasy staying under the same roof as Dragon Eye's teacher.

Ever since encountering Soke, the truth had been like shifting sands beneath his feet, and he wouldn't put it past the Grandmaster to be misleading him again. After all, the ninja *were* masters of deception.

Yet, in his heart, Jack felt certain he'd finally discovered the *real* reason why this ninja was helping him. It had nothing to do with the *rutter*, and all to do with guilt. He'd seen the sincere remorse in the old man's eyes. This at least explained why Soke had argued so adamantly for Jack to stay, in spite of the risks to the village. And the Grandmaster *had* fulfilled his promise to teach Jack *ninjutsu*. For that Jack was grateful; and with these new skills, he was ready to leave.

But he couldn't, could he? Not now he believed Hanzo was Akiko's lost brother, Kiyoshi.

Earlier that evening, he'd been struck by a dilemma as to whether to share this knowledge with Soke. He'd been about to make up his mind when Hanzo had begun jumping from the *doma* into the rain and back again.

'Look, I'm hardly wet,' Hanzo had cried excitedly.

'But why try to dodge raindrops?' Jack had asked.

'I'm perfecting my lightning-fast technique.'

Hanzo had insisted Jack join in and they both leapt in and out of the rain.

'Very amusing,' Soke had said, chuckling at their antics, 'but I'm even faster.'

The Grandmaster had then stepped out into the centre of the yard and promptly got soaking wet.

'What sort of lightning technique is *that*?' Hanzo had demanded.

'My speed doesn't depend upon a simple trick of avoiding raindrops. When it rains, you get wet. That's to be expected. The real test is whether you can avoid *me*!'

'*Of course* I can, Grandfather,' Hanzo had exclaimed, running around the yard with Soke play-chasing him.

That scene had brought home to Jack just how happy the boy was – as a ninja. Would it really be fair to turn Hanzo's world upside down?

On the other hand, Akiko was heartbroken and Jack's loyalty lay with her. She had a right to know her little brother was alive. Kiyoshi had been kidnapped. He justifiably belonged with Akiko and their mother, Hiroko, in Toba.

Jack had decided not to tell Soke. He didn't know how the Grandmaster would react. Soke, after all, loved the boy as his own. Besides, what if somehow he was wrong?

The only way to prove Kiyoshi's identity, beyond a shadow of a doubt, was for Akiko to see the boy for herself.

But how?

First, Jack didn't know *where* he was. Second, he had to get a message to Akiko. Third, he was sure the ninja wouldn't welcome another samurai in their village.

Until he worked out how to contact Akiko and reunite her with her brother, Jack had no option but to remain. He'd use the excuse of needing extra training. This would delay his journey but, if he was honest with himself, he *wanted* to stay. The possibility of seeing Akiko again filled him with joy.

With that pleasant thought, Jack stepped back inside the *doma* and quietly headed for bed. In the hearth room, the embers of the fire glowed red in the darkness and he noticed Soke's door ajar. Remembering the Grandmaster's challenge, Jack wondered if his stealth-walking was now good enough. After much practice, he'd managed to cross the rice paper without tearing it. This test would prove if all his extra training was paying off.

He slipped like a ghost into Soke's bedroom, his mind silent, his feet treading with the lightest touch.

The Grandmaster didn't stir. But the pillow was beneath his head.

How could he remove it without waking the old man?

Jack suddenly felt a drip of water run down his neck. Looking up, he saw the thatch was leaking slightly.

The Ring of Water, he thought.

Reaching up, Jack gently tugged at a loose piece of straw. He waited.

As the rain seeped through the thatch, a bead of water formed at the end of the protruding straw. It dropped on to Soke's forehead.

Moaning sleepily, the Grandmaster rolled aside, lifting his head out of the way. In that moment, Jack snatched the pillow.

Soke's head settled back on the *tatami* and Jack smiled to himself. He'd done it!

The Grandmaster's eyes blinked open. Looking at Jack, then at the pillow and finally at the roof where another drop of water had just fallen, he laughed.

'Jack, it appears you're ready for the Test of Truth.'

29

TEST OF TRUTH

This is madness, thought Jack as he knelt down upon the large flat rock that jutted out from the mountainside. Far below, he could see some villagers in the paddy fields, appearing as small as ants. Above was a cloudless sky. Behind him stood Soke, a sword in his hand.

Being in such a vulnerable position, Jack had little chance against the ninja.

The whole situation put him on edge and he still couldn't believe he'd been talked into it. Although he'd experienced some tough challenges during his training as a samurai – breaking wood with his bare hands, running the Gauntlet and even overcoming the limits of mind and body by standing beneath a raging waterfall – this topped them all.

A tense silence hung over the crowd of ninja as they waited for the Test of Truth to begin. To Jack's right, Shonin and Momochi observed him with interest, wondering how a *gaijin* would fare against such a ninja challenge. Jack glanced nervously over to the group on his right, spotting Hanzo, Tenzen and Miyuki at the front. She was taking some pleasure in Jack's discomfort, attempting to psyche him out by staring at him. Hanzo was fidgeting with excitement. Of all the other ninja students in attendance, Tenzen was the only one with an encouraging smile on his face.

Jack was already perspiring and his heart raced. He took several deep breaths, trying to calm himself. Soke had advised him to clear his mind of all thoughts, not even contemplate whether he would pass or fail. To do so would guarantee failure – and the consequence could be fatal.

The whole purpose of the Test of Truth was to enter the Ring of Sky – to experience the Void and channel the unseen power of the universe. It was necessary for him to enter a state of *mushin*, 'no mind'. He had to act without thinking – without relying on his physical senses.

'Let the Test of Truth commence,' announced Shonin.

Jack knew Soke held a razor-sharp *ninjatō* in his hands. Without warning, the Grandmaster would strike at his head. It was up to Jack to get out of the way. But, of course, he didn't know *when* to move. He had to *sense* the attack.

This was the Test of Truth.

Jack called upon all his meditation practice with Sensei Yamada. He closed his eyes, emptied his mind and slowed his breathing. Jack took comfort in the fact that he'd experienced *mushin* once before during a duel. He now sought that supreme mental state of a warrior in combat, one where he expected nothing, but was ready for anything.

For a brief second, Jack imagined Soke's sword slicing through his skull, but quickly pushed the gruesome image away. He *had* to focus.

The Grandmaster could attack at any moment.

Allowing his awareness of his surroundings to expand,

his survival instinct reached out like tentative fingers in the darkness. The air around him became motionless, time seeming to stand still.

It was no more than a sense of intent. But, in the space of a heartbeat, he felt a surge of energy push him to one side. He rolled with it, moving a fraction of a second before the gleaming blade of the *ninjatō* scythed through the air.

The Grandmaster had struck . . . and missed.

Jack came to a stop at the very lip of the rock, teetering on its edge.

'Congratulations!' said Shonin as Jack backed cautiously away from certain death. 'Not everyone survives that test unscathed.'

The students applauded Jack's success, while Hanzo bounced up and down in delight. Even Miyuki acknowledged the feat, begrudgingly clapping along with the other ninja.

Jack was too shaken up by the experience to do anything but breathe a long sigh of relief.

'This completes your initiation into the Five Rings,' said Soke, addressing Jack. 'Having experienced them all now, you're firmly on your way to learning how to endure like the Earth, flow like Water, strike like Fire, run like the Wind and be all-seeing like the Sky. Stay the path and you'll complete the journey.'

The Grandmaster turned to his students.

'Jack's no longer samurai,' he declared. 'From now on, he's a ninja.'

30

FIRST MISSION

Back in the village square, the students gathered round to personally congratulate Jack. Hanzo stood proudly beside him.

'Told you the *tengu* could do it,' he boasted to Kobei and his friends.

Tenzen clapped Jack firmly on the shoulder. 'I always knew there was ninja blood in you.'

Jack grinned in response. He never imagined in his wild-est dreams that he'd actually become a ninja, let alone feel *proud* of such an achievement. But during his time with the *shinobi*, he'd come to see them in a new light. While Soke hadn't been completely open with the truth, his intentions had proved honourable. The ninja had protected him from the samurai, taught him *ninjutsu* and even tried to make amends for Dragon Eye's sins. A single tree certainly didn't make a forest.

Deep down, Jack knew he'd always consider himself a samurai first and could never reconcile his father's death with being a *shinobi*. But he also realized that being a ninja could have its advantages.

The last to approach was Miyuki.

'You did well,' she said, almost managing a smile. 'But all this has just been practice. You're not a *true* ninja until you've completed your first mission.'

Jack gave Miyuki a questioning look.

'You need to prove yourself,' she explained. 'Come, Shonin has summoned you.'

Miyuki led Jack inside the farmhouse.

'This is an unnecessary risk,' Momochi was arguing as Jack entered the reception room. 'What if he makes a mistake? Or, worse, he's discovered?'

'It's a straightforward assignment,' replied Shonin. 'Besides, he'll be invisible.'

Shonin beckoned Jack to join them. 'Are you ready for your first mission as a ninja?'

Jack bowed his head in response, praying he wouldn't be required to assassinate anyone.

'Momochi's in charge. He will brief you.'

The second-in-command looked incensed, his moustache twitching in annoyance. He was clearly unhappy that Shonin had once again overruled him.

Jack was equally concerned. Here was Momochi's ideal opportunity to ensure he failed . . . or even orchestrate his capture by *daimyo* Akechi.

Grunting his disapproval, Momochi reluctantly addressed Jack. 'We believe *daimyo* Akechi is planning an offensive against the ninja clans in these mountains. We need to know what preparations he's made: how big his army is; when and where he will attack. The more we know about our enemy's plans, the easier it will be to stop him.'

Despite the risks, Jack realized this might be the opportunity he'd been looking for. Not only could he learn of his location in the Iga mountains, he might find a way to send a message to Akiko.

'I'll need to know where *daimyo* Akechi is,' said Jack.

'Maruyama Castle, two days' trek east.'

'Am I to go alone?'

'Of course not!' snorted Momochi. 'One of our most experienced ninja, Zenjubo, will lead the party, which will comprise Tenzen, Shiro, Miyuki and *you*.'

'So when do we leave?' Jack asked.

Shonin laughed. 'I *like* this new ninja!'

The next morning, they gathered in the farmhouse for their final briefing. Zenjubo, a tough, no-nonsense man of few words, handed out their supplies and equipment. He acknowledged Jack with a brief bow of his head, but made no comment as to his inclusion in the team.

Soke was at hand to ensure Jack was properly attired and prepared for the mission.

'What do you think?' asked Jack.

'Who said that?' Soke replied, glancing round as if Jack suddenly wasn't there.

Hanzo, who'd come along to wish Jack luck, giggled. 'The *tengu*'s invisible! It's magic!'

Jack joined in the laughter. He felt rather stupid wearing a basket on his head, but he couldn't deny the *komusō* outfit made the perfect disguise.

Soke passed Jack the *shakuhachi*. 'Remember it's not just about looking like a Monk of Emptiness, it's about acting the part,' he reminded Jack. 'That's why the *shakuhachi* practice was so important. Playing the flute will convince the samurai you're a real *komusō*.'

Zenjubo took his final instruction from Momochi and announced it was time to leave.

'Don't get caught, *tengu*!' Hanzo called cheerfully after him.

'I won't,' replied Jack, 'as long as you haven't set any traps for me!'

Momochi was standing at the main entrance. As Jack passed by, the ninja grabbed his arm.

'A word of warning,' he hissed. '*Shinobi* are everywhere. If you betray us, we *will* know.'

31

MONKS OF EMPTINESS

Jack paid careful attention to their route. He plotted the course in his head like entries in a ship's log, noting unusual features, memorizing distance, direction and time travelled by the position of the sun.

During the first morning, Zenjubo didn't follow any paths – not that there were many to follow. Jack realized this was another Ring of Earth defence to keep the village well hidden. But Jack was able to use a couple of distinctive outcrops to get his bearings. Around midday, they hit a main trail and thereafter Jack became more confident he could retrace his steps. The first night, they slept beside a river with a small waterfall, while the second night was located in a forest clearing marked by two fallen trees.

'With the war over, how can *daimyo* Akechi justify raising an army?' Jack asked as they broke camp on the morning of the third day.

Zenjubo looked at Jack, then nodded at Tenzen to explain.

'Officially,' said Tenzen, 'he's using the non-payment of rice tax as an excuse. At least, that's his reason for recruiting more samurai.'

'You samurai have an easy life,' commented Shiro, 'not even having to grow your own rice.'

Miyuki tutted in disgust. 'It's got more to do with his samurai sense of pride. *Daimyo* Akechi wants to finish what Nobunaga started. To achieve what the General failed to do. He's determined to wipe out the *shinobi* for good.'

'Quiet!' ordered Zenjubo as they came to the edge of the forest.

Ahead was a long road that led across a grassy open plain to the castle town of Maruyama. Upon a small hill at its centre, the fortress stood like a lone sentry. Encircled by a bailey wall, its base was constructed of coarse-cut stone upon which a four-storey keep had been built. Its walls were crisp cloud-white, topped with curving roofs of grey tile. Set off to one side was a wooden watchtower with unobstructed views of the plain.

'*Kasumiga Jo*,' whispered Tenzen. Mist Castle.

'Why's it called that?' asked Jack quietly.

'Legend has it that a fog descends to protect it in times of battle.'

'Let's go,' instructed Zenjubo, putting on his wicker basket. 'Shiro, stay here.'

'Why me?' complained Shiro. 'I always get the boring jobs on a mission. Why can't I go on surveillance for once?'

'Do as I say. Guard the packs. Act as lookout. If something goes wrong, tell Shonin.'

Shiro crossed his arms moodily, but did as he was told.

Zenjubo turned to Jack in his *komusō* disguise. He took one look and passed Jack a wet piece of bark. 'Rub your hands and lower arms with this,' he instructed.

'What's it for?' asked Jack, the bark leaving a light brown residue on his skin.

'The hairs on your arms give you away,' explained Zenjubo. 'They're too light in colour for a Japanese. Now, are you clear what you have to do on this mission?'

Jack nodded. They were to enter Maruyama in pairs, beg for alms in various locations, visit the temple, then leave. On their way through the town and castle grounds, they were to take note of the number of troops, horses, any artillery, the level of provisions and the state of readiness of the army. Jack had been partnered with Miyuki to investigate the town, while Tenzen and Zenjubo would infiltrate the castle.

A steady flow of traffic could be seen passing in and out of the main gate. Some merchants had packhorses, but most were on foot, bearing their loads upon their backs. Two men, sweating in the heat, shouldered a fancy palanquin and people stepped aside to allow the important dignitary to pass. Then a young man came running out of town, leaving a trail of dust in his wake as he sprinted down the road.

'He's in a hurry,' Jack commented.

'*Hikyaku*,' muttered Zenjubo.

Jack looked to Tenzen for an explanation.

'We call them "Flying Feet". He's a courier. Merchants rely on them for business. But judging by his speed, he's delivering a message for the *daimyo*.'

Jack was intrigued. Maybe he could hire one of these Flying Feet to contact Akiko. The problem would be finding one he could trust.

Zenjubo waited for a lull in activity before leaving the

cover of the forest. Walking slowly in a line, their *shakuhachi* in their hands, the four of them merged in with the traffic and approached the main gate.

Through the grille of his basket, Jack saw a number of samurai guards on duty. They were randomly checking the travel permits of merchants entering the town. Only now did it strike Jack just how risky this mission was. If he was discovered, all his ninja training would be for nothing. Jack felt a desperate urge to turn back while he could.

'Just remember,' hissed Miyuki from behind, 'I'll be watching your every move.'

Jack held his breath as they levelled with the guards, but the samurai allowed the four of them to pass through unopposed. Maybe this was going to work, after all.

Zenjubo led them up the main street. The wooden buildings on either side were a mix of shops, inns, houses and shrines. Various banners and lanterns proclaimed their wares and services. A ball of cedar branches hung outside one establishment, indicating *saké* for sale. The smells of cooking wafted through the air from countless food stalls. Jack spotted an old woman crouched beside a brazier, grilling pieces of chicken. Smiling, he remembered how his old friend Saburo had loved *yakitori*.

Zenjubo and Tenzen parted company with them in the market square. Miyuki found a spot beside a shrine, put down a small wooden bowl and began to play her flute. For the most part people ignored her, but then an old man tottered by and dropped in a copper coin.

While she was performing, Jack took the opportunity to gather the information they required. Glancing around, he was surprised at how busy the town was. Despite being in the middle of the Iga mountains, it was apparent that a large number of samurai had recently arrived. All the inns had signs declaring they were full and the main street was thronged with people, many carrying *katana* and *wakizashi*. There could be no doubt that *daimyo* Akechi was raising a second battalion.

Miyuki stopped playing. Bending down, she picked up her alms bowl.

'Only two coins and a rotten *daikon*,' she complained, holding up the browning radish in disgust. 'Let's see if you do any better, while I look around.'

Putting down his own begging bowl, Jack wet his lips and blew into the *shakuhachi*. The soulful languid notes of '*Hifumi hachi gaeshi*' floated over the hustle and bustle of the crowd.

Every so often a passer-by would drop a coin into his bowl.

As he reached the end of the piece, Miyuki stated, 'Time to visit the temple.'

Jack fished out his offerings. 'Five coins! And a bag of rice!'

'They were paying you to *stop*!' she muttered.

Walking through the town, they made note of what they saw, pausing to play and beg for alms at particular points of interest. They performed near the stables, counting at least two regiments' worth of horses and discovering a warehouse full of rice sacks. Even though they were on a mission, their competitive spirit simmered away as they compared takings for each performance.

After surveying the stables, they paid their respects at the temple in order not to arouse suspicion. Several other Monks of Emptiness were gathered there, passing through on their pilgrimage.

'You stay here and pretend to pray,' whispered Miyuki. 'I'm going to see what I can find out from the priest.'

Jack approached a large wooden effigy of the Buddha. Picking up a stick of incense, he lit it from a nearby candle and placed it in a bowl. The heady aroma of sandalwood filled the air. Bowing twice, he clapped his hands before bowing a final time.

'You travel far?' asked a soft voice from behind.

Jack turned to see another basket-headed monk. 'Two days,' he replied.

'Your journey has hardly begun.'

'And you?' asked Jack.

'My pilgrimage is never-ending. I'm visiting all the temples in Japan.'

All the temples, thought Jack, wondering whether this monk could possibly deliver the message to Akiko. He'd surely be more trustworthy than a courier.

'Including the Ise shrine near Toba?' Jack asked innocently.

'Of course,' he replied. 'I've already prayed there. I'm now heading south.'

Jack was glad to be wearing the basket, otherwise the monk would have seen the disappointment on his face.

'Journey well,' said the monk, bowing as he departed.

'What do you think you're doing?' demanded Miyuki, suddenly appearing at Jack's side.

'Just being friendly,' said Jack.

'Well, don't. You're risking our mission.'

The two of them returned to the central square and found a spot to perform in sight of the main gate while they waited for the others to return.

'Time to go,' Miyuki whispered, indicating with her flute the appearance of Zenjubo and Tenzen. The two of them were already heading down the main street.

Jack came to the end of his song and a few more alms dropped into his bowl.

'I think that settles it,' he said, depositing the proceeds into his bag. It jingled with considerably more coins than Miyuki had collected.

'You can celebrate when we're out of here,' she replied testily.

Miyuki led the way through the busy main street, the townsfolk giving them a respectful berth. As they passed a stall selling fans, Jack overheard the merchant talking to a finely dressed woman.

'The one with pearl inlay comes from Toba . . .'

His attention caught, Jack slowed his pace, trying to eavesdrop further.

'Do you have any others like this?' the lady asked.

The merchant shook his head. 'But I can send for more. My son travels the Tokaido Road regularly. He'll be passing Toba next month.'

This merchant could deliver the message to Akiko, thought Jack. *For the right money, of course.*

By now, Miyuki was approaching the gate. She looked back impatiently, wondering what was holding Jack up. Not wanting to be left behind or rouse her suspicion further,

Jack quickened his pace. Then he realized this would look odd. He was supposed to be a monk in meditation. His haste could attract the unwanted attention of a samurai. As hard as it was, he walked slowly and with great deliberation. Through his wicker basket, Jack eyed the guards. But they were paying him no interest. He reached the gate and almost wanted to skip down the road. The mission had gone without a hitch *and* he'd found a way of contacting Akiko.

'*Komusō!*'

Jack froze, his heart leaping into his throat.

Miyuki, further down the road, glanced back but didn't stop.

'I'm talking to you, monk. Come here.'

Jack's first instinct was to run. But he'd have little hope of escaping with a basket on his head. Keeping his cool, he turned to face the guard. The man beckoned him over.

'Play us a song.'

Jack almost wanted to laugh out loud with relief. The samurai appeared relaxed, not at all suspicious. Obediently, Jack raised the *shakuhachi* to his lips and began to play '*Hifumi*'.

The guard groaned. 'Not *that* one,' he said, rolling his eyes. 'I want to hear "*Shika no Tone*".'

Jack hesitated. Soke had once played the tune for him, but he'd never been able to master it.

'I'm sorry,' Jack admitted. 'I don't know that tune.'

The guard's eyes narrowed. Without warning, the samurai drew his sword.

'A *real komusō* would!'

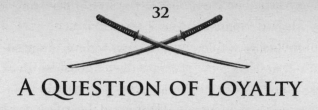

32

A QUESTION OF LOYALTY

'The infamous *gaijin* samurai in my castle!' mused *daimyo* Akechi, stroking the tips of his neatly trimmed moustache. 'Or are you now a ninja?' he laughed.

Jack kept his silence, his head bowed as he knelt before the samurai lord. Two guards were stationed either side of him. Four more were lined against the back wall. All were impatient to execute him on the *daimyo's* command.

Outside, birds were twittering and chirping in the bright summer sunshine, oblivious to Jack's predicament. Following his capture, the gatekeeper had almost dropped his sword as he ordered Jack to remove the basket and was greeted by a foreign face. The other guards had jumped to their feet, surrounding him in a matter of seconds. In the uproar, Miyuki had vanished from sight. Jack had been swiftly escorted to the fourth floor of the castle and presented to *daimyo* Akechi.

The samurai lord was immaculately attired in a sheer black *hakama* and *kataginu* winged jacket, his family *mon* of a dragonfly woven in gold thread upon his chest. Handsome and self-assured, his hair was tied tightly into a topknot and oiled smooth. The *daimyo* was also vain, judging by the immense silk-screen painting in the room, depicting him larger than life and victorious in battle.

'Only *shinobi* would consider such a clever disguise,' he went on, indicating the *komusō* basket and robes. 'But I'm intrigued to know why the ninja are helping you.'

'The ninja are my enemy, Akechi-sama,' said Jack, bowing even lower.

'If that's the case, then how come you're still alive? Where have you been hiding all this time? My patrols have searched for you in every known valley, forest and village of my province.'

'I've survived in the mountains, avoiding everyone I could.'

'Please don't insult my intelligence,' sighed the *daimyo*. 'You're too well fed to have lived like a wild animal. Now, just tell me, where is the village that took you in?'

'I . . . can't tell you,' Jack replied.

'Can't or won't?'

Akechi studied him for a moment.

'I'm not an unreasonable lord,' he said with a smile as smooth as silk. 'I'll make a deal with you. In return for telling me the location of your ninja village, I'll grant you your freedom.'

Jack didn't trust the samurai lord. The man's promise seemed as unconvincing as his silk-screen painting. 'What about the Shogun's orders?'

'I'll inform the Shogun you rendered me a great service. Your safety's assured. To my borders, at least.'

Jack thought carefully before replying. 'I still can't tell you. The ninja captured and blindfolded me.'

The *daimyo* raised his eyebrows sceptically.

'This is a question of loyalty, Fletcher-san, a matter of *bushido*!' asserted *daimyo* Akechi, now using the respectful etiquette to address Jack. 'Are you samurai . . . or ninja?'

Even Jack was unsure of that answer. A few months before, there would have been no doubt he was a samurai. *But now?*

'I've heard great things about you,' admitted Akechi, suddenly adopting a flattering tone. '*Daimyo* Takatomi, once your lord in Kyoto, has spoken highly of your samurai arts. I believe you saved his life, preventing an assassination by Dragon Eye? And didn't that same ninja kill your father?'

'Yes,' replied Jack through gritted teeth, trying not to let emotions cloud his judgement.

'Then *why* are you protecting the *shinobi*?'

'Dragon Eye's dead. I just want to go home,' said Jack, avoiding the question.

'Don't be a fool! Dragon Eye lives on through the ninja. They're all the same. Devils! That's why they hide their faces.'

The *daimyo* leant forward confidentially, his expression sorrowful.

'My father was murdered by ninja too,' he said, speaking quietly as if divulging some great secret to Jack. 'I don't know which *one*, though. So I have to kill them *all* to regain my family's honour.'

Jack saw the venomous hatred in the man's eyes. He realized the *daimyo* was so consumed with vengeance he'd lost all reason. Just like Dragon Eye.

'I intend to hunt down every last ninja, burn their villages to the ground and end their evil ways, once and for all.

Imagine that, Fletcher-san. No more ninja. Your father's enemy wiped from the face of the earth.'

Jack resolved, there and then, he could *never* let this man discover the village. He'd slaughter every innocent man, woman and child he found. Miyuki would be faced with the same awful tragedy all over again. Wherever his loyalties lay, Jack couldn't allow *that* to happen, especially with Hanzo – or Kiyoshi, as he now thought of him – as part of the village.

'A single tree doesn't make a forest,' said Jack.

'What?'

'Not all ninja are like that. Many are simply farmers, just trying to survive –'

The *daimyo* cut him short with a dismissive wave of his hand. 'You've clearly spent too long among them. The ninja have bewitched your mind with their magic.'

He clicked his fingers and the two guards hauled Jack to his feet.

'Perhaps you need time to think about where your loyalties lie, *gaijin*,' snapped *daimyo* Akechi, his previous charm giving way to displeasure. 'Gemnan!' he called.

A thin-faced man with sallow skin and narrow eyes slipped through a side door into the room. Shuffling up to his lord, he gave a crooked bow.

'You have a choice, *gaijin*,' stated the *daimyo*. 'If by tomorrow morning you haven't revealed the location of the village, Gemnan will help you remember. He can be *very* persuasive.'

Gemnan, his lips parting into a sadistic grin, scrutinized Jack the way a snake might its prey. Jack felt a shiver of dread run down his spine. Whatever means this man had of persuading him, it wouldn't be pleasant . . . or painless.

33

HELL'S GARDEN

'Welcome to my garden,' wheezed Gemnan as the two guards threw Jack roughly to the ground.

The courtyard, located to the rear of the castle, was a barren, sunbaked patch of earth. There were no flowers, no bushes, just a lone tree from which a man hung, suspended by his arms behind his back.

'It's quite beautiful, isn't it?' said Gemnan proudly.

Jack's eyes widened in alarm as he looked around the high-walled yard. Another prisoner was tied to stakes driven into the ground. He lay spread-eagled in the sun, groaning feebly, his skin red-raw and bloodied. To Jack's left, an immense black cauldron stood over a fire, steam rising from the bubbling water. But Jack didn't think for one moment Gemnan ever cooked food in it.

At the far end of the yard, a wooden crucifix had been erected. It stood ominously vacant, its shadow stretching towards Jack like a beckoning skeletal hand.

'Follow me,' ordered Gemnan.

Getting to his feet, Jack was violently shoved in the back by one of the guards. He staggered forward as if in a nightmare, the gruesome garden a vision of Hell on earth.

'Mind where you're walking, *gaijin*,' said Gemnan. 'We were testing swords this morning.'

'On what?' asked Jack, horrified, as he stepped over a pool of blood drying in the midday heat.

'Prisoners,' replied Gemnan. 'We'd run out of corpses.'

Seeing the shock on Jack's face, he let out a callous laugh. 'Don't worry, I have *other* plans for you.'

Gemnan led Jack past a large iron grille set into the ground. The pitiful sound of moaning could be heard coming from below. Jack glanced down into a large stinking pit. Several emaciated men lay in a heap, flies buzzing around them.

'There's a dead man down here!' cried one unfortunate soul.

'And there'll be another soon if you don't shut up!' replied Gemnan, spitting on the prisoner from above.

Even in his perilous state, the prisoner couldn't help but gawp at the bizarre sight of a blue-eyed, blond-haired foreign boy in their midst.

Gemnan walked over to the crucifix. Panicking, Jack began to look for a way of escape. But the two guards behind him were watching closely, their hands ready on their swords. Jack wouldn't stand a chance. He'd be cut down in an instant.

'The cross would be a fitting punishment for a Christian like you,' Gemnan considered, clearly relishing Jack's grow-ing fear. 'Perhaps *that* will be your end. For the time being, though, I've been told to treat you well. So I've arranged for your own private chamber.'

Producing a set of keys, Gemnan made his way over to a small metal cage in one corner and unlocked the door. Bowing, he gestured politely. 'Your room for the night, young samurai.'

Before Jack could protest, he was seized by the arms and forcibly pushed inside. The cage was barely big enough to contain him. He couldn't stand up or lie down. He could hardly turn round. All he could do was squat. And the cage was in the full glare of the sun.

'Would you like some water before I leave you to think over your situation?' asked Gemnan.

Jack nodded warily. The sadistic smile returned to his jailer's face.

'I'm sure you would,' he laughed. 'By tomorrow, you'll be *begging* for it.'

Gemnan instructed one of the guards to remain behind should Jack decide to talk, adding, 'I hope he doesn't, though. It'll be most interesting to see how long a *gaijin* survives the cauldron.'

As Gemnan went to depart, he turned back to Jack.

'Oh, I almost forgot. Do you want to know the *real* reason you were discovered?' The man's eyes once more had the look of a snake about to strike as he cackled, 'A ninja betrayed you.'

34

FINGER NEEDLE FIST

The screaming didn't stop all afternoon. Jack thought he'd go to his grave with those cries still ringing in his ears. The man who'd been hanging in the tree had been cut down, only to be submerged in the boiling waters of the cauldron.

Gemnan had stood by, observing the man slowly die. The intense fascination the torturer had displayed sickened Jack to the pit of his stomach. And Jack knew that by sunrise he might be suffering the same fate.

His mind was in turmoil. Had a ninja *really* betrayed him?

He wouldn't put it past Momochi. The man had been keen to strike a deal with *daimyo* Akechi. But why, then, did the *daimyo* still want the location of their village? And how had Momochi got a message through so quickly? He'd only known of Jack's inclusion in the mission at the last moment. It was possible Momochi had instructed Miyuki to inform the guards. But this seemed reckless for a man so intent on protecting his village. Momochi surely realized that by going on the mission Jack would learn of the valley's location and be questioned upon capture. Or perhaps Miyuki had acted on her own initiative? She'd been against him becoming a ninja from the very start. This could be her attempt to get rid of him . . . permanently. But again this put her and her village at great and unnecessary risk.

The other option was that Gemnan was lying. The samurai was clearly an experienced interrogator and torturer. Maybe this was one of his techniques? To make Jack *think* he'd been betrayed – to get him to talk. Looking back on his capture, the guards on the gate had been utterly shocked at their discovery – not the reaction of informed men. It could be just pure bad luck on Jack's part that the guard had chosen him for a song. If only Jack had practised '*Shika no Tone*', he wouldn't have been caught.

Whatever the truth was, Jack wouldn't be betraying *anyone*.

He had to protect Akiko's brother, and all the other innocent villagers. Besides, as Soke had said, there was no bargaining with this samurai lord. So revealing the village's location wouldn't change his fate. And all his efforts to survive and protect the *rutter* were to come to nothing. He'd endured years of gruelling samurai training, overcome insurmountable challenges, finally defeated his nemesis Dragon Eye, fought through a civil war and even become a ninja – only to die in this hellhole.

He was destined for a painful death . . . *unless* he could escape.

But how? The cage was locked; the bars solid. He was now stiff and dehydrated from squatting for hours in the sun. By morning, he'd be too weak to put up any resistance.

As dusk fell, Jack knew this would be his best, and possibly only, opportunity. The samurai who'd been ordered to watch him was tired. Judging by his expression, he wasn't enjoying his duty and couldn't wait for it to be over.

'Guard,' croaked Jack, his throat parched.

'What?' he answered irritably.

Jack managed hardly more than a whisper in response.

'Speak up!'

Jack tried again.

'I can't hear you,' the man complained, stepping over to the cage. 'Are you ready to confess?'

Jack croaked an unintelligible reply.

The samurai leaned in closer. As the guard's ear drew level with his mouth, Jack thrust his arms through the bars, seizing the man's head and inserting Finger Needle Fist deep into the guard's ear canal. He shuddered with pain and tried to pull away, but Jack drove a Finger Sword Fist hard against the man's throat, striking a pressure point Miyuki had shown him. The guard crumpled against the bars, groaning with agony.

'Open the door.'

'I don't have the key . . .' he moaned. 'Gemnan has it . . .'

Jack saw the guard reaching for his *tantō*. Without hesitating, Jack hit him with Fall Down Fist across the neck. The guard collapsed, unconscious. Jack reached through the bars and took the knife. Using the tip of the blade, he jimmied the lock open, just as his father had once shown him back in England.

Jack tumbled out of the cage. He was so stiff he could hardly stand, let alone run. The samurai was still out cold. Whether Miyuki had betrayed him or not, he definitely had one thing to thank her for – the Sixteen Secret Fists. But he knew the man would soon come round. He took the guard's *katana* along with his knife.

Keeping to the wall, Jack darted silently through the darkness, the blood beginning to flow back into his legs. As he reached the gate to the courtyard, Jack spotted the prisoner who'd been staked to the ground. Whatever crime he may have committed, Jack couldn't leave the poor man like that. Not at the mercy of the vicious Gemnan.

Crouching down beside him, Jack cut loose his bonds. 'You're free,' he whispered.

The man didn't reply. It was at that point Jack realized the prisoner had died. Not only had he been staked to the ground in the blazing heat but he'd been tied over a bamboo plant, its sharpened stems allowed to grow into him. Jack couldn't believe the brutality of Gemnan.

He remembered the other prisoners in the pit and considered trying to release them too. But before he could act, Jack heard the sound of the gate being unlocked. Sprinting for the cover of the tree, he used his Ring of Earth skills to blend in with the trunk, ensuring his arms covered his blond hair.

Two samurai guards entered the courtyard, passing so close that Jack could have reached out and touched them.

'I hate night duty,' one of them mumbled.

As soon as they had their backs to him, Jack silently climbed the tree. Once he was high enough, he leapt to the top of the nearest wall, landing with cat-like grace.

'BREAKOUT!' cried one of the samurai, discovering the unconscious guard and empty cage.

Jack jumped from the wall as several samurai, carrying flaming torches, burst into the courtyard. He landed in an alleyway and ran for his life. As more shouts broke out around the castle, he scaled the bailey wall and dropped down the other side. He zigzagged through the town trying to avoid any samurai. Entering the market square, Jack saw the orange-red glow of torches heading his way. Samurai were converging on him from both directions.

Desperately looking around, Jack spotted a water barrel beside a storehouse. Dashing over, he climbed in. Expelling all the air from his lungs, he took three deep breaths. The barrel was nearly three-quarters full, so by the time he'd submerged himself the water was over his head.

Holding his breath, he waited. By the reflected light of their torches, he knew at least two samurai had stopped next to his barrel. As his breath ebbed away, Jack willed them to move on.

But they didn't.

His lungs were approaching their limit and Jack screwed his eyes shut, drawing on all his ninja breathing training. *An unconsciousness ninja is as good as dead.*

He couldn't hold his breath any longer. Bursting from the barrel, he emerged, sword drawn.

But all the samurai had gone.

Clambering out, Jack gulped down several mouthfuls of water to slake his thirst from his day in the sun, before taking to the backstreets. Keeping to the shadows, he worked his way to the town's outer wall. More a boundary than a barricade, Jack scaled it with little problem and dropped down on to the edge of the plain.

Stealing himself for a suicidal dash to the safety of the forest, he prayed they wouldn't spot him. Jack broke from the cover of the wall and ran hard. The earth pounded beneath his feet. The tall grass whipped past.

'There he is!' came a cry.

A moment later, an arrow shot by, barely missing him, followed by another. But he daren't look back.

All of a sudden, he was aware of the sound of horses' hooves. He'd never be able to outrun a mounted samurai. The darkened forest was drawing closer with every step. If he could reach it, he might just have a chance.

Remembering his Dragon Breathing, he put on a burst of speed.

35

A FALSE ACCUSATION

The shouts of the samurai were coming nearer and nearer with every step. Jack could almost feel the snorting breath of the horses upon his neck.

He wasn't going to make it.

With one last desperate effort, he lunged forward and the undergrowth enveloped him. Slipping through the bushes and vaulting a fallen log, Jack entered the forest. He weaved between the trees, the dense foliage and darkness covering his escape.

Only when he was sure the samurai had lost his trail, did Jack slow his pace. He took a moment to catch his breath in a small clearing and gather his bearings. It was virtually pitch-black in the forest, but Jack identified the northern star through a gap in the canopy and calculated the direction he should head in.

Suddenly he was seized from behind and thrown to the ground, a blade held to his throat.

Jack smiled. 'Miyuki,' he said, more relieved than he could ever have imagined at seeing the girl.

'How did you manage to escape?' she demanded, the knife still at his neck.

'Good to see you too,' replied Jack, wondering if she *had* actually betrayed him. 'I knocked out the guard.'

'Just the *one* guard?' she queried.

Jack nodded. 'I used a technique *you* taught me. Fall Down Fist. Then I evaded the other guards.'

Miyuki reluctantly let him up.

'Where are the others?' asked Jack.

'Shiro's gone to inform Shonin of your capture. Tenzen's with him. Zenjubo went to find you in the castle. Let's go,' she said, shouldering her pack.

'Shouldn't we wait for him?'

Miyuki shook her head. 'Zenjubo can look after himself.' She strode off, heading south.

'But isn't the village that way?' said Jack, pointing east.

Miyuki glared at him. 'Don't think like a samurai. Think like a ninja. Do you want to lead the whole of Akechi's army there? Do you? Why do you think he let you escape so easily?'

'*Easily?* I was held in a cage. I had to pick the lock, leap a castle wall, hide in a water barrel and run for my life!'

'The *daimyo* isn't stupid. A *single* guard for a sworn enemy of the Shogun? Akechi *let* you escape.'

She looked him straight in the eye, as if trying to peer into his heart. 'I bet you struck a deal with him for your freedom.'

Jack stared aghast at Miyuki. 'I didn't betray *anyone*!' he protested.

'We'll see about that.'

Shonin, Momochi and Soke held council. Jack knelt before them in the farmhouse reception room. Miyuki, Shiro and

193

Tenzen, having already given their account of the mission, sat at the back listening to Jack's story of his escape. Zenjubo had yet to return.

'And you did not reveal the location of our village?' asked Shonin.

'No,' replied Jack.

'He's lying,' said Momochi. 'Are we to believe he overcame a guard and escaped from a locked cage all by himself? He *must* have betrayed us.'

'NO!' Jack insisted. 'If anyone was betrayed, it was *me*.'

'Please explain,' said Shonin, holding up his hand to silence Momochi's objection.

Jack took a second to compose himself. Momochi had been undermining his defence from the very start, pushing for his immediate execution as a traitor. Now he wanted to turn the tables. To discover whether Momochi had betrayed him, or Gemnan had lied.

'The *daimyo*'s torturer said a *ninja*,' Jack looked directly at Momochi, 'had informed them of my presence.'

A moment of shocked silence passed between the three men. Soke looked at Momochi questioningly.

'If you're accusing me,' contested Momochi, 'then think again. From the outset I've made my disapproval clear, but I would *never* jeopardize the safety of our village. My family are here, remember. Shonin, I respect your authority and would have informed you of any such plan.'

Jack was almost convinced Momochi was telling the truth. And so too, it appeared, was Shonin. That left Miyuki. But she'd been with him throughout the mission. *No, that wasn't entirely true*, Jack realized. Miyuki had gone on her own to see the priest at the temple – at least, that's what she said she was doing.

'Perhaps it was someone else,' suggested Jack, glancing over his shoulder at Miyuki.

'Nonsense!' snapped Momochi. 'A ninja would know better than to endanger a mission like that. This samurai Gemnan was obviously trying to get you to talk. And I suspect you *did*!'

'That's not true. I was willing to give my life to protect this village,' declared Jack.

'I believe you, Jack-kun,' said Soke.

'You would!' Momochi shot back irately. 'But your judgement of character has been called into question once before –'

'Enough!' interrupted Shonin, seeing the old wound open up in the Grandmaster. 'I've heard both of you and listened to Jack's recount. What we need is an informed judgement. Where's Zenjubo?'

Miyuki bowed and spoke. 'He returned to the castle. His plan was to rescue Jack – or ensure he didn't talk.'

Jack understood the cold-blooded implication of that statement. If he hadn't managed to escape, he'd have been the victim of a ninja assassination.

'Shonin,' called a ninja in the doorway. 'Zenjubo's just coming into the square.'

A moment later, Zenjubo walked in, dirty and travel-worn. He barely looked at Jack as he passed by. Bowing before the council, he made his report.

Shonin listened without comment, then asked, 'Has the village been compromised in any way?'

Zenjubo shook his head. 'The boy said nothing.'

36

ONE OF THE CLAN

'I owe you an apology,' said Miyuki.

Jack was startled by the admission. She stood before him, her head bowed in respect. Miyuki had found him by the village pond, where Jack had gone after the council meeting to recover and gather his thoughts. The question of who'd betrayed him still remained unanswered. Although it was more than likely a ploy by Gemnan, Jack as a samurai was yet to be convinced of a ninja's loyalty and honour to him. *Shinobi* may follow *ninniku*, but they weren't bound by the code of *bushido* like the samurai were.

When he'd seen Miyuki approach, Jack had tensed for yet another confrontation. But her remorseful attitude took him completely off-guard.

'Apologize?' said Jack.

She looked up at him, her dark eyes, once so full of hatred, seeming to have thawed.

'I was wrong,' she confessed. 'My bitterness at my family's fate would only let me see you as samurai.'

Jack listened, speechless. *Was this the same girl who had*

thrown him into a manure heap? Knocked him out cold? Put a knife to his throat, twice?

Miyuki continued. 'Soke once told me that a single tree doesn't make a forest. But I thought all samurai trees grew from the same seed. You proved me wrong. The spirit of *ninniku* is within you.'

She placed a hand over her chest. 'Jack, you have a pure heart. You didn't betray us to the *daimyo*. In my eyes, that makes you a *true* ninja.' She bowed low, this time holding it.

'Can you find it in your heart to forgive me?' she asked in a tremulous voice.

Jack knew the Japanese valued apology highly. A sincere and respectful one was considered to wipe away all transgressions. He also realized it took Miyuki great courage to admit she was wrong, considering all the hostility that had passed between them. He wasn't one to hold grudges. Besides, hadn't he also been guilty of misjudging the ninja? Unless Miyuki was attempting a very cunning deception, it seemed doubtful that she'd betrayed him. And it would do him no favours to throw her apology back in her face. He decided to take the risk and trust her sincerity.

'Of course,' said Jack. 'On condition that you'll accept my apology for breaking your water pot.'

'Yes,' she replied, a smile lighting up her face.

That evening, Shonin arranged for a celebration of Jack's official induction as a ninja. He held a formal dinner in his farmhouse, inviting all the heads of family, as well as Tenzen, Miyuki and Hanzo. To Jack's surprise, Miyuki chose the seat beside him.

'May I?' said Miyuki, offering to pour Jack his tea.

Jack hesitated. After all the antagonism between them, he still couldn't quite believe she was acting so amicably. He also recalled her lethal answer to the Ring of Water.

'I haven't poisoned it, if that's what you're thinking,' she laughed.

'No, of course not,' Jack replied, and, hurriedly thinking of an excuse, added, 'It's just, in England, a man pours his own drink.'

'Well, you're in Japan,' she said, filling his cup.

'What's England like?' asked Hanzo, who sat on Jack's other side.

Jack thought for a moment. An unexpected wave of homesickness hit him. He could recall green fields, dirty streets, bustling ports, the smell of baking bread, the stink of the tanneries, the peel of church bells on a Sunday, the laughter of his little sister. But these memories of home were fading like a ship in fog. He'd been gone too long, far too long.

'Very different from Japan,' he replied, a faraway look in his eyes. 'But some things are the same. It's an island like Japan. We have castles. Farms. But we grow wheat, not rice. No one drinks tea, though we do eat fish. Just not like this.' He picked up a slice of raw salmon with his *hashi* and popped it in his mouth.

'Do you have samurai and ninja too?' asked Hanzo eagerly.

'No,' replied Jack, smiling at the idea. 'But we used to have knights who fought for the King. They followed a code much like *bushido* called chivalry.'

'But if you don't have rice, tea or ninja, why would you

want to go home?' asked Hanzo, his brow creasing in bewilderment.

Jack almost laughed out loud at Hanzo's childlike logic, and was only stopped by the nagging worry tugging at his heart.

'Jess . . . she's waiting for me.'

'Jess?' queried Miyuki. 'She's your . . .'

'Little sister,' said Jack. 'She was left in the care of an old neighbour. But I've been gone so long I worry she's now on her own or in a workhouse.'

'I'm sure she's fine,' consoled Miyuki, hearing the anxiety in his voice. 'If she's half as resilient as you, she'll have found a way to survive.'

Jack bowed his head in acknowledgement of Miyuki's kind words, but the gesture was more to hide the tears welling in his eyes. When he and his father had left Jess in England, she was barely five years old, innocent and vulnerable. That was how he still pictured her; and as her older brother and only surviving relative, it was his duty to look after her. He *had* to continue his journey to Nagasaki and home.

Jack tried to put his concerns to the back of his mind. If he was worried for Jess, then Akiko was equally grieving for Kiyoshi. Somehow, Jack vowed, he would reunite them.

Hanzo, in his youth and enthusiasm, was oblivious to Jack's moment of sadness. Shovelling down another mouthful of rice, he said, '*Tengu*, tell me again how you escaped the samurai. Are you *sure* you didn't use magic and fly out?'

Turning to Hanzo, Jack prepared to regale his story of escape for the umpteenth time when Shonin clapped for attention.

'Tonight is for celebration and reflection,' he announced. 'I admit my judgement was misguided in sending Jack upon this mission. Momochi, please accept my apology. But even monkeys fall from trees.'

There was some laughter at this, and Momochi seemed satisfied that his opinion had been publicly and respectfully acknowledged.

'But I have been proved right,' continued Shonin, 'in agreeing to Soke's request to train Jack as a ninja.'

All heads turned towards Jack, who felt slightly embarrassed at being the centre of attention. Hanzo, though, beamed proudly on his behalf.

'Our foreign friend has proved himself, beyond doubt, to be loyal to our clan. Not only that, his incredible escape is a credit to the boy's *ninjutsu* skills – and our Grandmaster's tuition.'

There was a murmur of approval and Soke bowed humbly in response.

'I realize some of you may question the fact that Jack was caught in the first place. But his experience has taught us an important lesson.'

Shonin paused to ensure he had everyone's undivided attention.

'The samurai are getting wise to our tricks. Seeing through our disguises. We *must* take more care in the future. As you know, *daimyo* Akechi is planning to invade the Iga mountains once again. Thanks to Jack, we've learnt it's a matter of personal revenge, and Zenjubo has confirmed Akechi *doesn't* have the support of the Shogun.'

Intense whispering broke out among the ninja. Shonin

waited for silence before continuing. 'We're already using this information to our advantage. Momochi has sent emissaries to the Shogun's court in Edo. Covertly, they will petition against *daimyo* Akechi, spread rumours he's intending to enlarge his province by force. We'll also remind the court officials of the *shinobi's* loyal service in the recent war, seeking for that debt to be recognized. With any luck, the Shogun will put a stop to Akechi's plans without a single sword being drawn.'

A round of applause greeted this strategy and Shonin smiled, satisfied with the approval his clan had given him. Jack remembered how Soke had told him the *shinobi* only sought combat as a last resort, preferring espionage to warfare. Here was the proof.

'But enough of such dark thoughts; it's time to accept Jack as one of the clan,' Shonin declared. 'The sparrow never lands where the tiger roams.'

Immediately everyone got to their feet. Except Jack.

'Stand up,' Miyuki whispered. 'That's our clan's secret password. Anyone who doesn't stand reveals themselves as the enemy.'

Shonin raised his cup. 'Jack has woken from death and returned to life. His old path as a samurai is his new road as a ninja.'

Shonin and all the heads of family then toasted Jack.

'Ninja Jack! May the Five Rings guide you!'

37

THE NOTE

Jack felt like the frog that had finally seen the great sea. Although he was still honour-bound to the samurai, Jack couldn't deny his pride at being accepted as one of the ninja clan.

Throughout his training he'd wrestled with his conscience, struggling to justify his association with the *shinobi* against his father's death at their hands. To begin with he'd rationalized his decision as a matter of survival, then as a means to knowing his enemy. But as time had gone on, Jack realized the ninja were perhaps no longer his foe and that he enjoyed *ninjutsu*. Not only that, he'd discovered certain skills were *better* and *more* effective than the samurai martial arts.

At first, he'd considered this a betrayal of the teachings of Masamoto whose sword work was unparalleled. But now he saw the two styles could be complementary to one another. Just as he'd come to terms with balancing Buddhism and his own Christian beliefs – *they're all strands of the same rug, only different colours*, as Sensei Yamada had once said – perhaps *ninjutsu* and the samurai arts could exist side by side. Maybe he could be *both* samurai and ninja. That combination had certainly made Akiko a formidable martial artist. He hoped the same would apply to him and that his father up in Heaven would understand his decision.

Whatever, Jack knew his loyalty – his soul – would always remain with Masamoto and the samurai. But the spirit of *ninniku*, the pure heart of the ninja, was undoubtedly becoming part of him. This was why he was finding it so hard to write the note to Akiko.

Sitting upon the steps of the village temple, shaded from the sun, the white sheet of rice paper he'd taken from Soke's house remained blank in his lap. Jack couldn't simply write down the directions to the village for her. If the note fell into the wrong hands, he *would* be a traitor and Akechi's army would come and destroy the clan.

The message had to be encoded. He understood the principles of making a cryptogram, since his father had instructed him on how to decipher the code that hid the most important information in the *rutter*. However, the difficulty in this instance was creating a cipher that Akiko could understand and work out on her own.

After a great deal of thought, Jack decided to use a combination of the Japanese *kanji* Akiko had taught him, the few English words he'd shown her and references to their training at the *Niten Ichi Ryū*.

Picking up the piece of charcoal he'd acquired from Soke's furnace oven, Jack began to write. It was laborious work. Not only did he have to code the message accurately, but Jack had to remember all the necessary *kanji* symbols and the correct order of their strokes.

The note took him several attempts to get right, but by

mid–morning he had the finished article. Now he just needed to find someone to deliver it for him.

'What are you doing?' said a voice from behind.

Jack, guilty, hid the note inside his jacket as Shiro emerged from the forest.

'Nothing,' replied Jack breezily.

'Looks like you were writing something,' said Shiro, eyeing him suspiciously.

How long had Shiro been standing there? wondered Jack with growing concern.

Jack had chosen the temple for its seclusion and when he'd arrived earlier that morning, he'd been careful to ensure the place was deserted. Throughout his task, he'd kept one eye on the path leading up from the village. For whatever reason, Shiro must have been out in the forest before dawn.

'I was practising my *kanji*,' replied Jack, holding up one of his crumpled earlier attempts. 'But I'm not very good.'

He screwed up the paper, collected the other pieces and got to his feet. 'So what are you doing here?'

'Looking for you,' said Shiro. Pursing his lips, he asked, 'You've lived with the samurai – what's their life like?'

Something about Shiro's question put Jack on his guard. 'I was treated well. Samurai school was disciplined, but I learnt a great deal.'

'Did you have to work?'

'Not really, we trained most of the time,' admitted Jack. 'Our duty was to Masamoto and our lord, *daimyo* Takatomi. I suppose we earned our keep by fighting on his side when the time came.'

Shiro smiled appreciatively.

'What's Kyoto like? That's where you lived, wasn't it?'

'Busy. There are always festivals, crowds, markets. It's so much more hectic than your village.'

'Sounds exciting . . .' said Shiro, gazing into the peaceful valley below.

'It can be,' Jack replied, making a move back towards the village. 'I'd better go. Hanzo will be waiting for his sword lesson.'

Shiro nodded noncommittally and Jack just prayed the boy wouldn't mention their encounter to Momochi. But as he headed down into the village, he felt Shiro's eyes on him all the way.

38

NINJA MAGIC

'No, like this,' said Miyuki, gently repositioning Jack's fingers into the hand sign for *Rin* – strength.

As one of the clan, Jack now found himself being taught the ninja's hidden knowledge, the secret teachings of the *densho* scrolls. A week in, he was still familiarizing himself with the intricate finger-knitting patterns of *kuji-in*. These nine secret hand signs, each with their own mantras, triggered extraordinary powers in the ninja.

Magical powers.

Jack had been sceptical. Soke had claimed *kuji-in* could give a ninja great strength, forewarn of danger, read another person's thoughts, even control the elements of nature. Although Jack had witnessed his Zen master, Sensei Yamada, perform some astonishing feats at the *Niten Ichi Ryū* school, he could not bring himself to believe in these mystical arts. They seemed *too* far-fetched.

That was until Soke, invoking *Rin*, had lifted a tree trunk above his head. Now he was a believer.

'Can you remember the mantra?' asked Miyuki, who sat beside him in the lee of the Buddhist temple.

Jack nodded. '*On baishiraman taya sowaka.*'

'Perfect,' she said, smiling her approval.

Having made the correct hand sign, Jack closed his eyes and repeated the mantra over and over. He visualized a flame within him growing brighter, spreading throughout his body, filling him with energy.

During their first lesson in the clan's hidden knowledge, Soke had explained, '*Kuji-in* is a combination of hand posture, meditation and focus. Together they unlock the powers of the mind and tap into the energy of the Ring of Sky.'

Jack had yet to achieve this. But he thought it was possible. He'd experienced the power of *ki*, his own spiritual energy, during his meditation training as a samurai. So he knew what to strive for. *Kuji-in*, however, was on a far higher level and would need a lot more practice.

Out of nowhere he felt a hot rush and a burst of energy. It was very brief – like a bolt of lightning.

'Are you all right?' asked Miyuki.

Jack opened his eyes.

'You shook like a tree in a storm.'

'I'm fine,' Jack replied, his body tingling all over.

'You just channelled into the Ring of Sky,' explained Soke, walking over to check on their progress. 'It can be a bit unnerving first time, but you'll learn to control it. Even a brief connection can be useful, though, giving you a vital burst of energy in times of crisis.'

Soke beckoned the other students together in front of the temple.

'Now I wish you to focus on *Sha*, healing. This is the hand sign,' he instructed, clasping his hands together, his fingers interlaced, the index finger and thumb both extended. 'Of all the *kuji-in*, *Sha* is the most worthy of your attention. The ability to heal is far more valuable than the ability to kill.'

He formed his students into a semi-circle overlooking the village.

'For the time being, concentrate on self-healing. Once you've mastered this, you can bestow your healing properties on others.'

One by one, the students settled into their postures and began their meditation.

'*On haya baishiraman taya sowaka . . .*'

The chanting of the *Sha* mantra echoed out across the valley as the sun slowly set over the mountains. Jack could smell a mix of jasmine and sandalwood incense drifting upon the breeze, and soon fell into a deep trance. The peace and serenity of his surroundings seeped into him, easing his mind, body and soul.

By the time the sun dropped behind the mountains, Jack felt reborn.

39

MOVING TARGET

'Welcome to my hideout,' said Tenzen proudly.

Jack gazed around in awe at the grotto, its high ceiling glimmering with quartz and crystals. He'd been surprised enough when Tenzen had led him to a waterfall in the mountains for his *shuriken* training. But then he'd been astounded as Tenzen had stepped through this cascade and into the hidden cavern behind. The bright sunshine filtering through the waterfall made the grotto appear light and airy, though the cavern receded into darkness.

'How far back does it go?' Jack asked.

'These mountains are riddled with caves, tunnels and passageways,' replied Tenzen. 'I've yet to fully explore them.'

'Who else knows about this place?'

'It's my secret. But I *know* I can trust you not to tell anyone.'

'So why bring me here?' asked Jack.

'Target practice,' he replied, handing Jack three *shuriken*.

'What's wrong with the posts back in the village?'

'They don't move, and samurai do,' replied Tenzen, walking over to a small log resting upon a ledge. 'We need a more realistic test for your *shuriken* skills. You can hit stationary objects almost every time, but can you hit a moving target?'

Tenzen pushed the log off the ledge. As it swung across the grotto and back again, Jack saw it was attached by a rope tied to a stalactite in the ceiling.

Taking careful aim, Jack threw his first *shuriken*. It didn't even come close, clattering into the rock wall behind. As the log continued its arc, Jack took a second shot. Again the throwing star missed, this time disappearing into the grotto's black hole. He cursed in frustration. With all the training Tenzen had given him, Jack thought he'd mastered this skill.

'Anticipate the target's movement,' advised Tenzen, giving the log another push.

Following the sweeping trajectory of the log, Jack flicked his third and final throwing star. It flew through the air, just ahead of the target and . . . shot past.

Jack watched as his *shuriken* rebounded off the cave wall and vanished into the waterfall. A second later he was knocked off his feet. Jack sat up, dazed and confused. Then he saw the offending log spinning above his head.

'Always keep one eye on your target,' said Tenzen, laughing. 'Especially when you miss.'

Tenzen produced three more *shuriken* from his pouch. 'Let me demonstrate the technique.'

As the target arced across the grotto, Tenzen launched his throwing stars one after the other. The first two struck the wood, the third sliced through the rope, sending the log crashing to the ground.

'That's incredible!' exclaimed Jack, his admiration for the ninja increasing.

'Just takes a little practice,' Tenzen replied, retrieving his *shuriken*.

'But you're so good at *everything*. Concealment, speed-running, ninja swimming, *shuriken-jutsu* . . .'

'I've no choice,' replied Tenzen, sighing as if some great weight rested upon his shoulders. He looked at Jack, seemingly unsure whether to confide in him or not. Then, pulling the last of his throwing stars out of the wood, he sat down upon a rock and faced Jack.

'As Shonin's son, I'm destined to lead the clan one day,' he began. 'That means I *have* to be the best.'

'You've nothing to worry about,' said Jack. 'Your *ninjutsu* is faultless.'

'Being a leader's not just about fighting and throwing *shuriken*. I'll have to coordinate missions, organize the farming, negotiate with samurai for our services, manage the politics of the village, maintain defences, avoid war with *daimyo* Akechi and plan for the future. My father is *brilliant* at all these things. You saw how he handled Momochi at the dinner, admitting his mistake yet still appearing in total control. That takes true skill – diplomacy that I don't naturally have. The entire village admires Shonin. I still have to *earn* that respect.'

'You'll make a brilliant leader,' reassured Jack.

'But what if I can't rise to the challenge?' said Tenzen, driving the blade of a *shuriken* into the log. 'What if I make a wrong decision under pressure?'

'I'm sure you won't,' said Jack. 'My father used to say, *In a storm, a ship that turns from a wave will flounder, but a ship that attacks the wave will rise and conquer.* I've no doubt you'll rise to the challenge when the time comes.'

'I hope so, because I sense a storm is coming.'

40

BANDITS

Hanzo sneaked through the forest, his eyes scanning for the slightest movement. He was oblivious to Jack, who crouched high in a tree, his black *shinobi shozoku* rendering him invisible in the twilight.

After a further week's intensive training in *kuji-in*, Soke had decided his students required a more physical activity. He'd instructed them to practise their Ring of Earth concealment skills and avoid detection by the best tracker, Hanzo.

Jack thought he'd evaded his friend, when Hanzo stopped and looked round.

'Soke's called us back!' Hanzo called out.

Jack formed the hand sign *Jin*, silently mouthing its mantra. This *kuji-in* enabled him to read the thoughts of others. He understood the result would be little more than suggestion, a feeling; but it could help him judge whether someone was lying or not.

Hanzo was *definitely* lying. The boy knew Jack was close. Jack had seen him also use *Jin* to sense his presence within the forest. Now Hanzo was trying to draw him out.

Jack slowed his breathing, not moving a muscle and becoming one with the tree.

'I'll eat your dinner, *tengu*!' said Hanzo, giving the area another sweep.

'Over here,' called a hushed voice that Jack recognized as Miyuki's. 'I've found his trail. I told you he's as subtle as an elephant.'

Clearly, Miyuki had been caught and was now part of the tracking team.

Jack grinned to himself. She'd fallen for his ploy – he'd left broken stems along a small forest track. Hanzo darted from the clearing in Miyuki's direction. Jack waited before dropping noiselessly to the forest floor. He thought about cutting across the ridge and backtracking to the temple, when he suddenly sensed danger.

Before Hanzo's appearance, he'd been practising the hand sign *Kai*. This enhanced a ninja's intuition, forewarning them of threats. However, Jack got the feeling he wasn't the one in danger. Someone else was, possibly Hanzo. Following his instincts, Jack ran through the forest. The sensation became stronger. Eventually reaching the furthest boundary of the village's domain, he heard voices.

'Hand it over,' growled a man, 'and we'll let you live.'

Coming to a rocky outcrop, Jack looked down to see three men on a forest path surrounding a fourth younger man. Judging by their appearance – shabby kimono, unkempt beards, wooden clubs and knives in their hands – the three men weren't samurai. Or ninja. They were bandits.

Their victim was better dressed, in a plain travelling kimono and wooden sandals. A merchant or craftsman, Jack guessed. The young man held out a pouch with a trembling hand and threw it to the middle bandit, a brawny, hard-faced man with a flattened nose.

'Is that all?' the bandit demanded, feeling the weight of the coins in his hand.

The victim mutely nodded his head.

The bandit snorted his disgust. 'Kill him.'

'But you said you wouldn't,' cried the man.

'I lied.'

The two other bandits, grinning maliciously, converged on their victim. One wielded a wooden club; the other had a rusty knife.

Jack knew the next few seconds would decide the poor man's fate. He couldn't stand by and allow him to be murdered. Quickly pulling a *shuriken* from a pouch on his waist, he flicked it at the bandit with the club. Blood spurting from his wrist, the man dropped his weapon and screamed. Unseen, Jack leapt from the rock, landing between the second bandit and his victim.

Blocking the knife attack, Jack grabbed hold of the bandit's arm, twisted it and threw him to the ground. There was a sharp crack as the man's arm broke, leaving him writhing in agony.

'Oi, ninja! Try this for size.'

Jack looked round just in time to see a massive cudgel being swung towards his head. Ducking, he simultaneously elbowed the leader in the stomach, but the man hardly flinched. As the bandit prepared for another bone-breaking swing, Jack drove in with Demon Horn Fist, sending him colliding into a tree and the cudgel flying from the leader's grasp.

'You don't scare me, ninja,' the bandit wheezed, now drawing a vicious knife from his belt. Then he stopped in his tracks as if he'd seen a ghost.

'*Blue eyes?*' he muttered, and began to edge fearfully away. 'You're no ninja. You're a *demon*!'

Turning on his heels, the leader fled down the path, his two companions following close behind.

'P-p-please don't kill me,' stuttered the young man, who'd fallen to his knees, his face ashen with fear at the strange sight of a ninja with blue eyes.

Jack retrieved the purse the bandit had dropped in his haste.

'Take it! Take it all!' the man pleaded.

'It's yours,' replied Jack, placing the purse into the man's begging hands. 'And you're free to go.'

'Th-th-thank you,' stuttered the man in astonishment. He bowed his head to the ground. 'It's my father's takings from Maruyama.'

'Your father's a merchant?'

'Yes, he sells fans,' the young man replied, warily getting to his feet.

'Tell me, where are you headed?'

'Shono . . . But I left late and decided to take a short cut to the post station . . . Stupid idea. I should have listened to my father . . .'

'And after that?'

'Kameyama . . . Tsu . . . Toba . . . Why?'

Jack smiled behind his hood. Here was the opportunity he'd been waiting for.

'I need a favour,' said Jack, deciding to trust his instincts with the man.

'My life is yours to command,' replied the merchant's son, bowing solemnly.

Jack reached into the folds of his *shozoku* jacket and removed the note. 'Can you deliver this message to Date Akiko in Toba?'

Taking the folded slip of rice paper, the merchant bowed again. 'It would be an honour to be of service.'

'This message is very important,' Jack insisted. 'It has to be given to Akiko and *no one* else.'

'I'll guard it with my life,' promised the merchant.

Jack watched the young man depart and prayed the message would reach its intended destination.

41

WAITING

As dawn broke, Jack sat beside the temple overlooking the valley. The sun, peeking above the mountains, welcomed a new day and the village awoke to the sound of a cockerel crowing. Kajiya's forge burst into life and a few farmers emerged from their homes, stretching themselves in readiness for the hard work ahead.

Jack waited, as he'd done every day for the past few weeks. In that time, the rice had turned from a vibrant green into a light brown, the fields had been drained and the seed heads had slowly drooped with the weight of their crop. They now shone like gold in the early morning sunshine.

Sighing, Jack reconciled himself to the fact that Akiko wasn't coming. Maybe she hadn't got his message, or hadn't been able to work out the code, or else couldn't follow his directions to the temple. If she didn't appear in the next few days, Jack decided he would have to make the journey himself to tell her about Hanzo. He couldn't leave Japan now without imparting this knowledge, which would mean so much to his closest friend. Although he didn't like the idea of having to retrace his steps and pass through Shono again, there was no alternative.

'You've been visiting the Buddha a lot recently.'

Jack looked up and was glad to see Miyuki. He'd been concerned it might be Shiro again, the boy having appeared unexpectedly on several other occasions. Each time he'd interrogated Jack about the samurai and their way of life. Try as he might, Jack didn't warm to Shiro. But apparently the boy hadn't mentioned to Momochi any suspicions regarding the note. And for that Jack was thankful.

Miyuki was dressed in a simple white *yukata* and held in her hands a round straw hat with a wide brim for keeping the sun off. Clearly, she wasn't training today and would be working in the fields like everyone else.

'I've been praying for my sister,' replied Jack.

This was true, since each day he spent waiting for Akiko was another day Jess had to survive. He also took the time to call upon the spirits of his mother and father for their support in the journey ahead.

Miyuki nodded sympathetically and sat down next to him. 'I pay my respects to my family here too,' she revealed.

'Is this where they're buried?' asked Jack, glancing over at the small graveyard.

'No, but I put up a grave marker in honour of them.'

It was now Jack's turn to nod sympathetically.

They both lapsed into silence and gazed pensively across the valley.

'I miss . . . my family,' whispered Miyuki, her voice small and choking with emotion.

Jack realized, despite the tough exterior she presented,

Miyuki was vulnerable inside. He recognized the lonely emptiness she felt in her life. 'I miss my parents too,' he admitted.

Miyuki looked at him, her eyes wet with tears.

'At least your father's killer is dead. You've had revenge. I've had nothing,' she said, clenching her fists in her lap. 'But one day I'll punish the samurai for what they did.'

Jack saw the flame of hatred reignite in her eyes. It wasn't directed at him this time, but he knew the damage it could do to a person.

'Revenge doesn't solve anything. It'll eat away at you until there's nothing left,' said Jack, remembering his Zen master's words the time he'd announced his intention to avenge his father. 'I didn't kill Dragon Eye. My friend honourably sacrificed his life to do that. But Dragon Eye's death brought me no comfort. I still grieve for my father every single day. You should focus on living, not killing.'

'But how can I? When every night I go to sleep, I see my mother dying before my eyes . . .' Miyuki once again lapsed into silence. She trembled as if wanting to speak, but was unable to.

'Do you want to tell me what happened?' Jack suggested, understanding Miyuki desperately needed to talk through her grief. Possibly she'd never spoken of it to the others, afraid they might think she was weak and unworthy of being a ninja.

Eventually she plucked up the courage.

'I was eight at the time. It was summer. Jun, my brother, was playing outside with my father. I was in the house, helping my mother with the chores. The samurai attacked without warning. They rampaged through our village. Killing . . . killing everyone . . .' Miyuki gave a shuddering breath as she relived her nightmare. 'My father was shouting for us to run. My mother, hearing him shriek in pain, quickly pushed me under the floorboards. Jun ran in, screaming. My mother tried to shield his little body, but the samurai just kicked her away and cut him down. He was only five! What harm could he do them?'

Miyuki began to sob. 'My mother collapsed to the floor where I lay hidden. I think she did it on purpose, to stop the samurai discovering me. She wasn't even trying to fight back, but the samurai still killed her. I saw the sword go in!'

Jack felt compelled to comfort Miyuki. He too had seen his father run through with a sword. The horrifying memory was burnt into his soul. Jack put an arm tenderly round Miyuki. She stiffened, then accepted his kindness, crying on his shoulder.

'Your mother sounds very brave,' said Jack. 'Like my father, she sacrificed her life so *you* could live on. That's why you must let go of these thoughts of revenge. Your mother wouldn't want you to spend the rest of your life consumed with hatred.'

'But that samurai actually stayed to *watch* her die! I'll never forget the glee on his face. And all the time, my mother's blood was dripping on to me!'

Jack could think of nothing to say that would comfort her. He just let her cry, tears long overdue streaming down her cheeks. Eventually, she became self-conscious of Jack's arm round her. Sitting up, she wiped her eyes with the back of her hand.

'It's an early harvest this year,' she announced, standing up. 'We should go and help bring it in.'

Nodding, Jack got to his feet.

'You'll need a hat, by the way,' said Miyuki, offering him the one in her hand.

'Thank you,' replied Jack, and put it on. 'It's a perfect fit.'

42

HARVEST

The heat stretched the day into an endless toil. Sweat poured off Jack and he was glad for Miyuki's hat. Though the work was arduous, Jack also found it satisfying. They worked in teams, bent over the crops, sickles in hand. The blades, glinting in the sun, swooped like silver swallows through the paddy fields. Some of the villagers sang while they worked, and a real sense of community spirit bound them all to their task. Every hour produced more and more sheaves of rice ready for threshing.

Tenzen had shown Jack how to cut the rice at its roots and tie the stalks into bundles. Then they laid them in rows for Hanzo and the other children to carry away. As midday approached, Tenzen suggested they take a break beneath the shade of a tree.

'Any further news on *daimyo* Akechi's plans?' asked Jack, offering round his water gourd. He was concerned that the samurai lord would attack before Akiko managed to get to the village.

Tenzen gratefully took some water before passing it on to Shiro and Miyuki. 'The last intelligence we received was that *daimyo* Akechi had recruited enough samurai and was impatient to begin his offensive. But without knowledge of our village's location or the Shogun's support, his generals were advising against a blanket invasion. They don't want him to make the same mistake as General Nobunaga's son.'

'Which was?' asked Jack.

'Attacking several villages at once,' explained Tenzen. 'By dividing his forces, his troops were too widespread. Our ninja used this to their advantage and decimated the invading samurai.'

'They were put into such a panic,' Miyuki added, 'some even turned on each other by mistake.' With a barely concealed smile, she returned the water gourd to Jack.

'Unfortunately,' Tenzen continued, 'his humiliating defeat brought the wrath of Oda Nobunaga upon the ninja clans.'

The terrible consequence for the *shinobi* of that battle was left unsaid, but it hung heavy in the air.

'The good news is that the longer Akechi deliberates, the greater the chance our emissaries have of influencing the Edo court and persuading the Shogun to intervene. Whatever happens, we have to get the harvest in first.'

With that thought, Tenzen led them back to work.

'Come on, Shiro!' called Tenzen. 'We'll get it done a lot quicker if you put your back into it too.'

Shiro wearily got to his feet, grumbling, 'A ninja's work is never done!'

Earlier that day, Jack had discovered the harvest was a time of ritual celebration. The head of each family had gone into the fields and made offerings to a stone shrine in honour of Ta-no-kami, the god of the rice fields. After presenting *saké*, flowers and other small gifts, the men had pulled out three plants each with fine heads of rice.

That evening, Jack sat with Soke and Hanzo, and they enjoyed a simple but solemn meal together. The rice Soke had selected was laid out upon a small shelf that acted as the farmhouse's *kami* shrine. Everyone washed their hands and Soke led them in prayer for a good harvest. Then in reverential silence he presented himself, Hanzo and Jack with a few grains. In turn, they tasted the rice.

A satisfied grin appeared on Soke's face. 'The rice has grown well again this year,' he announced.

That night Jack went to bed content, but utterly exhausted. However, by the afternoon of the third day, Jack *really* knew what it meant to be tired. His muscles were knotted and aching, and the sapping heat had drained his strength. He'd thought being a rigging monkey on-board the *Alexandria* had been tough work, but that was nothing compared to the backbreaking labour of a rice harvest.

Matters weren't helped by the weather. There wasn't even a breeze to alleviate the unrelenting heat of the sun. And the ground, baked hard, was now cracking into a dusty-brown mosaic.

Jack took a water break, resting under the feeble shade of a tree. Shiro was already there, apparently dozing.

'I warned you your arms would drop off,' Shiro muttered from beneath his straw hat. 'You should conserve your energy. Never know when you might need it.'

Miyuki joined them.

'It's *so* hot today,' she gasped, wiping her brow.

Jack nodded, taking a long swig from his water gourd. As he did so, he noticed a column of hazy smoke rising from the ridge into the cloudless blue sky. 'Too hot,' he said. 'Looks like a forest fire's started.'

Miyuki squinted in the direction Jack was gazing.

'That's no fire. It's a smoke beacon!' she said, her eyes widening in alarm. 'We're under attack!'

43

INVASION

'How did they find us?' Miyuki exclaimed as the alarm was raised throughout the village.

'Who knows?' said Shiro, glancing sideways at Jack.

Jack felt a cold slither of dread run through him. It *can't* have been his fault. Even if *daimyo* Akechi had somehow got his hands on the note, the message had been carefully coded.

'All that matters is they have,' stated Tenzen as he kicked away at a dam and allowed the paddy fields to flood again.

'But why now?' asked Miyuki. 'When we're in harvest?'

'That's exactly why. Our guard is down. We're tired. Akechi's been waiting for this moment.'

A battalion of armoured samurai materialized from the forest to stand upon the ridge in one unbroken line. Raising their swords aloft, the countless blades catching the blazing sun, they gave an almighty battle cry. It echoed through the valley.

This was answered by another.

Jack was almost stopped in his tracks at the sight of a second battalion marching up the valley road, the column stretching into the distance like an immense dragon's tail.

'They certainly haven't come to negotiate a surrender,' said Tenzen. 'This'll be a fight to the death. Gather your weapons. My father will need us all in the village square.'

Splitting from the others, Jack ran to Soke's farmhouse. The first wave of troops had already begun to descend the slopes. But the Ring of Earth was proving an effective defence. The steep valley sides and lack of paths hampered their advance. Some samurai were even falling over them-selves, their armour hindering them.

Jack flung open the door to the *doma*. In the hearth room, Soke had raised a section of the floorboards, beneath which Jack could see a whole host of hidden weapons – swords, knives, *shuriken*, *shuko* claws, chains, and even a small bow and quiver of arrows. The entire time Jack had been living in the house, he'd had no idea this compartment existed. The shock on his face must have been apparent.

'Although I hope for the best,' said Soke, fishing out a large *katana*, 'I've always prepared for the worst.'

He offered the weapon to Jack, unsheathing the blade to reveal a jagged, saw-like edge. 'It's a *shikoro-ken*,' he explained. 'A Sword of Destruction.'

Jack tried not to imagine the damage such a weapon could do.

'Thank you,' he replied, handing it back, 'but I'd prefer my own swords.'

Soke nodded. 'Better the devil you know.' He put the *shikoro-ken* together with the other weapons he was collecting.

Hanzo appeared, a bag in his hand, and began to stuff as many *shuriken* as he could into it. He glanced up at Jack with fearful yet determined eyes.

'Are they in the village?' he asked.

'Not yet,' replied Jack, hoping his voice didn't give away the dread he felt.

He squeezed the boy's shoulder reassuringly and hurried past into the bedroom. Grabbing his *katana* and *wakizashi*, Jack slipped them firmly into the *obi* of his farming trousers. Even though he wasn't dressed for combat, with his swords he felt ready to confront the samurai.

His pack was stashed in the corner. All his possessions and, most importantly, the *rutter*. He couldn't leave that behind. Snatching up the bag, he ran back into the hearth room. Soke and Hanzo were waiting for him at the *doma* entrance.

'Hurry!' urged the Grandmaster.

As Jack passed the hidden compartment, an idea struck him. However important the contents, his pack would compromise his fighting ability. He dropped it into the hole and slammed the floorboards shut. At least the *rutter* would be safe until he returned . . . if he ever did.

Jack joined Soke and Hanzo in the yard. The first line of samurai had reached the village boundary, weaving along the network of pathways, while some struggled through the flooding paddy fields. A vanguard of ninja rushed to meet them, hoping to give the other villagers time to marshal in the square.

Soke handed Jack a bundle of weapons.

'Let's go,' he ordered, moving with astonishing agility.

They sprinted along the path and on to the road. Other ninja joined them in their dash to the relative safety of the square. Ahead, Jack saw the second samurai battalion approaching. Only three men wide, due to the deliberately narrow road, the column was having to fight every step of the way as a small party of ninja battled to hold them back. But it would be touch and go whether Hanzo, Soke and Jack made it to the square's gate before the samurai did.

Suddenly the column surged forward as the ninja fell beneath the blades of the samurai. It was now an all-out race to reach the wooden gate. Putting on a burst of speed, Jack sprinted up the rise with Soke and Hanzo. Behind them, the pounding of feet and shouts of the samurai pursued them. Risking a glance back, Jack saw a warrior, his sword raised in one hand, about to cut him down.

Then a flash of silver shot past Jack and struck the samurai in the throat. He let out a guttural cry, stumbled and fell, blood gushing from his mouth. Tenzen, standing by the gate, launched another *shuriken* to take out the next samurai in line. Jack shot through the entrance, one of the last before the gate was slammed shut and barred.

The samurai troops began to hammer against the barrier. For the time being it held, but Jack knew they were on borrowed time.

'Thanks for saving me back there,' he gasped as Tenzen helped bolster the gate with wooden staves.

'You'd have done the same for me,' Tenzen replied, then in jest added, 'If you could hit a moving target, that is!'

'Distribute the weapons, Jack,' instructed Soke, before going to report to Shonin.

Handing out the few weapons he had, Jack was disheartened to see that barely half the villagers had made it. But he was glad to see Miyuki among the survivors.

'Here,' said Jack, offering her the *shikoro-ken*. 'It's the ideal weapon for you.'

Miyuki took it, smiling grimly when she drew the blade. 'Thanks, but we'll need more than a Sword of Destruction to get out of this alive.'

'I've been in worse situations,' said Jack, thinking of the Battle of Osaka and his encounter with the Red Devils.

'Are you so sure?' she replied, looking out across the paddy fields – not with despair, but resignation.

The fields swarmed with samurai, the rice crops the villagers had been working so hard to harvest now trampled underfoot. Any pockets of resistance were being swiftly crushed. From all directions, *daimyo* Akechi's forces closed in upon the central square. At a guess, the ninja were outnumbered ten to one. With such a force, Jack realized *daimyo* Akechi intended to wipe out the entire village, just as he'd vowed to.

Jack never imagined he'd find himself on the side of the ninja, fighting against samurai. *Perhaps this is one battle I won't survive*, he thought.

As the samurai gathered for their main assault on the square, Jack spotted the *daimyo* Akechi on his horse. Dressed in full ceremonial armour, he looked like the warrior in his painting – except he was safely at the rear, letting his troops take the fight to the ninja.

Inside the square, Shonin was rallying everyone together. The heads of family were taking up their stations to defend the four corners. Mothers with their children were being shepherded inside the farmhouse by Momochi.

Jack looked down at Hanzo, who stood by his side, silent

yet resolute. 'You should go too,' he said, hoping against hope that the women and children might be spared.

Hanzo shook his head. 'I'm not scared,' he said, drawing a short sword from his hip. '*This* is what I've trained for.'

Jack couldn't help but smile. The boy had the heart of a ninja and the samurai courage to match.

But as Jack prepared to face their enemy, he was terrified the so-called tuition he'd given Hanzo wouldn't be enough to repel the attack of a fully armed warrior. He could only pray he was wrong.

44

THE VILLAGE SQUARE

To Jack's surprise and relief, the samurai's initial offensive was repelled. The village square, built as it was upon a bank and with one side buffered by the pond, was proving to be an effective stronghold. Ninja armed with bows shot arrows into the samurai horde, picking off those who attempted to scale the steep bank. Any warrior managing to do so was confronted by the impenetrable thorn hedge, while samurai reaching the inner fence found themselves skewered by spears and *naginata*.

The supreme confidence of Akechi's troops was then dealt another blow.

Jack was helping defend the eastern corner, when Hanzo called out, 'Look! They're fighting among themselves.'

Jack was stunned to see he was right. A company of samurai was in utter disarray, blood flowing as they slaughtered one another for no apparent reason.

Tenzen laughed, though his eyes betrayed a deeper sorrow.

'That will be my uncle, Ishibe, and his men,' he said with pride. 'They've been hiding out in the storehouse, disguised in samurai armour.'

Jack now understood. A Ring of Wind tactic. *A ninja's presence should be like the wind — always felt but never seen.* It was a suicide mission. By infiltrating and killing the samurai from within their own ranks, Ishibe and his men had turned the samurai upon themselves. Not knowing who was friend or foe, each soldier now fought for his own life.

Chaos reigned and it sent ripples of mistrust among the other companies. But the commanders rallied their troops and enforced order upon them. The infighting petered out, the imposters exposed. Only one remained alive. He was dragged to the front of the column for all to see.

'Ishibe,' breathed Tenzen.

A samurai soldier forced the ninja to his knees. Then the commanding officer approached, withdrew his *katana* and cut off Ishibe's head.

'NO!' cried Tenzen.

Jack grabbed hold of Tenzen's arm, fearing his friend was about to leap the fence to wreak revenge.

The officer picked up Ishibe's severed head by the hair and held it aloft. Pointing his sword at the villagers in the square, he shouted, 'THIS IS THE FATE OF ALL NINJA!'

'*And yours too!*' screamed Tenzen as his *shuriken* struck the commander in the face a second later.

Blood gushing from his eyesocket, the commander bawled, 'ATTACK! ATTACK!'

The samurai, rattling their swords, gave a deafening battle cry, and in one unstoppable wave stormed the barricades. The wooden gate disintegrated under the force of the assault. As the troops poured into the square, Jack now withdrew *both* his swords. If there was ever a time he needed the Two Heavens, this was it.

'Stay by my side,' Jack told Hanzo.

'Are we going to die, *tengu*?' he asked, his voice wavering.

Jack didn't want to lie to Hanzo, but neither did he want him to give up hope. '*Tengu* can't die, remember!'

Hanzo looked up at Jack, his tender years all too visible in his terrified face. 'But I'm not a *tengu*.'

'Well, I am. And I'm going to protect you with my life.'

The first samurai through the gate were slain immediately. But for every one killed, two more appeared. The ninja were driven back. Reinforcements rushed to their aid. Soke swung his cane and chain with devastating results. Despite his years, his lethal skills dealt death to any samurai who approached.

A group of soldiers broke through, charging towards Miyuki, Jack and Hanzo. Raising their swords, Jack and Miyuki prepared to defend themselves. But before the enemy had got within reach, five blades flicked through the air. They struck within the space of a single breath.

Ikki goken.

The five samurai collapsed to the ground, screaming in agony.

Tenzen held out his hand to Hanzo. 'More!'

Hanzo hastily passed him another five throwing stars from his bag.

The screaming samurai were put out of their misery by ninja with spears. But these kills were small victories in a battle the *shinobi* could only lose. It was immediately apparent to Jack that, forced to fight on samurai terms, the ninja were outskilled in the sword and outnumbered in men. Only their sheer bravery and determination held back the inevitable slaughter.

Shonin fought alongside his men, splatters of blood staining his kimono. His bodyguards fell one by one under the swords of the samurai, but he wouldn't yield.

The fighting spread throughout the square, the cries of battle now joined by the screams of the wounded and dying. A unit of samurai carved their way through the ninja defence. In its midst was their commanding officer, his face dripping with blood, his eye a gruesome hole. The unit purposefully fought its way over to Tenzen.

'You take my eye, I take your head!' the commanding officer declared, swinging his sword.

Tenzen threw a pointed *shuriken*, but the samurai was ready for him this time. Deflecting the spike with his blade, he drove forward with his *katana*.

Drawing his *ninjatō*, Tenzen fought for his life.

Jack and Miyuki rushed to his defence, but the samurai's escort engaged them in combat, leaving Tenzen to struggle on alone. As Jack clashed with two warriors, through the chaos of battle Hanzo saw Soke surrounded by samurai. A glancing blow from one of his attacker's swords dug deep into the Grandmaster's thigh and he dropped to the ground.

'*Grandfather!*' cried Hanzo, running to his aid, his sword held high.

'NO!' shouted Jack. But it was too late. The boy was no longer under his protection.

In that moment of distraction, Jack was caught across the arm by one of the samurai's blades. It was only a flesh wound, but it roused his fighting spirit. Side-kicking the first samurai hard in the chest, he simultaneously hobbled the second with a lightning strike to the knee. Jack barged through them, rushing across the square in pursuit of Hanzo. But another samurai, broad as an ox and with a terrifying *menpō* mask of gold and black serrated teeth, blocked his path.

'The infamous *gaijin* samurai!' he grunted in satisfaction. 'You're *my* prize.'

The samurai wielded a deadly *nagamaki*, a weapon with a lethal *katana*-length blade and an extended shaft equally as long.

Jack barely avoided his thrust and was almost hacked in two by a second sweeping attack. Deflecting the blade, Jack attempted a counter-cut across the man's chest, but he couldn't get close enough. The *nagamaki*'s extra reach kept his swords at bay. Driven backwards by a series of sweeping slices, he stumbled over the dead body of a ninja and fell to the bloodsoaked ground.

As Jack instinctively rolled to his feet, the samurai seized upon the advantage and thrust for his heart. There was no time for Jack to evade it. But then a jagged-edge sword cleaved through the *nagamaki*'s shaft *and* the samurai's lead hand – severing them both.

Holding his stump before his eyes, the samurai's cry of shock was cut short when a ninja's arrow lodged itself in his throat. The samurai collapsed in a juddering heap at Jack's feet.

'Come on,' Miyuki insisted, dragging Jack towards the farmhouse. She too was wounded, blood running down her arm.

'But Hanzo!' he protested. 'Soke!'

Mounting the embankments on all sides, Akechi's army surged into the square and overwhelmed the remaining ninja. Neither Hanzo nor Soke were anywhere to be seen.

'It's too late!' cried Miyuki. She pulled Jack inside the farmhouse, where a handful of ninja were making a last stand. Stumbling down the corridor, Miyuki led Jack into the reception room. As she hurried towards the dais, two samurai – one wearing a red *menpō* with a hooknose, the other a helmet with two spiked horns – burst through a *shoji* to their left.

'At last, I've caught up with you!' snarled the horn-headed samurai.

Jack couldn't believe it, though he recognized the man's rat-like moustache and bushy eyebrows. It was the samurai from the inn at Shono.

'You won't escape me this time, *gaijin*,' he growled, raising his *katana*.

Jack and Miyuki, side by side, swords in hand, confronted their enemy.

Miyuki glanced at Jack with grim finality. 'To the death!'

45

FIRE IN THE FARMHOUSE

The two samurai bore down on them. Without warning, the one wearing the *menpō* attacked his leader. In a lightning strike, he chopped at his neck with the edge of his hand. The samurai collapsed to the ground, unconscious.

'*Fall Down Fist?*' uttered Miyuki, more stunned at the technique than their sudden change of fate.

Their samurai saviour pulled off his mask to reveal a girl's face. The long dark hair was hidden by the helmet, but the half-moon eyes, dark as black pearl, and the rose-petal lips were instantly recognizable.

'Akiko!' cried Jack in astonishment and delight.

He rushed forwards, embracing her. For that brief moment, the battle receded into the distance and he was back in Toba.

'*Forever bound to one another,*' she whispered in his ear, returning his embrace.

'You *know* this samurai?' exclaimed Miyuki, her sword still raised.

'This is Akiko,' said Jack, as if that explained everything. 'My closest friend.'

Akiko bowed her head respectfully, though she kept her eyes on Miyuki throughout.

'We don't have time for formalities,' responded Miyuki, barely acknowledging Akiko's bow. 'We have to get out of here.'

Their innate distrust of one another was immediately apparent. For one brief moment, Jack wondered whether Akiko, as a samurai, had revealed the location of the ninja village to *daimyo* Akechi. But Jack trusted her implicitly. Besides, Akiko wouldn't have wanted to risk her little brother's life in a mass attack upon the village.

'I can take you prisoner,' Akiko suggested, overlooking Miyuki's slight. Glancing at Jack, she added, 'Just like Sensei Kyuzo did at Osaka Castle.'

Miyuki laughed at the idea. 'No samurai will ever take *me* prisoner.'

'And I'm afraid it wouldn't work,' said Jack. '*Daimyo* Akechi intends to kill us all. And he *definitely* wants to kill me.'

'You can't fight your way past a thousand samurai,' Akiko argued.

'We don't need to,' shot back Miyuki.

Jack wondered what she had in mind. Escaping disguised as samurai warriors was out of the question. They were trapped in the farmhouse, lacked a second set of armour and, besides, Akechi's army was on the alert for imposters.

'You trust this *samurai*?' Miyuki asked of Jack.

'With my life,' he replied.

'Then I suppose I'll have to,' she said, sheathing her sword. 'Follow me.'

Miyuki stepped on to the dais. The sounds of fighting drew nearer. Suddenly a figure staggered into the room.

'Tenzen!' said Jack with relief, having given him up for dead.

The ninja was battleworn and bloodstained, a nasty gash on his forehead. Seeing Akiko, he went to throw his last remaining *shuriken*.

'NO!' Jack shouted, jumping into his line of sight. 'She's with me.'

Tenzen shot Jack a disbelieving look, but Miyuki gave an affirmative nod and he lowered his hand.

'Where's Shonin?' asked Miyuki urgently.

'I don't know,' Tenzen replied with dismay. He pressed his hand to his wound. 'I took the commander's other eye out and my father took his head. But I lost him after that. The battle was too chaotic.'

'And Soke? Hanzo?' asked Jack.

Limping over, Tenzen put a hand on Jack's shoulder, both for comfort and support. 'I'm sorry. I haven't seen them.'

'We have to go,' Miyuki urged.

At that moment, Kajiya the bladesmith ran in. 'They've set fire to the farmhouse!' he shouted.

Behind him, Shiro and two other students appeared, Danjo and Kato, panic etched on their faces. Smoke was already billowing from the corridor into the room.

'Good,' said Miyuki to everyone's surprise. 'It will cover our escape.'

She pushed at the wall panel with the painting of the kingfisher. It pivoted open to reveal a secret corridor. Jack stared open-mouthed, but he didn't know why he should be surprised. This was a ninja house after all.

'Who's the samurai?' Kajiya demanded as Miyuki disappeared down the passageway.

'A friend of Jack's,' replied Tenzen, limping after Miyuki. 'On our side, supposedly.'

Kaijya stared at Akiko. 'You picked a fine day to visit,' he said, ushering her and Jack ahead of him.

The corridor led through a door into a small hidden room. They crowded in, barely enough space for the eight survivors.

'We'll be burnt alive in here!' commented Akiko.

'Out of the way,' Miyuki ordered, pushing Akiko to one side.

Bending down, she removed the *shoji*'s wooden runner and lifted a square section of the corridor's floor to reveal a secret passageway.

Now Jack *was* surprised.

'Go!' beckoned Miyuki as the sound of flames crackled above them. 'Kajiya, you lead the way.'

The bladesmith jumped into the hole, swiftly followed by the other ninja and Tenzen. Miyuki, affecting a bow, stepped aside to allow Akiko down. '*Samurai* first.'

'Thank you,' replied Akiko, equally civil.

'You next, Jack,' said Miyuki. 'I'll protect your back.'

Jack landed in a narrow passageway that led down and away from the farmhouse. The floor was wooden, but the walls and low ceiling were hard-packed earth and rock, reinforced by beams. He had to crouch and shuffle along. Up ahead, he could just make out the faint light from Kajiya's candle and the sound of running water. Behind him, it was pitch darkness as Miyuki shut the trapdoor.

'Hurry,' she whispered, 'and be quiet as we pass under the well shaft.'

When they reached the bottom of the slope, they entered the water. Jack went waist deep, its chill almost taking his breath away, but at least he could now stand. Passing through a patch of pale light, the sounds of cheering could be heard echoing down the shaft.

'It's all over,' said Miyuki in a quiet voice.

Jack looked back to see her face ghostly in the reflected light, a single tear running down her cheek. Once again, her life had been destroyed by the samurai.

They forged on, the slope rising slightly beneath their feet. The current became stronger as the sound of running water grew louder in the darkness.

'Where are we?' whispered Jack.

'Under the mountain,' replied Miyuki. 'Shonin came across an underground stream when digging the well.'

'Why didn't everyone use this escape route?'

'It's a secret only known to a select few. The holding of the square was to give the children and their mothers time to escape. Shonin wasn't going to let the samurai slaughter them this time.'

Jack was amazed by the ninja leader's cunning and sacrifice. Akechi and his samurai saw all the villagers run for the square. With everyone dead there and the farmhouse burnt down, the *daimyo* would believe he'd wiped out this ninja clan.

Miyuki sighed. 'Unfortunately, we didn't hold out long enough to get Shonin, Soke and the other heads of family through.'

Or Hanzo, thought Jack desperately. *How am I going to tell Akiko I've lost her little brother to the fight?*

'We should keep mov–'

Miyuki stopped and listened. The sounds of splashing were approaching fast from behind.

'Go!' said Miyuki in alarm.

Quickening their pace, they entered a rift in the rock. The stream cascaded down and they had to climb against the flow. Tenzen slipped and tumbled past Akiko. But she grabbed him, halting his fall. Recovering his footing, Tenzen nodded his appreciation, clearly surprised at her reactions and strength, and resumed his climbing.

Near the top, Kajiya reached for a ladder that led into a wooden shaft. In turn, they scrambled up the steps towards another trapdoor. Jack clambered out after the others, emerging behind the statue of the Buddha. As Miyuki exited, she drew her *shikoro-ken* in readiness to cut down their pursuers. Out of the darkness, a sword red with blood rose to meet Miyuki's blade.

THE NINE NINJA

Black with smoke, Zenjubo's face appeared, his eyes narrowing when he spotted Akiko. 'Prisoner?'

'No, friend,' answered Miyuki, though her hostile expression suggested otherwise.

'Did anyone else make it?' asked Tenzen. 'Momochi? *My father?*'

Zenjubo shook his head.

Distraught at the news, Tenzen stormed out of the temple, Miyuki hurrying after him. Zenjubo nodded for everyone to follow as he closed the trapdoor behind them.

Gathering outside where Tenzen was slumped on the steps with Miyuki, the survivors gazed in stunned silence at the devastation. A plume of smoke rose from the flaming farmhouse into the clear blue sky. Samurai swarmed over the village like a nest of angry wasps, and the bodies of friends and family lay scattered in the dust. Seeing the soldiers ransack the farmers' homes, Jack's anguish intensified, his concern for the *nutter's* fate adding to his grief at losing Soke and Hanzo.

Akiko, noting Jack's distress, took him gently to one side. 'How did you end up *here*? As a *ninja*?'

'It's a long story,' sighed Jack. 'But I ran into trouble in Shono and it was Soke, the Grandmaster, who saved me.'

Akiko gave him an incredulous look. 'But the *shinobi* are our enemy!'

'A frog in a well does not know the great sea,' he replied.

'When did *you* become Sensei Yamada?' she said, shaking her head in wonder.

'The ninja aren't who you think they are.'

'I realize that truth more than any samurai,' she replied. 'I trained as one. All the more reason *not* to trust them.'

Akiko held Jack's gaze. 'You've changed.'

'Perhaps,' admitted Jack. Then, smiling warmly at her, he added, 'But I'm glad you haven't.'

She returned his smile with equal warmth. 'I see you still have my father's swords. In my eyes, you'll *always* be a samurai.'

For a moment, neither spoke, simply content to be in each other's company again.

Finally, Jack broke the silence. 'I was beginning to worry my message hadn't got through.'

'I came as fast as I could. The merchant you sent was held up in Kameyama. He apologized profusely. Then it took time to figure out your message. These mountains are a maze, one rocky outcrop looks like another. I had no option but to return to Maruyama. There I discovered *daimyo* Akechi was mobilizing for an attack on a *shinobi* village, and it was rumoured there was a foreigner . . . a *gaijin* ninja.'

Akiko raised her eyebrows at Jack knowingly.

'With a reward on his head, I joined the army to capture him for myself.'

'Lucky for me you did!' replied Jack. 'I'm just sorry there's no reward.'

Akiko's expression became serious. 'Your message said you think you've found Kiyoshi. Where is he?'

Jack, unable to meet Akiko's eyes, sadly shook his head.

'Hanzo . . . who might be Kiyoshi, insisted on staying to fight.' He gazed across the smoke-filled valley, remorse overwhelming his heart. 'I tried to protect him, but in the middle of battle he ran to save his grandfather, Soke. Kiyoshi's a brave soul. But I fear he's . . . dead.'

A wave of grief struck Akiko as all her hopes were dashed. Her face drained of colour and Jack reached out a hand to steady her.

'I'm too late . . .' she wept, her eyes welling with tears as Jack took her in his arms.

Miyuki glanced over at them, then quickly looked away when Jack caught her gaze.

Their sorrow was interrupted by Danjo, suddenly exclaiming, 'Look, they've taken prisoners!'

The boy pointed into the valley, where a detachment of samurai was returning victorious to Maruyama, *daimyo* Akechi at the head. Trailing behind was a sorry line of ninja. Not many, perhaps twenty or so.

Jack's heart lifted at the idea that Hanzo might be among them. Then it immediately went cold.

'*Daimyo* Akechi vowed to kill everyone. Why's he taken prisoners?'

'Torture,' Zenjubo said bitterly.

'But he's won!' exclaimed Jack.

'He'll want the locations of the other ninja clans in his province,' explained Tenzen, getting to his feet.

Zenjubo turned to him. 'Your eyesight's better than mine. Who's survived?'

Squinting into the distance, Tenzen's expression turned from dejection to delight. 'My father's at the front with Momochi!' he exclaimed. 'And I think that's Soke at the back.'

Jack strained to make out any of them. Then he spotted Soke's bald head towards the rear of the line. Beside him, a small figure was helping him along.

'*Hanzo's alive*,' breathed Jack, turning to Akiko with relief.

But their joy was cut short as they recalled the fate awaiting her little brother. Now Jack only felt sick, shuddering at the thought of Hanzo imprisoned in Gemnan's garden of Hell. The pit. The hanging tree. The bamboo spikes. The boiling pot. The crucifix.

'We *must* rescue them!' said Jack.

Shiro, who had been silent until now, laughed scornfully at the suggestion. 'What can we possibly do? There's only *eight* of us.'

'Nine,' corrected Akiko.

'When did *you* suddenly become a ninja?' Miyuki snapped.

'I've trained in your ways.'

'So you're a spy!'

'Take's one to know one.'

Miyuki stared daggers at her. 'What do you care anyway?'

'I care more than you know!' retorted Akiko, the jibe breaking her usual calm demeanour.

'I find that hard to believe,' shot back Miyuki, squaring up to her. 'Samurai lack heart.'

'And you lack –'

'Enough!' said Tenzen, stepping between them, all of a sudden taking charge. 'This isn't helping matters.'

'What I don't understand is why *she's* here in the first place,' said Miyuki, glaring at Akiko over Tenzen's shoulder.

'Jack must have sent her a message,' said Shiro, his eyes narrowing in suspicion.

Horrified, everyone turned to Jack.

'Did you?' demanded Tenzen.

Jack nodded, mortified at being exposed in such a way. 'I asked Akiko to come.'

'So you did betray us!' seethed Miyuki.

'NO! My message was coded. *Daimyo* Akechi had no idea of its existence. There was no way he could have found out,' Jack argued. 'Akiko joined the army as a disguise. Besides, she would *never* reveal the location.'

'Why should we believe that?' said Tenzen.

'Because I believe Hanzo is her lost brother.'

For a moment, no one spoke, stunned by the revelation. Tenzen stared at Akiko, clearly weighing up whether this was true and if he could trust her.

'*That's* why I care,' said Akiko ardently.

'But you're samurai,' Miyuki reminded her spitefully. 'Hanzo's a ninja.'

Akiko didn't back down. 'My little brother, Kiyoshi, was kidnapped by Dragon Eye and hidden with a ninja clan in these mountains. If there's even the slightest possibility Hanzo is Kiyoshi, I'll risk my life to save him!'

'There's more fire in this samurai than in my furnace,' commented Kajiya, who sat on the temple steps. 'If we're going to rescue Shonin and the others, then I want this one on our side.'

Zenjubo grunted his agreement.

'It's settled then,' said Tenzen, bowing formally to Akiko. 'A samurai could prove very useful in our rescue mission.'

'You're not seriously considering attacking *daimyo* Akechi's army, are you?' interrupted Shiro, his eyes wide with disbelief.

'I realize the odds are stacked against us,' replied Tenzen. 'But the *shinobi* faced far greater challenges against Nobunaga's son – and won.'

He looked at each of them, testing their resolve. Jack recognized in Tenzen's eyes the hawk-like intensity and inspiring conviction of his father. Without dispute, Tenzen had become the natural leader of the group. He'd risen to the challenge.

'Remember, we're not just rescuing friends and saving lives,' Tenzen continued, spurring their motivation. 'We're rescuing the clan, saving Shonin and Soke's knowledge. But we'll be fighting back on *our* terms – stealth, not strength, will win the day.'

47

AN UNLUCKY NUMBER

'We've got no chance like *this*,' said Shiro, forcing them to take a look at themselves.

Apart from Akiko, they were a ragged bunch in their tattered, bloodstained work clothes with only a handful of weapons between them. It was apparent to all they were ill-equipped for any sort of mission.

'You're right,' conceded Tenzen. 'We'll have to return to the village for equipment and supplies.'

He looked down into the valley, where the samurai were still pillaging the houses and checking for survivors. 'It'll be dangerous, though. Any volunteers?'

Jack was about to put up his hand, the chance of retrieving the *rutter* foremost in his mind, when Miyuki interrupted.

'All we need is a little faith,' she said, striding over to the temple. The others followed, bemused.

Inside, she knelt as if to pray before the Buddha, then, reaching forward, she pressed both hands against the wooden base. There was a soft click and a secret compartment opened. Miyuki pulled out the drawer to reveal a number of black *shinobi shozoku*.

'How come only *you* knew about this?' asked Kajiya, amazed.

'I came to pay my respects to my parents one evening, when I found Soke checking their condition,' Miyuki explained, distributing the outfits to all but Akiko. 'Sorry, none left for you.'

'No matter, I've come prepared,' replied Akiko, smiling politely.

'We'll still need weapons,' pointed out Shiro.

Miyuki rolled her eyes. 'Don't you ever stop moaning? I sometimes wonder if you really *are* a ninja.'

Ignoring his protests, she led them over to the far corner of the graveyard.

'But . . . this is your family's marker,' said Tenzen.

Miyuki nodded. 'Read the inscription.'

Tenzen grinned and began digging in the earth with his knife.

'What does it say?' whispered Jack to Akiko.

'Hope for the best, prepare for the worst.'

Now Jack smiled too and knelt down to help Tenzen.

The two of them dug down until a large lacquered box was revealed. Tenzen and Jack pulled off the lid. Inside was a carefully considered collection of weapons and equipment. Two *ninjatō*, four pairs of *shuko* claws and *ashiko* foot hooks, a bag of *tetsu-bishi* spikes, a varied selection of *shuriken*, two *kaginawa* climbing ropes, a blowpipe complete with poisoned darts, a sickle and chain and some explosives.

Reaching down, Miyuki picked up the blowpipe. 'Even from the grave, my parents *will* have their revenge.'

The rest of the equipment was handed out and the ninja

prepared themselves for the mission. As Jack was getting ready, the cut on his arm opened up again.

'Let me bind that for you,' said Akiko, who was packing her armour into a sack for the journey.

He sat down on the temple steps, letting her clean and bandage the wound with strips torn from their discarded work clothes. Jack had missed her kindness and compassion. What a fool he'd been to leave her that day in Toba. But what choice did he have, with the Shogun banishing foreigners and his sister alone in England? If *only* circumstances had been different, he'd have followed his heart.

'That should do it,' she said, smiling sweetly at him.

'Thank you,' replied Jack, though he wanted to say so much more. By the look in her eyes, she did too, but they both knew this wasn't the time or place.

'I'd better get changed,' he mumbled.

At that moment Miyuki passed by. She gave Jack a cold, hard stare, before turning it on Akiko.

'Tenzen, do you *really* think we should be taking this samurai along with us? Nine is an unlucky number. She'll bring misfortune upon the mission.'

'Miyuki,' said Tenzen, gently leading her away, 'this samurai could be Hanzo's sister. If that's the case, she deserves the chance to help save him. And if we're going to succeed, we'll need *everyone*.'

Akiko looked at Jack. 'I can understand her hating samurai, but why does she have such an issue with me? We're on the same side.'

'Miyuki takes a while to warm to people,' he replied in her defence. 'But she's a good person once she trusts you.'

'Really?' said Akiko, giving Jack a dubious look.

While they'd been getting organized and their injuries tended to, Kajiya had lit a small fire in the woods and cooked some of the rice he'd found stored in a large temple pot – another of Soke's secret stashes. Their morale and strength were soon boosted by the warm meal.

'We have food, clothes and weapons,' Tenzen announced. 'Now all we need is a plan.'

48

MIST CASTLE

The crucifixes lined the road like dead trees. Leading in an avenue up to the main gate of Maruyama, they offered a grim welcome to any traveller. A group of workmen laboured hard to erect the last cross before sundown. The sound of their hammering was faint but insistent to the ears of the ninja, who lay hidden at the forest edge.

It had been three days since the attack on the village. They'd caught up with Akechi's army on the second day and followed them through the mountains, but the prisoners had been well guarded and there were simply too many troops to stage an escape attempt. Tenzen suggested they wait until the samurai were no longer expecting trouble. 'Akechi's too arrogant to believe anyone would attack his castle. We'll have the element of surprise,' he argued, and they'd all agreed.

They watched the last crucifix being raised. It was smaller than the others.

Child-size.

Akiko let out a gasp of horror. So did Miyuki. Jack felt his blood run cold. This samurai lord was cruel and heartless. No wonder the ninja despised him so.

'Akechi's making an example of them,' said Tenzen with disgust. 'To warn the other *shinobi* villages not to resist.'

A rustling in the undergrowth alerted them to the return of Kajiya, Danjo and Kato. Only their eyes showed in the gathering darkness.

'All set?' asked Zenjubo.

The bladesmith nodded.

'We attack tonight,' announced Tenzen.

'Shouldn't we at least reconnoitre the town first?' suggested Shiro.

'No time. And we know the layout from the last mission.'

'But we're rushing into this without enough preparation,' Shiro argued.

'We've already discussed this,' snapped Tenzen, his patience having worn thin with Shiro's objections. 'They could be dead by the morning.'

'What are we waiting for then?' urged Jack, plagued by visions of Soke hanging from Gemnan's tree and Hanzo boiling in his cauldron. Jack pulled down his hood and adjusted the *katana* on his back. As a ninja, Tenzen had told him it would be too cumbersome to carry two swords for such a mission, so the *wakizashi* was left with the rest of their equipment, back at the temple.

'Wait,' said Zenjubo, much to Shiro's evident relief.

Sitting cross-legged, his eyes closed, Zenjubo spread his hands out in front of him, the thumb and index finger touching. '*On chirichi iba rotaya sowaka . . .*'

Jack recognized the *kuji-in* chant and hand sign for *Zai*. Despite his impatience to leave, he forced himself to wait for Zenjubo to complete his meditation. Zenjubo continued to chant the mantra under his breath. But whatever ninja magic he was summoning, it appeared to be having little effect.

Still they waited.

As dusk fell, Jack noticed it was getting colder in the valley basin and a mist rolled in, settling like dragon's breath across the plain. Eventually the town disappeared from view and only the castle poked through, a single jagged tooth in the valley's mouth.

'*Kasumiga Jo*,' Tenzen whispered, smiling knowingly at Zenjubo. 'He's using Mist Castle's legendary defence against itself. Now we'll be no more than phantoms in the night. Not even the sentries in the watchtower will spot us.'

Jack turned to Zenjubo in awe. He knew *Zai* gave control over the elements, but he'd never imagined such power. '*You* did this?'

Zenjubo shook his head. 'Merely encouraged it.'

This, Jack realized, was the Ring of Earth in action again.

'Now we go,' Zenjubo announced.

The first to depart were Tenzen and Akiko.

'See you in the castle,' said Akiko, her eyes fixing Jack with the steely determination he knew so well. Kitted out in her armour again, she was eager to find her little brother and, if necessary, fight for his life.

'Good luck!' whispered Jack as he watched her disappear into the mist.

All of a sudden, he felt a chill run through his body – a foreboding that things would go terribly wrong. Only now did he question what he'd got Akiko into. What if he was wrong about Hanzo? He'd be risking Akiko's life for no reason. Jack almost cried out for her to return. But it was too late for that. Whatever course he'd set them both upon, there was no turning back.

'Are you ready?' asked Miyuki.

Jack nodded, shaking off his sense of dread. It wouldn't do any good to share such concerns before the mission.

Miyuki drew closer. 'Sorry if I've been a little on edge lately,' she admitted quietly.

'I understand,' replied Jack. 'We're all upset after the attack.'

'It's not only that,' she continued. 'I know that girl's your friend . . . but I just can't like samurai.'

'Akiko's different, though.'

'Not like you,' she replied, her eyes catching the moon-light as she met Jack's gaze.

'Let's move,' Zenjubo ordered, coercing the obstinate Shiro to his feet.

The four of them left the cover of the forest, melting into the mist like ghosts. The final group of Kajiya, Denjo and Kato would stay back until they'd reached the town's boundary.

Jack followed the fleeting shadows across the plain. It was eerily quiet, only the sound of their breathing and their feet rushing through the long grass. With no sense of distance in the enveloping mist, Jack felt as if he was running through a dream, no end in sight. He was beginning to think Zenjubo had led them in the wrong direction, when out of the mist loomed a large black cross. Zenjubo immediately cut a diagonal away from the main gate and the town wall materialized before them.

Not slowing her pace, Miyuki shot ahead, turning to

offer the cradle of her hands to boost them over. Zenjubo flew into the air, leaping the wall in a single bound. Shiro followed close behind. As Jack approached, he recalled the devious grin on Miyuki's face the time she'd thrown him into the manure heap.

Always look before you leap.

Heeding that advice, Jack sprang on to the top of the wall, pausing briefly to adjust his landing and avoid an open water barrel. He dropped safely into a deserted alleyway.

Zenjubo and Shiro were waiting for him in the shadows. The ninja uncoiled the rope of his *kaginawa* and threw one end back over the wall. A moment later, Miyuki was by their side. The first stage of entry had gone without a hitch.

Jack just hoped it had been the same for Akiko.

49

DRUNKARD

In town, the mist hadn't taken hold. Their black *shinobi shozoku*, however, allowed Jack and the others to pass unseen as Zenjubo guided them through the warren of alleys and passageways, the castle dark and foreboding against the night sky. The side streets were unusually quiet, but ahead Jack could hear the sounds of revelry. As they passed near the central square, he caught glimpses of drunken samurai high on victory.

'What've they got to *celebrate*?' spat Miyuki.

At that moment, a samurai burst into their alley.

Jack was pulled into the shadows by Zenjubo and they all watched as the samurai swayed on his feet, staggered in their direction, then leant against a wall. He'd clearly had one too many *saké*. A glint of light caught Jack's eye. Zenjubo held a *tantō* in readiness. Jack shook his head in silent protest.

The samurai took a couple more steps towards his doom – then vomited over his own feet.

'Hidori!' called a slurred voice from the inn. 'It's your round!'

The samurai, wiping his mouth with the back of his hand, cursed and tottered back inside. Jack breathed a sigh of relief; their mission had been almost ruined by a drunkard.

Rapidly moving on, they slipped into a side street and ran upslope towards their intended destination: Mist Castle. Its outer walls rose above them, an insurmountable barrier to most attackers – but not to ninja. The four of them huddled in the corner where the main bailey wall of the rear courtyards met the castle base. Further along, flaming torches flickered beside a fortified gateway.

Like the entrance to Hell, thought Jack, his concern mounting for Hanzo the closer they came to Gemnan's garden.

Two sentries stood dutifully by, oblivious to the assassins. Opening his pack, Zenjubo passed Miyuki, Shiro and Jack a pair of *shuko* claws and *ashiko* foot hooks each. Slipping them on, they silently scaled the wall in turn.

Jack discovered the claws and hooks dug into the smooth plastered wall with little trouble. At last he knew the secret to the extraordinary climbing ability of his old enemy Dragon Eye. Jack too could now scale buildings like a black widow spider – except he wasn't here to kill; he was here to save his friends.

Keeping to the corner where it was darkest, Jack pulled himself up. He was making good progress when the plaster under his right foot gave way. Fragments tumbled to the ground. The noise wasn't much more than a trickling of dust, but it sounded like an avalanche to Jack – and it was loud enough to capture the attention of a guard.

'Did you hear that?' he asked the other sentry.

Jack clung to the wall, trying to melt into the shadows. He didn't move a muscle, not even daring to look round when he heard the scuff of feet approach.

A bird called out, cawing three times before flapping its wings.

'It's just a crow,' said the guard.

Jack remained where he was, hugging the wall like a limpet. His arms were beginning to tremble when he heard a whisper from below.

'*Get moving!*'

Climbing again, Jack joined Zenjubo and Shiro on the small tiled roof that topped the wall. Miyuki was right behind him. They flattened themselves against the slope, becoming one with the roof.

'It's lucky that bird called,' said Jack under his breath.

'That was no bird!' corrected Miyuki.

Jack stared at Zenjubo in amazement. The ninja's reserved nature gave little indication of his remarkable and diverse skills.

'Where are they?' said Miyuki impatiently, looking around for Tenzen and Akiko.

Her question started Jack worrying too, the ominous sense of dread returning.

'I *knew* we couldn't trust that samurai,' she muttered.

Before Jack could reply, Zenjubo put a finger to his lips and pointed.

Akiko was marching up the road, dragging Tenzen behind her. Limping badly, his face bloodied and his arms bound behind his back, Tenzen looked thoroughly beaten.

Miyuki turned on Jack. 'What she's *done* to him?'

50

KACHIMUSHI

Presenting her captive to the guards, Akiko was let through the gate without question. One of the sentries accompanied them in the direction of Gemnan's garden.

'She's leading us into a trap!' insisted Miyuki.

Although Jack trusted Akiko implicitly, he too was shocked by Tenzen's appalling condition. *What's gone wrong?*

Following from above, the four ninja observed Akiko and her prisoner being led up to a second gate, where they were handed over to a guard of more senior status, a brute of a man with a thick beard and heavy fists. He grabbed Tenzen by the throat, inspecting the gash on his forehead with amusement.

'Might not need a crucifix for this one!' he laughed, spitting into Tenzen's face. 'Looks like a corpse already.'

Tenzen barely reacted, managing little more than a groan as his head lolled in the samurai's grip.

'This way! Before he drops dead.'

Grabbing Tenzen by the shoulder, Akiko roughly shoved him through the gate to the inner courtyards. The four ninja climbed silently over the roof of the guardhouse and darted on ahead to Genman's garden. By the time the samurai reached it, Zenjubo and Miyuki were already in position, Jack and Shiro acting as lookouts. A jangle of keys preceded the click of the gate being unlocked.

'The pit's full. We'll put him in the cage,' the guard said, leading Akiko and her prisoner towards the far corner.

Before the guard had taken two steps, Tenzen straightened, the bindings round his arms falling away. As he seized the samurai in a death choke, Zenjubo and Miyuki leapt from the darkness and swiftly despatched the other two guards on duty in the courtyard.

Tenzen tightened his chokehold. The guard flailed his arms uselessly and was out cold in a matter of seconds, the blood to his brain cut off. Pulling a spiked *shuriken* hidden in his clothes, Tenzen thrust for the man's heart.

'No, you promised!' hissed Akiko, grabbing his arm. 'No killing unless absolutely necessary.'

Tenzen relented. 'Bind him then. But if he stirs, he dies.'

Akiko expertly tied the samurai, immobilizing and gagging him. Jack, leaving Shiro on lookout duty, dropped down beside her a moment before Miyuki ran over.

'Tenzen, what happened?' she demanded, shooting Akiko an evil glare.

'I'm fine,' Tenzen replied. 'We reopened my cut to look convincing.'

In the darkness, they heard a moan. But it didn't come from the comatose guard. Only now was their attention drawn to the figure hanging from the tree.

Hurrying over, they discovered Momochi, strung up by his arms. Zenjubo cut him down. In the pale moonlight,

Jack could see the man had been beaten to a pulp, his face barely recognizable beneath all the cuts and bruises.

'What . . . are you . . . doing here?' he slurred as Tenzen helped him to his feet.

'Rescuing you.'

'Who suggested . . . such a foolhardy plan?'

'Jack.'

Momochi turned his swollen eyes upon him. 'A brave move . . . or a clever trap . . .'

Reeling slightly, he grabbed Zenjubo's shoulder for support.

'They killed my son . . . boiled him in the pot . . .' he wept.

Everyone could see the embers still glowing red beneath the cauldron.

'They think I'm Shonin . . . Tried to get me to talk . . . But I didn't . . .'

'Where is my father?' asked Tenzen urgently.

'In the pit,' Momochi groaned as a fresh wave of pain and grief hit him.

'Hanzo and Soke too?' asked Jack.

Momochi nodded solemnly.

Leaving him in the care of Zenjubo, the others dashed over to the pit. Tenzen, Jack and Akiko crouched beside the heavy iron grille and peered into its depths. The moonlight barely reached the pale faces that stared up in disbelief from the stinking black hole below.

'Father!' whispered Tenzen.

The other prisoners parted to allow Shonin through. 'Tenzen, I *knew* I could rely on you.'

Then he spotted Akiko.

'Don't be alarmed,' said Tenzen. 'She's with us.'

'If a samurai is helping us, we must be desperate!' replied Shonin, smiling good-naturedly at Akiko.

'Hold on,' said Miyuki, taking the guard's keys from Tenzen. 'We'll have you out in no time.' She began to work her way through the set.

'Is Jack there?' croaked Soke from the dark depths of the pit, forced by his injury to sit on the fetid floor.

'I'm here,' he replied, glad to find Soke still alive. 'But where's Hanzo?'

Shonin lifted the boy upon his shoulders. Hanzo looked exhausted, dark patches beneath his eyes. To Jack's relief, he seemed relatively unharmed, except for a nasty bruise along his jawline.

'*Tengu*? I thought you'd died!' exclaimed Hanzo, tears running in rivulets down his grime-ridden face.

'*Tengu* can't die, remember!' replied Jack. 'I've brought someone to see you.' He moved aside for Akiko.

She removed her *menpō* and stared at the boy's face for a long time. Hanzo stared back, bemused by this lady in samurai armour.

'Well, is it?' asked Jack, the moment of truth causing him to hold his breath.

Akiko didn't reply.

'Perhaps you need to see the birthmark?' he whispered.

Akiko shook her head and broke into a tearful smile. 'My *kachimushi*!'

Hanzo immediately stopped crying. 'You . . . you're like the lady . . . in my dream.'

Jack could barely believe it. His instincts had been right. Bewildered looks were exchanged between the prisoners crowded in the pit. Weeping with joy, Akiko reached through the bars and gently stroked Hanzo's face. 'My *kachimushi*, what have they done to you?'

'I kicked a samurai warrior,' said Hanzo proudly. 'He tried to kill Grandfather.'

'Young samurai!' said Shonin, getting Akiko's attention. 'I don't know who you are or what this is about, but now isn't the time for explanations. We *need* to get out of here.'

Akiko immediately refocused on the task in hand, and turned to Miyuki. 'What's taking you so long?'

'None of the keys work!' Miyuki replied in annoyance. 'I've tried them all twice.'

Akiko snatched the keys from her, but she didn't have any luck either. In frustration she grabbed the bars, pulling futilely at them.

'I could pick the lock,' Jack suggested. 'Tenzen, have you got a needle *shuriken*?'

Tenzen handed him the thinnest one he had. But the lock proved more resistant than the one on the cage. The tip jammed and he almost broke it off.

'It's no use,' said Jack after his fifth attempt.

Akiko gripped the bars again in desperation, the torment of being so close yet so far from her little brother almost too much to bear.

'Who would hold the key?' asked Shonin calmly.

With cold certainty, Jack knew.

'Gemnan.'

51

Sleeping Samurai

'Time is not on our side,' Tenzen cautioned as Jack and Miyuki prepared for their mission to find the key. 'There could be a change of guard at any moment.'

'Are you *certain* you know where his room is?' asked Miyuki.

'It's on the second floor,' Jack replied, praying his memory served him right. 'After my meeting with *daimyo* Akechi, I was dragged out by the guards. But we briefly stopped on the stairs halfway down, while Gemnan went to his room. He'd joked he had to get the key to my lodgings!'

'Jack, *please* get the key,' implored Akiko, still kneeling beside the pit. 'I want my Kiyoshi out of this hellhole and home where he belongs.'

'Leave no trace and stay invisible,' said Zenjubo, handing Jack his *kaginawa* climbing rope.

Like Momochi, he was unhappy about sending Jack, but he was the only one with personal knowledge of the keep's layout. Miyuki had volunteered to go with him as her exceptional *shinobi aruki* skills would be required.

'Jack,' called Soke from the pit. 'I have faith in you, but remember the rice paper. A tear is a tear.'

'It'll be like stealing a pillow from under your head,' replied Jack, though in truth they both knew this wasn't the case. This time the lives and future of the clan were at stake.

'May the Five Rings guide you,' said Shonin as the two of them set off.

Miyuki led the way, vaulting on top of the wall and darting along its length. Jack followed close behind, leaping from wall to wall and roof to roof in the direction of the keep. They reached it without resistance, only encountering a samurai patrol in the last courtyard. Once the guards had turned the corner, the two of them jumped down and ran over to its base. The keep presented greater challenges than the castle wall had. The first-floor shutters were closed and the lower roof jutted out. Somehow they'd have to negotiate the overhanging eaves to reach the second floor.

Miyuki took the *kaginawa*, spinning its grappling hook in one hand, and threw it high into the air. The rope wrapped round a gargoyle of a tiger-headed fish that projected from the curved roof two storeys up. She gave the *kaginawa* a tug, checking it was secure, before climbing the rope. Jack held it steady as she hauled herself up. As soon as she had negotiated the eaves and got a footing on the roof, she beckoned him to follow.

Jack grabbed hold of the *kaginawa* and shot up the rope with practised ease. For one brief moment, he even imagined he was in the rigging of the *Alexandria*, the wind blowing in his face and the waves crashing far below. He was snapped out of his reverie by Miyuki urgently gesturing to him. Jack wondered why she was being *so* impatient.

Then he heard the voices. The patrol was coming back.

His muscles straining, one hand after the next, he shimmied up the *kaginawa* as if the rope was burning like a fuse behind him. The voices were getting louder, the footsteps closer. He leapt for the roof and Miyuki snapped up the rope seconds before the patrol rounded the corner. Breathing hard, Jack and Miyuki crouched in the shadows while the samurai passed beneath them.

Jack whispered, 'That was *too* close –'

Miyuki put a hand over his mouth, silencing him. She pointed to the open shutter to their right and Jack nodded, realizing his carelessness. Creeping along the roof, they approached the window and peered in.

The darkened room was full of samurai.

At a glance, Jack counted about thirty asleep on the floor. Miyuki indicated for the two of them to sneak through.

Bad idea, mouthed Jack.

Miyuki nodded, but crawled through the window anyway. Slowly and silently, she began to cross the room. Against his better judgement, Jack followed. He stepped lightly on to the wooden floor. Tiptoeing between the sleeping samurai, he prayed all his stealth training would pay off.

He was halfway when a loose floorboard squeaked under his weight. He stopped. So did Miyuki.

But all the samurai slept on, their snoring drowning out his mistake.

Carefully retracting his foot, Jack skirted the offending floorboard and joined Miyuki near the *shoji*. Her eyes were wide with alarm as she pointed to the floor.

Jack saw that a samurai had rolled over in his sleep and on to her foot. There was nothing she could do – unless they woke him. Miyuki signed for Jack to go on without her, but he shook his head, unwilling to leave her behind.

All of a sudden the man snored loudly like a pig.

This was enough for him to stir in his sleep, and he rolled off Miyuki's trapped foot. She hastily stepped away and over to the door. Keen to get out of the perilous situation, Jack reached for the *shoji*. But Miyuki stopped him.

Pulling a vial of oil from her pouch, she greased the runners first. The door slid silently open. Poking her head through, she checked the way was clear before stepping into the corridor with Jack and closing the door behind them.

Jack now took the lead, their way lit by candle lanterns set into the wall. Padding down the corridor, they bore right to a set of stairs. Jack recognized these as the ones he'd been dragged down from *daimyo* Akechi's floor. Having got his bearings, he was now able to guide Miyuki to Gemnan's room. Turning left, Jack found the corridor they'd been looking for.

He took one step then froze as a bird warbled.

It was a Nightingale Floor.

52

GEMNAN

'Gemnan must have a lot of enemies,' whispered Miyuki, studying the corridor before them.

Jack slid his foot off the Nightingale Floor and shook his head with dismay. Only now did it come back to him. Singing birds. He'd been so preoccupied with his fate at the time of his capture, Jack had thought all the sounds were coming from outside.

'It's impossible,' he said.

'For a samurai, yes. But not for a ninja.'

Miyuki placed her toes lightly upon the first floorboard. Silence.

She moved on to the next, her feet seeming to float above the surface.

'Follow in my footsteps.'

'But Soke said only one man has *ever* done this.'

'I'm not a man,' stated Miyuki.

Chastened, Jack did as he was told. Even though he'd perfected floating feet technique on rice paper, he'd never been taught the secret skills necessary to cross a Night-ingale Floor. Jack realized he'd have to match Miyuki's movements *exactly*. A single mistake – *a tear* – would bring their downfall.

Sweat beaded on his upper lip as he walked the invisible tightrope down the corridor. Progress was slow. And the longer they took, the more concerned Jack was that a guard would discover them. Distracted by this thought, he over-compensated mid-step and lost his balance. Teetering on one foot, his arms flailing, he fought to put his foot down in the right place.

Miyuki, concentrating on what lay ahead, was oblivious to his plight. Keeling sideways, Jack's hand found the wall and he managed to regain his balance. Breathing a silent sigh of relief, he continued to follow in Miyuki's footsteps, taking extra care now.

The corridor seemed to stretch on forever. Then Miyuki stopped.

Gemnan's door stood before them, the final barrier to their goal. Miyuki pointed to the floorboard bordering the *shoji*. 'This one will be fixed,' she whispered.

They both stepped on it; no sound of a nightingale.

As Miyuki took a moment to oil the *shoji*'s runners, Jack put his ear to the *washi* paper door. He heard a rhythmic wheezing from within.

Ever so gently, Miyuki slid open the *shoji*. A single gutter-ing candle lit the room. The floor was matted with finely woven *tatami*. In the centre, Gemnan lay upon a *futon*, a crumpled blanket covering his skeletal body. Protruding from beneath his pillow was the hilt of a knife. Next to it was a set of keys.

Jack just hoped one of them unlocked the pit cage.

Just like stealing a pillow, he reminded himself.

Stepping inside the room, Jack stealth-walked over to Gemnan. Miyuki, keeping one eye on the corridor, covered his back in case of trouble.

As silent as a ghost, he approached the sleeping torturer.

His skin crawled at seeing the man up close again. In the flickering gloom, the sallow-faced Gemnan looked like a corpse, only the sound of his laboured breathing indicating he was alive.

Reaching out, Jack's fingers closed round the keys. Very carefully, he picked them up, but still they made a slight jingling noise. Gemnan snorted and Jack froze as the torturer's head turned towards him. But the man was just settling in his sleep and his wheezing soon resumed.

Jack didn't want to linger any more than he had to. Pocketing the keys silently in his pouch, he turned to leave. Suddenly a *tantō* appeared, its blade catching the dying light of the candle. Jack seized the attacker's hand, trying to wrestle the knife away.

But Miyuki wouldn't let go. She was *determined* to kill Gemnan. Her dark eyes blazed with hatred. The tip of the blade hovered over Gemnan's heart as a mute battle was fought between Jack and Miyuki.

She's gone crazy! thought Jack. An unplanned assassination could jeopardize the entire mission. Releasing Hanzo and the others had to be the priority.

Miyuki made a final bid to thrust the *tantō* into the samurai's chest, but at the last moment Jack prised the knife from Miyuki's grasp. She glared at him, then at Gemnan. Miyuki looked ready to leap for the man's throat and Jack grabbed her, pulling her out of the room. He closed the *shoji* behind them, leaving Gemnan to sleep in blissful ignorance of his near death.

Miyuki fumed, but said nothing. Jack's heart was thumping in his chest, bewildered at what had just happened in there. Unable to ask for fear of waking the torturer, he merely signed for Miyuki to lead the way back over the Nightingale Floor.

A tense walk ensued. Jack was concerned that Miyuki might no longer be focused on the task in hand. He was right. She misjudged the last floorboard and it chirped loudly. Miyuki immediately corrected her step, but the damage had been done.

Reaching the stairs, Jack glanced back. Neither Genman nor a guard had appeared. *But a tear is a tear*, he thought.

Not wanting to risk the samurai's sleeping quarters again, Jack opened a shutter in the outer wall. They clambered out of the window and on to the roof. With the shutter closed, Jack could no longer hold back.

'What were you *thinking*?' he hissed. 'Zenjubo said leave *no* trace!'

Miyuki, seething, trembled all over. In a tense whisper, each word delivered with venom, she replied, '*That man killed my family!*'

Jack stared in shock. 'You're certain?'

She nodded once. 'That horrible, gloating face haunts my every dream.'

From his own experience, Jack knew that being so close to her family's murderer must have been insufferable.

'I understand your torment –'

'Then why did *you* stop me?' Miyuki whispered with icy malice.

'His screams would have woken the whole castle,' said Jack, trying to get her to see sense.

'I'd have slit his throat –'

'Assassination is *not* the mission,' Jack reminded her. 'Saving the clan is!'

'*I want my revenge!*' she said, tears welling in her eyes.

Jack took Miyuki's head gently between his hands, fixing her with his gaze.

'The greatest revenge you could have is for us *all* to escape.'

53

TRAITOR

'What took you so long?' demanded Momochi.

'A Nightingale Floor,' Jack replied, leaving out Miyuki's assassination attempt and their misjudged steps.

Tenzen found the correct key and had the grille open in seconds. 'Give me your *kaginawa*, Jack.'

Lowering the rope into the pit, Tenzen braced himself to take the strain as the prisoners climbed up. Shonin was first out, quickly followed by the others. The wounded Soke needed help, so Zenjubo jumped down and carried him up on his back. When Hanzo emerged, Akiko pulled him into her arms, much to his surprise. But there was no time for an explanation or prolonged reunion.

'Get the uniforms off those two guards,' ordered Shonin, then turned to address Takamori, one of the family heads renowned for his strength and combat skills. 'You and I will disguise ourselves as samurai. Together with this girl Akiko, we'll escort everyone out of the castle's main gate.'

'What about the sentries?' asked Tenzen.

'Zenjubo will scout ahead from the roof. The clan will stay back, while the three of us walk straight up to the gate.

You, Jack and Miyuki can hide behind us. At my signal, we'll silence the sentries, then escape through the town and into the forest.'

Changing into the samurai's clothes, Shonin nodded towards the gagged third guard. 'What's *he* doing still alive?'

'Akiko made me promise not to kill anyone needlessly,' explained Tenzen.

Shonin gave his son a disbelieving look. 'You've a far more merciful heart than I have.' Then turning sternly upon Akiko, he said, 'Your loyalty to your fellow samurai is admirable, but our clan's survival is at stake. You need to decide now – are you with us or against us?'

Akiko looked down at Hanzo, then back at Shonin. 'With you.'

'Good,' he said, slipping the guard's *katana* into his *obi.* 'Are we ready?'

The clan nodded as one.

'Leaving so soon,' said a sneering voice.

Daimyo Akechi stepped into the courtyard, Gemnan at his side, a malicious grin spread across his sickly face. A troop of heavily armed samurai surrounded the ninja in an instant.

'I'm so glad you could *all* join us,' announced *daimyo* Akechi. 'Just as planned.'

'What do you mean?' snarled Shonin.

The samurai lord paused, relishing his moment of conquest. 'A little bird warned us of your coming.'

Miyuki bowed her head in shame, the guilt of her mistake crushing her.

'Why do you think Gemnan kept the key to the pit by

278

his pillow? The Nightingale Floor thankfully proved its worth. Even though your ninja got in, they couldn't get out undetected. But none of you will be able to do either, once your feet are nailed to the cross!' He smirked, stroking the tips of his moustache. 'Admittedly, the rescue party arrived *earlier* than expected. Still, you can't trust everything a spy tells you.' *Daimyo* Akechi paused again, letting this piece of information sink into the ninjas' minds.

'A *spy*?' exclaimed Momochi.

'Yes, ironic, isn't it? A spy within spies. Gave us the location of your village. Told us the best time to attack. Even sabotaged your rescue mission.'

For a moment, no one spoke, all of them too shocked by the implications of Akechi's disclosure. Then Momochi, consumed with rage, launched himself at Jack.

'*You traitor!*' he cried, seizing him by the throat.

'But aren't you . . . the traitor?' Jack gasped, his fingers clawing at the man's iron grip as stars burst before his eyes.

'I'm going to kill you!' Momochi bawled. Tenzen, leaping to Jack's defence, fought to pull him away.

'NO, *she's* the spy!' screamed Miyuki, pointing at Akiko.

Akiko, holding Hanzo close, vigorously shook her head in denial.

A cruel high-pitched cackle broke the round of vicious accusations.

'The *gaijin* didn't betray you,' crowed Gemnan. 'Nor did that disloyal samurai.' Gemnan's eyes narrowed with pleasure as he delivered the painful truth. 'A ninja did!'

His callous laughter was joined by howls of mockery from the samurai troops.

The surviving group of ninja stared at one another, aghast that one of their own was a spy for the samurai. Momochi released Jack from his deathly grip. Despite their desperate situation, Jack was glad *he* hadn't been responsible for the village being found. *But who had? Momochi? Miyuki?*

'You brought your downfall upon yourselves,' scoffed *daimyo* Akechi.

A black-clad figure stepped out from behind the samurai lord. Jack was as shocked as the rest of the ninja.

'I thought you were my friend,' spat Miyuki.

Shiro stared at them, trembling but defiant.

'I'm sick to death of running and hiding all the time, standing knee-deep in mud for my food. That's not a life. I never asked to be a ninja. But I *choose* to be a samurai.'

Shonin glared at the boy, his fists clenched in white-hot anger. 'You sacrificed your village, your home and everyone, so you could become one of *them*! YOU TRAITOR!'

'That wasn't my intention, Shonin. I just wanted the *gaijin* captured, so I could claim the reward and be made a samurai. Yes, *I* was the one who told the guard about Jack while on our previous mission here. But he escaped. He *forced* me to reveal more,' Shiro cried.

'When did your heart turn rotten?' said Soke, sorrow-fully shaking his head at his former student. 'Have I not taught you the value of *ninniku*? No one forced you to do anything. You alone are responsible for your actions. Mark my words, you will *not* escape the consequences of your treason.'

'You're a fine one to talk, considering you're to blame for Dragon Eye and all he became,' Shiro shot back. 'Soke, you hardly ever acknowledged my abilities. None of you did. But I've proved to be a far greater spy than any ninja. I deceived you all.'

'You did well,' praised *daimyo* Akechi, a devilish smile upon his lips.

Shiro bowed in acknowledgement.

Gemnan grabbed the boy by the hair . . . and slit his throat.

He watched the life drain from Shiro's eyes. 'No more running, no more hiding . . . just as I promised.'

Shiro slumped to the ground, dead.

'You can *never* trust a ninja,' declared *daimyo* Akechi. 'Gemnan, crucify them now. Crucify *all* of them!'

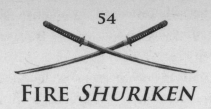

54

FIRE *SHURIKEN*

Kreee-eee-ar . . .

The shrill cry of a hawk pierced the night like a death knell. The samurai closed in to seize the ninja. A second screech, close by Jack's ear, was answered by a thunderous blast as the southern corner of the castle compounds exploded.

Zenjubo's signal had been heard and the ninja burst into action, rushing the troops and engaging in hand-to-hand combat. A smoke bomb landed in the centre of the courtyard, adding to the chaos of the situation.

Stunned by the surprise assault, the samurai lost their advantage and fought for their lives. Five fell in quick succession, a glimmering star protruding from each of their throats. Zenjubo whipped his chain and sickle through the air, ensnaring a fleeing samurai and dragging him to ground where he was swiftly finished off.

Shonin and Takamori clashed swords with their enemies, slaying them before seizing their *katana* and *wakizashi* for other ninja to wield.

In the confusion, *daimyo* Akechi had slipped unseen out of the courtyard, but Gemnan hadn't been so quick. Miyuki spotted him sneaking towards the gate, raised her blowpipe and fired a deadly dart. Catching the attack out of the corner of his eye, Gemnan grabbed the nearest samurai, shoving the unfortunate warrior into its path, then bolted for the gate. Miyuki, determined to reap justice on her family's murderer and without Jack to stop her, drew the deadly *shikoro-ken* from her back and raced to cut off his escape.

As the samurai forces became desperate, Hanzo was snatched by one of them as a human shield. But the warrior soon realized *that* was a mistake. Not only did his 'shield' fight back, but his action had also invoked the wrath of the samurai girl. Akiko drove him back, an Autumn Leaf strike disarming the warrior, at the same time as Hanzo put him in a crippling thumb lock. The samurai let go of the boy, but Hanzo didn't let go of him. Bringing the man to his knees, Hanzo cupped both hands and hit him with Eight Leaves Fist round the head. The samurai, his eyes rolling, reeled and collapsed face first to the ground.

Hanzo snatched up the samurai's sword.

'Let him live,' said Akiko.

'But he's samurai.'

'So am I,' she replied. 'Learn the value of life, before you take it so readily.'

Jack stood side by side with Tenzen, Akiko and Hanzo, protecting the injured Grandmaster. The few samurai who managed to evade Tenzen's lethal *shuriken* attacks were repelled by Jack and Akiko's superior swordsmanship. The one warrior who did get through was crippled by the unexpected power of Hanzo ramming straight into him with Demon Horn Fist.

Above, Jack glimpsed a flaming star as it shot through the night sky, rapidly followed by three more. *Fire* shuriken.

As they struck their target, small charges detonated, consuming the castle's watchtower in flames. Kajiya and his tiny team gave the impression of a mass assault on Maruyama's southern defences.

In the hellish orange glow of the blazing watchtower, Jack saw Miyuki cornered by Gemnan and another samurai. Gemnan now wielded a spear and Miyuki was battling to avoid its barbed tip as she simultaneously fought the two samurai. Jack shot a troubled glance at Tenzen, who'd just run out of throwing stars.

'Go! I'll be fine on my own,' said Tenzen, snatching up a discarded samurai *katana*. '*More* than fine!'

Jack rushed to save Miyuki.

'Slice her up for my pot!' sneered Gemnan, driving Miyuki towards the samurai's blade.

Jack leapt between them, forcing the samurai to retreat under the onslaught of his *katana*. Miyuki, deflecting Gemnan's spear thrust, swiped with the jagged edge of her *shikoro-ken* at his head. But Gemnan was surprisingly deft with his weapon. Dodging her attack, he drove the forked tip into Miyuki's shoulder. She screamed, thrown back into the wall.

Gemnan watched her struggle. 'Does it hurt?' he asked with a gleeful smile across his face.

As he went to thrust again, this time aiming for her heart, a chain whipped round his throat and he was yanked off his feet. Losing grip on the spear, he landed heavily on his back. Gagging, his face bright red, he managed to get his fingers round the chain and off his throat before Zenjubo could move in for the kill.

But Momochi was waiting for him.

The ninja, his rage entirely focused upon the torturer, seized Gemnan and lifted him high above his head. The man struggled futilely in his grip.

'This is for my son!' Momochi bawled, tossing the hated samurai into his own cauldron.

Gemnan, shrieking from the scalding water, flailed and writhed. His screams of pain pierced the shouts of combat, and the samurai Jack was fighting took one look at this horrific sight then fled from the courtyard.

Crawling out of the pot, Gemnan staggered around in maddened agony.

Miyuki was waiting for him now, wanting *her* revenge. 'You murdered my father! My mother! My little brother!' she cried, advancing on him.

Gemnan, seeing the bitter hatred in her eyes and the lethal Sword of Destruction in her hands, cowered from her. 'Devil! Devil! Everywhere devils!' he blurted, incoherent.

Stumbling in the darkness, Gemnan fell to the ground and gave a gut-wrenching moan. 'HELLLLLP me . . .'

His whole body twitched twice then fell still, the sharpened barbs of bamboo thrusting like a dozen spears through his chest.

Miyuki, her sword limp in her hand, stared coldly at the man who'd destroyed her life. Her eyes showed no joy, no pity, not even relief at his death. But there was no satisfaction either. His suffering was over far too quickly, but Miyuki's would remain with her for the rest of her life.

Jack, grabbing her arm, shook Miyuki out of her daze. 'It's time we got out of here,' he said.

The battle for the courtyard was over, but the ninja knew reinforcements would be on their way. Despite losing two in the fight, with another three injured, the *shinobi* hadn't lost hope.

'Let's go!' ordered Shonin, leading his clan out, with Soke helped by Hanzo.

They hurried through the castle compounds, heading straight for the eastern side gate. Thanks to Kajiya's efforts they met with little resistance, most of Akechi's troops having rallied to the defence of the castle's southern wall. Approaching the gate, another explosion ripped through the castle grounds. The five sentries stood awestruck, staring into the night at the raging flames.

'Seal the gate!' ordered Shonin as they marched purposefully towards them. 'We're under attack by ninja.'

The guards, shocked out of their trance, obediently followed orders. As they turned, Shonin drew his *katana* and drove it through the back of the first guard. Takamori brought down the second and third. Tenzen, appearing from behind Shonin, choked the fourth, leaving Akiko to deal with the last. Still unwilling to kill a fellow samurai, Akiko executed Fall Down Fist. Tenzen said nothing, knowing they'd be long gone before the man regained consciousness.

Meanwhile, Jack and Miyuki opened the gate and the clan, now guided by Zenjubo, fled the castle compounds. Disappearing into the backstreets, the band of ninja made for the town gate. Bypassing the main square, Jack saw the intoxicated samurai running in all directions, with no one sober enough to command them. The ensuing chaos gave the ninja vital cover and they quickly reached the main entrance of Maruyama. Shonin employed the same tactic at this gate, and in a matter of moments the sentries were overwhelmed.

Fleeing down the avenue of empty crucifixes and into the mist, Jack took a final glance back. The castle's watchtower, now an almighty flaming pyre, collapsed in upon itself, sending sparks like fireworks into the night. But a group of drunken samurai had rallied themselves and were charging after the escaping ninja. They reached the main gate, then suddenly all began hobbling and crying out in pain.

Tetsu-bishi.

Tenzen and Zenjubo had dropped the spiked caltrops before making their own escape. Warned of the trap, however, a group of mounted samurai, armed with bows, jumped their horses over the hazardous spikes and galloped on.

'*SCATTER!*' ordered Shonin as the samurai approached and arrows flew.

The ninja clan split into units, running in different directions through the mist. Akiko, bending to take Kiyoshi into her arms, was amazed when the boy put on a lightning burst of speed, dragging her along with him.

Takamori, as the strongest of the ninja, carried Soke over his shoulder. But despite his speed, he was felled by one of the samurai's arrows. They both went down. The Grandmaster rose to his knees, but Takamori lay still, the arrow having gone straight through his heart.

Jack and Miyuki rushed to Soke's aid as a samurai horseman bore down on him. Shouldering the Grandmaster under one arm, Miyuki taking the other, Jack hauled him to his feet and in the direction of the forest. The thundering of horses' hooves drew closer and the swish of arrows flew through the air like unseen hunting hawks. Only the mist prevented them being picked off one by one.

'Leave me,' gasped Soke. 'You've no chance of escape carrying me.'

'Every path has its puddle,' replied Jack, hurrying as fast as he could for the treeline.

Zenjubo appeared ahead, beckoning them towards him.

'You just have to learn how to avoid them,' said Jack.

As they ran up to him, Zenjubo cut a tether hidden in the long grass. Out of nowhere, two restrained bamboo stems sprang up either side of them, the rope of a *kaginawa* strung taut between their tips. Enshrouded in mist, the samurai behind didn't know what hit him as the cord struck his chest and threw him from his horse.

Soke grinned approvingly at Zenjubo's Ring of Earth tactic.

Only a few more strides separated them from the cover of the undergrowth.

Zenjubo was hard on their heels as the mounted archers converged on these last four fleeing ninja. Miyuki stumbled, but Zenjubo caught her and they all kept running.

The samurai were almost on top of them. Suddenly a huge wall of flame burst from the ground as they crossed into the forest. Jack praised Kajiya's foresight in planning a Ring of Fire defence. The horses whinnied in terror, the samurai cursing their steeds as they were thrown from their saddles.

Stumbling on through the undergrowth, Jack heard a final *swoosh* cut through the bushes. A second later, he was knocked to the ground by a crippling blow.

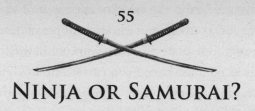

55

NINJA OR SAMURAI?

A searing pain, like a red-hot poker pushing through his body, broke the blackness. Jack's eyes flickered open. Beside him knelt Akiko, her face etched with concern as she tried to hold him up.

The red-hot poker returned with a vengeance, bursting though his left shoulder. Zenjubo, taking a grip on the bloody arrowhead, yanked the rest of the wooden shaft through and out. Jack moaned in sickening agony.

'Got it!' Zenjubo said triumphantly, holding up the arrow for inspection. 'All of it.'

Miyuki, a swatch of cloth at the ready, pressed hard on either side of Jack's wound to stem the bleeding. Jack cried out a second time.

'Don't make such a fuss,' chided Miyuki. 'I had a spear in *my* shoulder. Anyway, I thought you were a ninja, not a feeble samurai.'

Jack noticed she was already bandaged, a bloodstain seeping through the dressing. Groaning with the effort, Jack shifted into a more comfortable position. A second spike of pain caught him in the thigh. He winced, but kept his mouth shut, realizing the needle *shuriken* he'd used to try to pick the lock had stabbed through his pouch into his leg.

They were in a small clearing deep within the forest and Jack realized he must have been carried there. Tenzen was nearby, leaning against a tree, a bloodsoaked cloth held to his forehead. Other ninja were also recovering from their injuries and the frenzied escape. Shonin was tending to Soke's injured leg. Hanzo held his grandfather's hand, promising to look after him when they got back to the village.

'I'll be able to stop the bleeding,' explained Miyuki to Jack. 'But I'll need more time to heal the wound properly.'

Forming the hand sign for *Sha*, Miyuki positioned herself over the hole the arrow had gouged in Jack's flesh and began to chant, '*On haya baishiraman taya sowaka . . .*'

Jack felt a warm tingle settle over the stinging wound.

Akiko, relieved to see he was OK, excused herself. 'I think it's time I explained my presence to Kiyoshi and Soke.'

Jack watched as Akiko apprehensively settled down beside Hanzo. Like four seasons in a day, Hanzo's expression changed from shock to joy to sadness and then to disbelief.

'I'm a ninja, not a samurai!' he protested, looking to Soke for reassurance.

When he saw that the Grandmaster wasn't denying the story, just looking sad and accepting, Hanzo didn't seem to know whether to laugh or cry.

Akiko leant forward and whispered in his ear.

'You weren't, were you?' he replied, his eyes widening in astonishment. 'Can I be both too?'

Akiko nodded.

'I'll be just like the *tengu*!' he exclaimed. 'Do I get to use a samurai sword?'

Akiko smiled. 'Of course.'

'I *like* having a samurai sister,' said Hanzo, giving Akiko a hug.

'I love having my *kachimushi* back,' she sobbed, holding him so tight Jack thought she'd never let him go again.

As Jack followed this tearful reunion, Momochi strode over, his face puffy and blackened with bruises.

'Are you going to live?' he grunted.

Jack nodded, waiting for the next round of abuse from the man.

'Good. There'd be no point in apologizing to a dead person,' he said, bowing his head in repentance. 'Soke was right. You've got the heart of a ninja.'

Speechless, Jack returned the bow, wincing as his wound opened up again.

Miyuki grabbed his shoulder. 'Stop moving,' she complained, ripping a strip of cloth to bind his injury.

'Momochi!' called Shonin as more ninja in black *shinobi shozoku* emerged from the bushes. 'Kajiya's back. Gather everyone together.'

The group huddled in the centre of the clearing. Shonin looked dismayed at the pitiful number of survivors.

'Kajiya, where's the rest of your team?' he asked.

The bladesmith sadly shook his head. 'Only myself and Danjo remain. Kato didn't make it back and the others were killed in the attack on the village.'

There was a moment of grieved silence.

'We'll mourn our losses another day. But tonight we must

plan our survival,' stated Shonin with grave efficiency. 'First, we'll head back to the village. Akechi is bound to send his troops looking for us, but we should have enough time to gather supplies before retreating to our final refuge in the northern mountains. Zenjubo, send our fastest runner to the mothers and children, and tell them to prepare for the journey. We'll need everyone –'

'Shonin?' called out Jack, as Miyuki was tying off his bandage.

'What is it?' said Shonin tersely, unaccustomed to being interrupted.

'Am I right? The sparrow never lands where the tiger roams.'

Every ninja stood up – but one.

Realizing his error, this ninja lunged at Shonin, a blade drawn. The attack was so unexpected none of the other *shinobi* could react in time. But Jack was ready. He flicked his hand, sending the *shuriken* flying.

The needle pierced the outstretched arm of Shonin's assassin. The man yelled in shock, almost dropping the knife. He took a second swipe at Shonin.

By then the clan leader had rolled safely out of the way. The assassin dived after him, but Zenjubo leapt into the fray. The assassin fought back as they wrestled for control of the knife. Zenjubo, more skilled at hand-to-hand combat, broke the man's wrist, twisting his arm up and into his body. The assassin doubled over in pain as his own knife cut into him.

Collapsing to his knees, he let the bloodstained blade fall to the ground. Zenjubo ripped off the assassin's hood.

Blood oozing from his lips, his eyes wild, *daimyo* Akechi spluttered his last dying breath. 'You can *never* trust a ninja . . .'

56

THE RING OF EARTH

'How *did* you know?' asked Miyuki as she continued her daily healing, her hands hovering over Jack's wound.

Their escape, two nights ago, already seemed like a bad dream as they sat beside the village temple, letting the early morning sunshine warm their bodies.

'A ninja without observation is like a bird without wings,' grinned Jack, giving the same response he'd been giving everyone since Akechi's death.

'Stop teasing and just *tell* me!'

Jack finally relented. 'I wouldn't have known if Kajiya hadn't said Kato was dead. With Shiro gone too and you healing me, I couldn't work out why there were still five ninja in full *shinobi shozoku*.'

'It was lucky you were counting. Otherwise Shonin would be dead by now.'

'I was surprised it was *daimyo* Akechi himself,' Jack admitted. 'He struck me as a coward. But his obsession with revenge must have made him desperate.'

'You were right, by the way – revenge doesn't solve anything,' said Miyuki, her expression becoming sorrowful.

'Even though Gemnan's dead, I still miss my family just as much.'

'I miss mine too,' replied Jack, the void opening up in his heart as it always did when he thought of his mother and father.

For a moment, neither spoke, consumed by their grief, but comforted by each other's presence. Then Miyuki lowered her hands.

'That should do for now,' she said, forcing a smile back on to her face and gently touching his shoulder. 'It'll still be stiff for a few days. But as long as you rest, you'll be performing the Two Heavens in no time.'

'You definitely have healing hands,' said Jack as he took hers in his.

A forced cough alerted them to Tenzen walking over, a large pack on his back. 'It's time to go. Shonin wants to move before the sun's fully up.'

'Are you *certain* you don't want to come with us?' asked Miyuki. 'It'll be peaceful in the mountains and I can finish tending to your wound.'

Letting her hand go, Jack shook his head. 'You're very kind, but –'

'No . . . I understand,' she replied as Akiko appeared. 'Of course you can't.'

Miyuki stood and bowed at her approach. Akiko returned the greeting. Though there was no love lost between them, Jack saw there was now at least a sense of mutual respect.

'This is goodbye then,' said Miyuki, turning back to Jack.

'Yes, I suppose it is.'

Miyuki hesitated. Jack sensed she wanted to say more, but couldn't in Akiko's presence.

'I never did apologize for throwing you in the manure,' she said, flashing an embarrassed smile. And she still didn't. Blinking away a tear, Miyuki bowed a hurried goodbye, then walked purposefully over to her parent's grave marker.

'Will she be all right?' asked Jack, watching her with concern.

'Don't worry,' said Tenzen. 'I'll look out for her.' Reaching into his pouch, he produced five gleaming *shuriken*. 'These are for you,' he said, putting them into Jack's hand. 'A small token of thanks for helping me.'

'What did *I* do?' asked Jack.

'You were the one who told me a ship that attacks the wave will rise and conquer. I realized if I didn't take control at the temple we were all sunk,' he explained. 'And now I know you *can* hit a moving target, I'll challenge you to a *shuriken* contest the next time we meet. So you'd better practise.'

Jack laughed. 'I'd never beat you.'

'That's why I won't hold my breath!'

Tenzen bowed formally to both Jack and Akiko before joining the rest of the clan, gathering their belongings on the ridge.

Jack looked up at Akiko. Like Miyuki, she appeared to be on the verge of tears. 'Are you all right?'

Akiko mutely nodded, staring over to where Hanzo was playing with his friend Kobei, both thrilled at being reunited.

'Kiyoshi's happy,' she said, with forced joy in her voice.

Hanzo, noticing they were both looking at him, came

bounding over. Without thinking, he took Akiko's hand in his.

'*Tengu*, can you keep a secret?' he asked.

Nodding, Jack bent down close so Hanzo could whisper in his ear.

'*Soke says I'm going to be the next Grandmaster!*'

'Really?' said Jack, glancing up at Akiko and realizing she already knew this.

That was why she was upset.

'Yes!' Hanzo exclaimed, too excited to keep his voice down. 'I'll be allowed to see the *densho*, actually read the scrolls with all our clan's secrets!'

'That's a big responsibility,' said Jack.

'I know. Soke says it'll take a few years of preparation and then a lifetime of learning.'

'When are you starting?'

'As soon as we get to the refuge,' replied Hanzo.

Jack nodded his understanding of the situation.

'Come on, Hanzo!' cried Kobei, waving at his friend.

Hanzo smiled apologetically, as if he'd suddenly matured. Pulling Akiko by the arm, he said 'You can be on my side.'

Hanzo ran to rejoin his friends. '*Sayonara*, Jack!'

Jack couldn't help but laugh.

'What is it?' asked Akiko.

'That's the *first* time he's called me by my proper name!' he said, shaking his head in disbelief. He saw the sadness in Akiko's eyes. 'Are you not going with him?'

'No,' she replied in a quiet voice. 'Shonin says he can't risk *any* outsider knowing the location of their final refuge.'

'Then you should play with your brother while you have the chance.'

As Akiko went and shared her last moments with Hanzo, Shonin and Soke strolled over to Jack.

'I owe you my life, Ninja Jack,' said Shonin and inclined his head in gratitude. 'I wish there was more I could do for you, but we have to be gone before the samurai arrive.'

'You've done more than enough,' replied Jack, returning the bow.

Shonin clapped his hand upon Jack's good shoulder.

'You know you'll *always* have a place in my clan,' he said, smiling warmly. 'You just have to find us first!'

With that, Shonin left Jack and Soke to say their farewells.

'I'll be sad to leave here,' admitted the Grandmaster, gazing out across the valley. 'It was the perfect Ring of Earth.'

'What about the refuge?' asked Jack.

'The mountains are not kind to the old. I won't have so many years left up there.'

Jack went to dispute this, but Soke stopped him, and he could see the weariness and strain of the past few days engrained in the old man's wrinkled face.

'Why hide from the truth? It always finds you in the end,' Soke grinned. 'Life has worn me down like a rock in a river. My time has almost come.'

'Time enough to prepare Hanzo to become the next Grandmaster?'

Soke raised an eyebrow. 'He told you? I'll have to teach that boy discretion first.'

'A frog in a well does not know the great sea,' reminded Jack.

'How true,' said Soke, chuckling. 'Maybe the fact he's *really* a samurai will be good for all of us. Hanzo may be the saving of the ninja.'

'Soke!' called out Momochi, rounding up the clan. 'Shonin's keen to leave.'

The Grandmaster held his hand up, indicating he'd be with them shortly.

'Jack, you've come a long way since we first stood on this ridge, but you have a far longer journey ahead. Be guided by the Five Rings, and you *will* return home.'

'Your teaching has given me the hope that I will,' said Jack, bowing. 'You've also proved to me that a single tree doesn't make a forest. I swore the ninja would always be my enemy. Now the ninja will always be my friend.'

Soke nodded sagely.

'If you ever encounter a ninja, or believe they are one, then use this secret hand sign.' The Grandmaster clasped both hands together, middle fingers entwined, thumbs and little finger extended in a V shape. 'It's the Dragon Seal. A true ninja will recognize this and help you.'

Soke turned to go. 'A final piece of advice: to hide is the best defence.'

57

A HAPPY FAREWELL

Akiko and Jack walked slowly back into the deserted village. They passed through paddy fields, most of the crop trampled and unharvested. Thankfully, the clan had stockpiled food from previous years and hidden it beneath the temple. The smoky tang of burnt wood hung in the air, Shonin's farmhouse still smouldering away after five days. A number of other houses had been set on fire too, but most had just been ransacked for their rice and provisions.

Fortunately for Jack, Soke's house had been one of those pillaged but not set on fire. He'd found his pack safe and sound in the secret compartment beneath the floorboards, the *rutter* untouched within its protective oilskin. Beside it, Soke had left several rations of rice and some essential clothes.

Jack got changed for the journey, then joined Akiko out in the yard. It was sad to see the once thriving village so bereft of life, and neither he nor Akiko wanted to stay longer than they had to. The samurai could arrive at any moment.

Akiko hadn't spoken a word since she'd said goodbye to her brother.

'I'm sorry,' began Jack. 'Sorry he had to go.'

'I'm not,' Akiko replied, her voice subdued but resolute. 'Kiyoshi . . . I mean *Hanzo* is where he rightfully belongs. In the clan, with his friends. They're his family now.'

'But what about you?' asked Jack. 'You've spent the last five years looking for him.'

Akiko nodded. 'And *you* found him for me. My *kachimushi*'s alive and being cared for. That's all I need to know. It was a happy farewell.'

She looked at Jack, her expression hopeful.

'Soke's promised that Hanzo can visit us in Toba once the clan's resettled. I know he's eager to meet his mother.'

Akiko reached out and touched Jack's hand. 'I owe you so much.'

'I'm the one who owes *you*,' said Jack, gently taking her hand in his. 'It's the least I could do after all you've done for me.'

They gazed into one another's eyes, the connection between them more powerful than ever. This second farewell was proving even harder than the first. And now Jack knew what life was like without Akiko by his side.

'I should go,' she said, letting her hand fall away. 'My mother's waiting for me in Toba.'

'You could come with me,' Jack suggested, though he was well aware his journey took him in the opposite direction.

Akiko sadly shook her head. 'My mother *needs* to know about Kiyoshi. And I need to be there for her. It's a daughter's duty.'

'I understand,' said Jack, knowing it had been an impossible request.

Leaning in close, Akiko kissed him gently on the cheek.

'*Forever bound to one another*,' she whispered in his ear. Then she turned and walked away in the direction of the rising sun.

Jack, speechless, watched her figure recede down the village road, past the devastated square, round the pond and beyond. He realized he felt how Akiko must have done that day in Toba he left *her* behind. His heart reached out for his friend, begging her to come back.

Akiko kept walking, not even risking a glance over her shoulder. Maybe she was scared to. *Should he call to her?* But he didn't know what he would say. They were both leaves floating away on different streams.

When she disappeared from view, Jack still stood watching, his hand to the cheek she'd kissed. He dearly hoped to see her just one more time.

But Akiko was gone.

Once again, he was on his own. Perhaps better equipped than before for the hazardous journey ahead – but also more alone. He'd lost Akiko a second time. Then Jack reminded himself that, like Akiko, he had a duty to his family first. His love for his sister, Jess, while different, was equally compelling and she was waiting for him in England.

Gathering his things, Jack ensured the precious *rutter* was cushioned by the two kimono within the pack. On top was the little *inro* case containing Yori's paper crane and Akiko's pearl, the string of copper coins, and the straw containers of rice. Finally, he added a full gourd of water and Tenzen's five *shuriken*. Hanging from the strap was Sensei Yamada's *omamori*. Jack rubbed the amulet, praying for its continued protection, then slung the pack over his right shoulder.

Securing his samurai swords on his hip, Jack felt like a samurai again.

Picking up the last of his equipment, he felt like a ninja.

Jack was determined not to be caught out this time. Having adjusted the wicker basket on his head, he raised the *shakuhachi* to his lips and gently blew. The faltering first notes of '*Shika no Tone*' echoed across the valley as he resumed his solitary pilgrimage to Nagasaki, each step taking him closer to home.

NOTES ON THE SOURCES

The following quote is referenced within *Young Samurai: The Ring of Earth* (with the page number in square brackets below) and the source is acknowledged here:

1. [Page 77] 'The usefulness of a cup is its emptiness' by Lao Tzu (Philosopher and founder of Taoism, 600–531 BC).

Japanese Glossary

Bushido

Bushido, meaning the 'Way of the Warrior', is a Japanese code of conduct similar to the concept of chivalry. Samurai warriors were meant to adhere to the seven moral principles in their martial arts training and in their day-to-day lives.

Virtue 1: *Gi* – Rectitude
Gi is the ability to make the right decision with moral confidence and to be fair and equal towards all people no matter what colour, race, gender or age.

Virtue 2: *Yu* – Courage
Yu is the ability to handle any situation with valour and confidence.

仁

Virtue 3: *Jin* – Benevolence
Jin is a combination of compassion and generosity. This virtue works together with *Gi* and discourages samurai from using their skills arrogantly or for domination.

礼

Virtue 4: *Rei* – Respect
Rei is a matter of courtesy and proper behaviour towards others. This virtue means to have respect for all.

真

Virtue 5: *Makoto* – Honesty
Makota is about being honest to oneself as much as to others. It means acting in ways that are morally right and always doing things to the best of your ability.

名誉

Virtue 6: *Meiyo* – Honour
Meiyo is sought with a positive attitude in mind, but will only follow with correct behaviour. Success is an honourable goal to strive for.

忠義

Virtue 7: *Chungi* – Loyalty
Chungi is the foundation of all the virtues; without dedication and loyalty to the task at hand and to one another, one cannot hope to achieve the desired outcome.

A Short Guide to Pronouncing Japanese Words

Vowels are pronounced in the following way:
'a' as the 'a' in 'at'
'e' as the 'e' in 'bet'
'i' as the 'i' in 'police
'o' as the 'o' in 'dot'
'u' as the 'u' in 'put'
'ai' as in 'eye'
'ii' as in 'week'
'ō' as in 'go'
'ū' as in 'blue'

Consonants are pronounced in the same way as English:
'g' is hard as in 'get'
'j' is soft as in 'jelly'
'ch' as in 'church'
'z' as in 'zoo'
'ts' as in 'itself'

Each syllable is pronounced separately:
A-ki-ko
Ya-ma-to
Ma-sa-mo-to
Ka-zu-ki

ashiko	foot hooks
bō	wooden fighting staff
bōjutsu	the Art of the *Bō*

bushido	the Way of the Warrior – the samurai code
daikon	long, large white radish
daimyo	feudal lord
densho	the ninja book of secret techniques and principles
Dim Mak	Death Touch
dokujutsu	the Art of Poison
doma	the area within a building with a floor of packed earth
futon	Japanese bed: flat mattress placed directly on *tatami* flooring, and folded away during the day
gaijin	foreigner, outsider (derogatory term)
gotonpo	the Art of Concealment
hakama	traditional Japanese trousers
hanbō	short staff (90 cm) used in martial arts
hashi	chopsticks
Hifumi hachi gaeshi	alms-begging song, 'One, two, three, pass the alms bowl'
hikyaku	'Flying Feet' (a courier)
honkyoku	'original pieces' of music for the *shakuhachi* flute
ikki goken	the 'five blades in one breath' technique
inro	little case for holding small objects
Jin	ninja hand sign for reading the thoughts of others

kachimushi	old word for dragonfly, lit. 'victory bug'
kaginawa	three-pronged grappling hook on a rope
Kai	ninja hand sign for 'sensing of danger'
kajutsu	the Art of Fire
kama	sickle-shaped weapon
kami	spirits within objects in the Shinto faith
kanji	the Chinese characters used in the Japanese writing system
kataginu	winged, sleeveless jacket of the samurai
katana	long sword
kenjutsu	the Art of the Sword
kesagiri	double diagonal cut
ki	energy flow or life force (Chinese: *chi* or *qi*)
kissaki	tip of sword
koan	Buddhist question designed to stimulate intuition
komusō	Monk of Emptiness
kuji-in	nine syllable seals – a specialized form of Buddhist and ninja meditation
kusarigama	sickle and chain weapon
kyusho	vital or nerve point on a human body

manriki-gusari	chain weapon with two steel weights on the ends
menpō	protective metal mask covering part or all of face
metsubishi	blinding powder, used as ninja defence
mikan	satsuma, orange citrus fruit
mikkyō	secret teachings
mon	family crest
mushin	lit. 'no-mindedness'
nagamaki	large *katana*-style blade with an extended shaft.
nagare	flow or roll
naginata	long pole weapon with a curved blade on the end
nikkyō	wristlock move in *taijutsu*
ninja	Japanese assassin
ninjatō	ninja sword
ninjutsu	the Art of Stealth
ninniku	the philosophy of the ninja, 'cultivating a pure and compassionate heart'
Niten Ichi Ryū	the 'One School of Two Heavens'
nunchaku	a weapon comprising two sticks connected at the ends by a short chain or rope
obi	belt
ofuro	bath
omamori	Buddhist amulet to grant protection

origami	the art of folding paper
Rin	to meet or to face, but interpreted as strength for *ninjutsu* purposes
saké	rice wine
sakura	cherry-blossom tree
samurai	Japanese warrior
sarugaku	form of popular entertainment, similar to the modern-day circus,
saya	scabbard
sayonara	goodbye
sencha	green tea
sensei	teacher
Sha	ninja hand sign, interpreted as healing for *ninjutsu* purposes
shakuhachi	Japanese bamboo flute
Shichi Hō De	the 'seven ways of going' (disguises)
shikoro-ken	sword with a saw-like edge, also known as the 'Sword of Destruction'
shinobi	another name for ninja, literally 'stealer in'
shinobi aruki	stealth, or silent, walking
shinobi shozoku	the clothing of a ninja
shoji	Japanese sliding door
shuko	climbing claws
shuriken	metal throwing stars
shuriken-jutsu	the Art of the *Shuriken*
sohei	warrior monks

soke	title meaning 'head of the family' or grandmaster
sui-ren	water training
suizen	'blowing Zen', practice of playing flute for self-enlightenment
tabi	traditional Japanese socks
taijutsu	the Art of the Body (hand-to-hand combat)
Ta-no-kami	god of the rice fields
tantō	knife
Taryu-Jiai	inter-school martial arts competition
tatami	floor matting
tengu	a mythical Japanese devil bird or demon
tetsu-bishi	small sharp iron spike
ukemi	break falls
uki-ashi	floating feet technique
wakizashi	side-arm short sword
washi	Japanese paper
yakitori	grilled chicken on a stick
yamabushi	Lit. 'one who hides in the mountains'; Buddhist hermits who live in the mountains
Yama-no-kami	god of the mountains
yukata	summer kimono
Zai	ninja hand sign for sky or elements control
zazen	seated meditation

Japanese names usually consist of a family name (surname) followed by a given name, unlike in the Western world where the given name comes before the surname. In feudal Japan, names reflected a person's social status and spiritual beliefs. Also, when addressing someone, *san* is added to that person's surname (or given names in less formal situations) as a sign of courtesy, in the same way that we use Mr or Mrs in English, and for higher-status people *sama* is used. In Japan, *sensei* is usually added after a person's name if they are a teacher, although in the Young Samurai books a traditional English order has been retained. Boys and girls are usually addressed using *kun* and *chan*, respectively.

ACKNOWLEDGEMENTS

This fourth book in the Young Samurai series presents a new chapter in Jack's adventures. But the team behind it remains very much the same – only more dedicated than ever. My thanks go to all of them: Charlie Viney, my Loyal agent; Shannon Park, my Honourable editor at Puffin; Wendy Tse, my Honest copy-editor; Vanessa Godden, Lisa Hayden, Tania Vian-Smith and all the Courageous Puffin team; Francesca Dow, the *daimyo* of Puffin Books; Tessa Girvan, Franca Bernatavicius and Nicki Kennedy, my Benevolent overseas agents at ILA; Trevor, Paul and Jenny, my Respectful booking agents at Authors Abroad. You're all true samurai upholding the code of *bushido*!

There are so many other people I'd like to thank, but I would need a whole book for that. So I'll just mention these few in this edition: all the independent bookstores who have supported me from the start, including Mark at Mostly Books, Abingdon; David and Gill at The Mint House, Hurstpierpoint; and Vanessa and Julie at The Book Nook, Brighton; David Ansell Sensei of the Shin Ichi Do dojo (*www.shinichido.org*) for all his samurai sword training; Sensei

Peter Brown at the Shinobi Kai dojo (*www.shinobi-kai.net*) for all his ninja knowledge; the exceptionally dedicated Sensei Mary Stevens and Sensei Rob King at the Oxford School of Martial Arts (*www.schoolofmartialarts.com*) and, of course, Team Taurus – the real Young Samurai behind the book!; Rob Rose for your feedback and reviews (and for looking after Karen so well!); as promised, a mention to the Butcher Boys for all their sausages, steak and banter; and most importantly to my loving and supportive family, the Moles – Simon, Sue, Steve and Sam, and all the cousins – and especially my mum, dad and Sarah, I couldn't do it without you.

Lastly, I once again offer a bow of respect to all the librarians and teachers who have supported the series and to all the Young Samurai readers out there – thank you for your loyalty to the series. You can keep in touch with me and the progress of the Young Samurai series on my Facebook page, or via the website at *www.youngsamurai.com*

Arigatō gozaimasu!

CAN'T WAIT
FOR THE NEXT
JACK FLETCHER
BLOCKBUSTER?

THE RING OF WATER

Here's a **sneak preview** . . .

1

THE AMULET

Japan, autumn 1614

For one terrifying moment, Jack remembered *nothing*.

He had no idea where he was, what had happened to him, what he was supposed to be doing. He didn't even know *who* he was. Desperately, like a drowning man, he clung on to any memory he had.

My name is Jack Fletcher . . . from London, England . . . I'm fifteen . . . I have a little sister, Jess . . . I'm a rigging monkey on-board a trading ship, the Alexandria *. . . No! I'm a samurai. I trained at a warrior school in Kyoto . . . the* Niten Ichi Ryū *. . . BUT I'm a ninja too . . . That can't be right – the ninja Dragon Eye killed my father!*

Jack's head throbbed and he felt himself blacking out again. He tried to fight the sinking sensation, but didn't have the strength to resist. His fragmented mind was slipping away, dragged back into unconsciousness.

An incessant *drip . . . drip . . . drip* of water brought him round. Through the dense fog clouding his mind, Jack became aware of rain. Heavy rain, pummelling the wet earth and drowning out all other sounds. Forcing his eyes open,

Jack discovered he was lying on a rough bed of straw. Water was seeping through a thatched roof and falling on to his face.

The drip was infuriating. But Jack's body ached so much he struggled to shift himself out of the way. Turning his head to one side, he groaned with pain and came face to face with a cow. Chewing morosely on some cud, the animal stared back at him, clearly begrudging the fact that she had to share her lodgings. As far as Jack could tell, the cow was the only other occupant of the small stable.

Painfully easing himself up on one elbow, the room swimming before his eyes, Jack felt a wave of nausea wash over him. He retched on to the straw-strewn floor, green bile spewing from his mouth. The cow was even less impressed by this undignified display and moved away.

Beside the improvised straw bed, someone had left him a jug of water. Jack sat up and gratefully had a drink, washing his mouth out before taking a large gulp. Swallowing proved difficult. His throat was raw, the acidic contents of his stomach having burnt its way out. He took another sip, more carefully this time, and the pain eased a little.

Jack realized he was a mess. His lower lip was split, his left eye swollen. Dark bruises covered his arms and legs, while his ribs felt sore, though on inspection thankfully not broken.

How did I get like this?

He was dressed in a dirty ragged kimono that certainly wasn't his. The last time he could recall he was wearing the blue robes of a *komusō*, a Monk of Emptiness, as part of a ninja disguise allowing him to pass freely through Japan.

He'd been making his way to the port of Nagasaki in the south, hoping to find a ship bound for England and home to his little sister, Jess.

Panic overwhelmed him. *Where are all my belongings?*

Jack's eyes darted around the stable in search of his swords and pack. But apart from the cow, a pile of straw and a few rusty farm tools, they were nowhere to be seen.

Calm down, he told himself. *Someone has been kind enough to leave me water. That someone might also have my possessions.*

With a trembling hand, Jack took another swig from the jug, hoping the drink would clear his head. But try as he might, he had no memory of the last few days. Jack knew he'd left the ninja village in the mountains and was sure he'd managed to reach the borders of Iga Province unopposed. But beyond that he had no recollection.

Outside through the open doorway, Jack noticed the rain was letting up. He assumed it was morning. Although the sky was so dark with thunderclouds, it could easily have been the evening. He had a choice – he could wait for whoever had given him the water to appear, or he could take action and find his possessions himself.

As Jack sat there, summoning up the energy to stand, he vaguely became aware of something clasped in his left hand. Opening his fingers, he found a green silk pouch embroidered in golden thread with the emblem of a wreath and three *kanji* characters: 東大寺. Inside the little bag was what felt like a rectangular piece of wood. Jack recognized the object, but for a moment its name eluded him . . .

An omamori. *That's it! A Buddhist amulet.*

Sensei Yamada, his Zen philosophy master at the *Niten*

Ichi Ryū, had given him before he'd set off on his journey. It was meant to grant him protection.

But this wasn't his *omamori*. His amulet had a red silk bag. So whose was this?

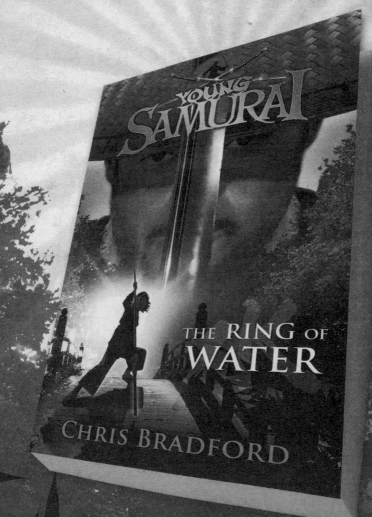

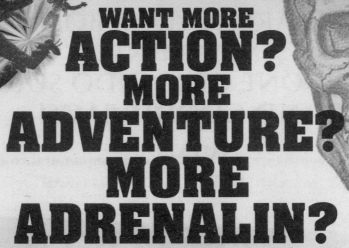

WANT MORE ACTION? MORE ADVENTURE? MORE ADRENALIN?

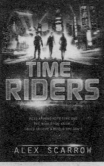

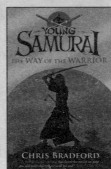

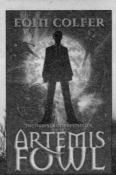

GET INTO PUFFIN'S ADVENTURE BOOKS FOR BOYS